SIDEWINDERS:
DEADWOOD GULCH

SIDEWINDERS:
DEADWOOD GULCH

William W. Johnstone
with J. A. Johnstone

PINNACLE BOOKS
Kensington Publishing Corp.
www.kensingtonbooks.com

PINNACLE BOOKS are published by

Kensington Publishing Corp.
119 West 40th Street
New York, NY 10018

PUBLISHER'S NOTE
Following the death of William W. Johnstone, the Johnstone family is
working with a carefully selected writer to organize and complete Mr.
Johnstone's outlines and many unfinished manuscripts to create addi-
tional novels in all of his series like The Last Gunfighter, Mountain
Man, and Eagles, among others. The novel was inspired by Mr. Johnstone's superb storytelling.

All Kensington titles, imprints, and distributed lines are available at special quantity discounts for bulk purchases for sales promotions, premiums,
fund-raising, educational, or institutional use. Special book excerpts or cus-
tomized printings can also be created to fit specific needs. For details, write
or phone the office of the Kensington special sales manager: Kensington
Publishing Corp., 119 West 40th Street, New York, NY 10018, attn: Special
Sales Department; Phone: 1-800-221-2647.

PINNACLE BOOKS and the Pinnacle logo are Reg. U.S. Pat. &
TM Off.
The WWJ steer head logo is a trademark of Kensington Publishing Corp.

ISBN-13: 978-0-7860-2347-9
ISBN-10: 0-7860-2347-3

First Printing: June 2011

10 9 8 7 6 5 4 3 2 1

Printed in the United States of America

*Satan finds some mischief
for idle hands to do.*
—Isaac Watts

*Bo and me, we try to stay busy
and dodge that ol' Devil.*
—Scratch Morton

CHAPTER 1

Six sturdy mules pulled the wagon along the trail that followed a winding gulch through the Black Hills of the Dakota Territory. Off to the right of the trail flowed a narrow, brawling creek lined by cottonwood, aspen, and box elders. The pine-covered sides of the gulch rose steeply and cast a pall of gloom over the trail despite the sunny day. Winter wasn't far off, and a chill hung in the air.

Breath fogged in front of the faces of the driver and the three guards on the wagon. The guards wore sheepskin jackets, while the driver was bundled in an old mackinaw. The man on the seat next to the driver had a shotgun across his knees. The two guards in the back of the wagon, with the sacks of gold dust bound for the Stebbins & Post Bank in Deadwood, clutched Winchesters. Deadwood was four miles away along this narrow gulch, and lately every foot of the way had been dangerous. Time was, these runs from the mine to the bank had been made by just two men, a driver and a guard, but with the latest outbreak of lawlessness and violence plaguing the area, the mine owners had increased their precautions.

The driver hoped having three tough men along with him would be enough. He wasn't in any mood to die today, and he dang sure didn't want any devil's pitchfork carved into his forehead.

His name was Chloride Coleman. He had followed the lure of gold and silver from one end of the frontier to the other for more than twenty-five years, after first heading for California during the Gold Rush of '49. Since then he had been a lot of places, including the rough mining camp of Deadwood when gold seekers first flooded into the Black Hills. He had spent part of the intervening years searching for his own fortune before finally coming to the realization that he wasn't fated to find it. He could make a living, though, working for men who had been more fortunate.

"Can't you get those jugheads moving a little faster, Chloride?" Mitch Davis, the guard on the seat beside him, asked. "This place gives me the fantods."

"Hold your horses," Chloride said. He chuckled. "Of course, them ain't horses I'm drivin', are they?"

He turned his head to spit a stream of tobacco juice into the weeds beside the trail. Steaks of brownish-yellow in his white beard testified to the thousands of other times he had done the same thing.

"I'll feel better when we get to Deadwood," one of the men in the back said. Chloride didn't know them very well. The one who had spoken was called Turley. His more taciturn companion was Berkner. Like Mitch Davis and Chloride himself, they had come to the Dakota Territory in search of their fortune, only to find that the big mining concerns had gobbled up the best claims already, squeezing out the individual miners. The days of some prospector striking it rich were as dead as Wild Bill Hickok, shot in the head from behind in the Number 10 Saloon about four years earlier.

Davis lifted his shotgun and said, "I don't like the looks of that deadfall up ahead. I don't think it was there the last time we came through here. There might be half a dozen of those Devils hiding behind it. Better steer around it as much as you can, Chloride."

"Now how am I gonna do that?" Chloride asked. "The trail goes right beside that big ol' tree, and the way the side of the gulch comes crowdin' in, there ain't no way to go except right past it."

"Yeah, well, maybe not, but don't waste any time getting by it. Better whip up that team a little."

Chloride sighed and reached for the whip socketed into a holder next to him. With skill born of long experience, he popped the blacksnake over the heads of the mules and yelled, "Gee up, you varmints! Gee up!"

The stolid mules leaned into their harness and moved a little faster, but not much.

"Keep your guns on that deadfall," Davis told Turley and Berkner. He was nominally in charge of the guards. Both men lifted their rifles to their shoulders and trained the weapons on the huge log lying a short distance to the left of the trail. Davis was right, Chloride thought. Several of the outlaws who called themselves the Deadwood Devils might be hiding behind it, lying in wait to ambush the wagon carrying the gold shipment.

Davis got up on one knee on the seat so he could fire the shotgun over Chloride's head if he needed to.

"Careful with that," the old-timer urged him as the wagon started past the deadfall. "I ain't partial to havin' greeners go off right next to my ear. I'm already deaf enough from old age."

"Better deaf than dead," Davis told him. "If there are any road agents behind that tree, you'll be glad I've got this shot—"

He didn't get to finish his sentence, because at that moment a shot rang out, but not from behind the deadfall. Instead it came from the other direction, from the trees on the other side of the creek.

Davis grunted and toppled over, falling against Chloride. He rolled off the startled driver and landed on the floorboards at Chloride's booted feet. Chloride's rheumy eyes widened in shock at the sight of the grisly mess that the back of Mitch Davis's head had turned into. A bullet had blown away a fist-size chunk of his skull and some of the brain underneath.

More shots blasted from across the creek as Turley and Berkner tried to swivel around and return the fire. Chloride slashed frantically at the backs of the mules and shouted at them, trying to get them to break into a run.

Turley and Berkner got several shots off. Flame spouted from the muzzles of their Winchesters. But then Turley slumped back onto the chests that held bags of gold dust and chunks of gold ore. Blood welled from a hole in his chest where bushwhack lead had found him. He dropped his rifle and pawed frantically at the wound for a second before his head slumped back and his eyes began to glaze over in death.

That left just Turley to fight off the attack, and he was badly outnumbered. Several outlaws burst from the trees on horseback and splashed across the creek to give chase to the wagon, which was rattling and bouncing along faster now as Chloride finally got the mules to run. Smoke puffed from the six-guns wielded by the men, who had bandanas pulled up over their faces to conceal their identities.

Chloride yelled encouragement to the remaining guard. "Hold 'em off, Turley!"

"Get this wagon moving faster!" Turley shouted back as he levered another round into the Winchester's chamber. Both men knew the odds of the wagon team being able to outrun the desperadoes' horses were mighty slim. The outlaws were closing the gap by the second.

A gurgling cry came from Turley. Chloride glanced over his shoulder and saw the man thrashing around as blood poured from his bullet-ripped throat. Chloride bit back a curse. Turley would be dead in seconds, Davis and Berkner had already crossed the divide, and that left Chloride alone against a horde of bloodthirsty outlaws. For a second he thought about reining in the team, bringing the wagon to a stop, and throwing himself on the mercy of the gang if he turned the gold shipment over to them.

He discarded the idea almost instantly. Those varmints were cold-blooded murderers and had proven that on several occasions in the past. They had earned the nickname of Devils they had given themselves. If he surrendered, they'd just put a bullet in him.

Besides, he was too old and stubborn to quit. Holding the reins in his left hand, he used his right to fumble the old cap-and-ball revolver from the holster at his waist. He twisted around on the seat and lifted the gun, earing back the hammer. It went off with a loud boom as he aimed at the riders thundering along right behind the wagon and pulled the trigger.

None of the outlaws even slowed down.

Because Chloride was turned around on the seat, he didn't see the sharp bend in the trail coming up as it followed the winding course of the creek. The mules didn't slow down as they raced around the turn. Chloride felt the wagon lurch and sway underneath him. Something in its underpinning gave way with a loud snap, and Chloride yelled as he suddenly found himself sailing through the air. The wagon overturned with a crash behind him.

Branches clawed at his face as he landed in a thick clump of brush. That was probably all that saved him from a broken leg at best or a broken neck at worst. The impact knocked the breath out of him. He lay there unable to move, unable to do anything except gasp for air. That probably saved his life, too, because the outlaws' guns continued to roar and bullets whipped through the brush all around him and just over his head.

Chloride squeezed his eyes shut. He and the Good Lord weren't exactly on the best of terms, due to Chloride's fondness for whiskey, cards, and, when he was younger, wicked women, but with all that lead flying through the air, the old-timer didn't hesitate to offer up a plea for help to *El Señor Dios*.

"That's enough!" a man ordered. "Hold your fire, blast it!"

"But the driver fell off the wagon and landed in that brush," another man protested as the guns fell silent.

"I saw what happened," the first man said. "He

probably broke his neck when he landed, and even if he didn't, you've thrown enough lead in there to turn him into a sieve. Let's go on about our business."

Chloride held his breath now, even though he felt like he was half-suffocating from lack of air. He knew that if they heard him gasping, he'd get a bullet in a hurry.

At the same time, he knew he couldn't stay here. The outlaws might take it into their heads at any second to search the brush and make sure he was dead. Moving slowly and as quietly as possible, he began working his way backward, inching along so he wouldn't cause the branches to wave around and give away his position. It was nerve-racking, especially because he could hear the killers moving around only a few yards away.

His feet bumped against something. Carefully, he turned his head and saw that he had reached a cluster of large rocks at the base of the slope forming the northern wall of the gulch. Chloride crawled among the rocks, confident that they would offer him better shelter. He lay there on his belly for a long moment as his heart pounded furiously in his chest. He started breathing again, shallowly so it wouldn't be too loud

After a while he lifted his head. He had lost his battered old hat with the turned-up brim when he went flying off the wagon, so he didn't have to worry about that. He stayed low, edging his head up just enough so he could see part of the trail.

The outlaws were moving the gold from the wrecked wagon. They had busted open the chests and were loading the pokes of gold dust into their saddlebags. The sacks of nuggets were slung onto the backs of a couple of pack animals and lashed in place. Chloride didn't see the wagon team. The mules must have broken loose from the wagon when it crashed. They were probably still running toward Deadwood.

Those outlaws were crafty varmints, Chloride thought. They had dragged that deadfall up by the trail and then left it there as a distraction for the guards on the wagon, and all the while they were hidden in the trees on the other side of the creek, ready to ambush and hijack the gold shipment.

The old-timer counted eight men, all of them still masked and wearing their hats pulled low. He couldn't see enough of their faces to have even a hope of recognizing them. They went about their business with swift efficiency, and when they had transferred all the gold to their horses and the pack animals, one of the men reached under the long duster he wore and drew out a knife. Even in the gulch's gloom, the blade glittered.

The bodies of the three guards had also spilled out of the wagon when it overturned. They sprawled limply on the trail not far from the wrecked vehicle. In the concealment of the rocks, Chloride swallowed hard as he watched the man with the knife go over to Turley's body. He hooked the toe of his boot under Turley's shoulder and rolled the corpse onto its back, then knelt beside it. Sunlight flashed on the knife again as the man got to work.

And once again, Chloride closed his eyes tightly. He didn't have to watch to know what the man was doing. The tip of that razor-sharp blade would slice through Turley's forehead and cut a vertical line down it. Then, part of the way down that line, two more lines would be carved into Turley's skin, curving up on either side of the first wound to form a symbol that looked roughly like a pitchfork.

It was the bloody mark of the Deadwood Devils, the calling card of the gang that had descended on the Black Hills. Chloride had seen it before on bodies brought into Deadwood after previous robberies.

When the old-timer forced his eyes open, he saw that the outlaw with the knife had finished his grim work. The bodies of the three dead guards lay on their backs, their eyes pointed sightlessly toward the sky and blood seeping from the grotesque markings on their foreheads.

"What about the driver?" one of the men asked as the one who seemed to be in charge wiped his knife on Mitch Davis's shirt.

The man straightened and sheathed the weapon. "I told you, he's probably dead."

"But he might not be. We ought to take a look."

Chloride held his breath.

"No," the boss said. "If he's alive, we'll leave him that way."

"But he'll head for Deadwood and tell folks what happened."

"They'll find out soon enough. There'll be another wagon or a rider come along this trail before the day's over, more than likely. And it's pretty obvious what happened here, don't you think?"

The man who had wanted to search for Chloride shrugged his shoulders. "If you say so."

"I do say so," the boss snapped. "It might be better if the driver *is* still alive. Then he can tell what he saw here, and everybody in Deadwood will be even more afraid of us than they are now. We want everybody in this part of the country to know that if you cross paths with the Deadwood Devils . . . you're going straight to hell."

After what he had seen today, Chloride Coleman didn't doubt it a bit.

CHAPTER 2

"Place has changed quite a bit since the last time we were here," Scratch Morton said to Bo Creel as the two Texans rode along Deadwood's Main Street.

"What did you expect?" Bo asked. "The place was just a raw mining camp then. It had only been here a couple of months. It's a real town now. Not only that, but I remember hearing something about a big fire they had here a year or so ago that burned down some of the buildings. They've rebuilt since then. The saloon where Bill Hickok was shot isn't even there anymore."

"Well, *I* recollect we didn't find no gold when we were here before. So what are we doin' here now?"

Bo shrugged. "Everybody's got to be somewhere."

That was especially true of these two wandering sons of the Lone Star State. Best friends for fifty years, Bo and Scratch had met when they were both youngsters, so long ago Texas had still been part of Mexico . . . but not for much longer. That was during the middle of the Runaway Scrape, when Sam Houston's ragtag army and most of the Texican civilians had been fleeing from the inexorable advance of the dictator Santa Anna's forces. An even smaller and more ragtag group of volunteers had delayed the Mexicans by luring them into a siege of an old mission near San Antonio de Bexar, but a lot of scared people believed that was just postponing the inevitable.

Of course, it hadn't turned out that way. Houston's men, among them the barely-old-enough-to-shave Bo and Scratch, had won a stunning victory at San Jacinto, and Texas had become an independent republic for nine years before joining the Union.

Although they were still friends, Bo and Scratch had gone their separate ways after that monumental battle and might have lived out their lives like that if sickness hadn't claimed the lives of Bo's wife and their young children several years later. Heartbroken by the loss, Bo had wanted to be anywhere but Texas, and his friend Scratch, who hadn't settled down yet, had been glad to go with him.

Somehow or other, they had just kept on drifting ever since then. Through the long decades, they had been almost everywhere west of the Mississippi, had worked at a wide variety of mostly honest jobs, and had managed to stay out of jail except for every now and then when some lawman got overzealous.

Despite the fact that they were now in late middle-age, the rugged lives they had led meant both Texans were still vigorous, active men. Bo, who favored a black Stetson, a long black frock coat, and a string tie, reminded some people of a traveling preacher with his solemn face and graying hair. That is, until they caught a glimpse of the well-worn walnut grips of the Colt he wore holstered on his right hip.

There was no mistaking Scratch for any sort of sky

pilot, not with the gaudy, long-barreled, ivory-handled Remington revolvers he carried in fancy holsters. Scratch's big, cream-colored hat and fringed buckskin jacket gave him the look of a dandy. His hair under the hat was pure silver. If he hadn't been clean shaven, folks might have mistaken him for the famous buffalo hunter and showman William F. Cody.

"How are we fixed for dinero, Bo?" Scratch asked as he nodded toward a sign on a business building that said RED TOP CAFÉ.

"We have a little left from that poker game in Cheyenne," Bo replied.

"Enough for a good meal after a long ride?"

"Yeah, but I thought you wanted to start saving up our pesos so we could try to make it south to some place warmer before winter sets in."

"Well, I did," Scratch admitted. "It's hard on these old bones of mine to spend the cold months this far north. But I got to thinkin' . . . what are the chances we'll really come up with enough money to do that?"

Bo shook his head. "I don't know. You can't ever tell. We might find something that would make us some money."

"Yeah, and we might starve to death before then, too," Scratch pointed out. "So we might as well get us a good meal now and postpone that terrible end."

Bo laughed. Scratch was a creature of the moment, and he could usually find some way to rationalize giving in to whatever impulse gripped him. And it was true, too, that Bo was hungry and would enjoy an actual hot meal for a change, instead of the skimpy trail grub they'd been making do with.

"All right," he said as he reined his horse toward the café. "Reckon we might as well."

They rode over to the hitch rail in front of the café and dismounted. A low boardwalk ran in front of the buildings on this side of the street. The Texans stepped up onto it and were about to enter the place when they heard a commotion coming from inside.

"Blast it!" a man yelled. "I said I was havin' a kiss with my piece of pie, and I meant it!"

Bo and Scratch exchanged a glance. "Maybe we ought to find some other place to eat," Bo suggested.

"I don't think so," the silver-haired Texan shot back with a quick, eager grin. Before Bo could stop him or say anything else, Scratch pushed the door open and stepped inside.

Bo was well aware that his old friend had a tendency to rush into trouble. In this case, that was all right, because Bo had to admit he was curious about what was going on inside the Red Top Café, too.

As he came through the door, his gaze flicked back and forth and instantly took in the scene before him. The Red Top was a neatly kept place with a number of tables covered by checkered tablecloths. To the right was a lunch counter with stools along it. Behind the counter, a pass-through was cut into the wall between the dining room and the kitchen. Also on that wall were a blackboard with the day's menu and prices chalked on it and a couple of shelves with several pies and cakes sitting on them. A small wood-burning stove behind the counter kept a pot of coffee warm. Another stove squatted in the rear corner of the dining room, giving off enough heat to keep out the chill from the wind blowing outside.

Since the hour was getting close to the middle of the day, quite a few of the tables were occupied by men eating lunch. Some of the stools at the counter had been until recently, too, judging by the abandoned plates half-full of food and the men he saw standing back along the wall. Some of them were still clutching napkins, as if they had just gotten up and hurried out of harm's way.

"Harm's way" was a good description of the man who stood in front of the counter, glaring across it at the woman behind it. He was tall and broad shouldered, with heavy muscles that bulged the flannel shirt he wore. His thick legs were like the trunks of trees, and the lace-up work boots he wore were some of the biggest Bo had ever seen. The clenched fists at his side reminded Bo of hams. He wasn't sure if either of them would fit in a two-gallon pail. The man was hatless, revealing a tangled thatch of dark hair that fell forward over an ape-like brow. Dark beard stubble grew on the slab-like jaw he thrust out defiantly.

That was the monster Scratch was about to confront.

The giant rumbled, "Come on, Sue Beth. It's not gonna hurt you, and you know it. One kiss, that's all I'm askin'."

"And it's one more kiss than you're going to get, Reese Bardwell," the woman behind the counter shot back at him. "I'll sell you pieces of pie all day long if you want, but my kisses are not for sale, sir!"

Bardwell snarled and stepped closer to the counter. He lifted arms that were so long there was no place back there the woman called Sue Beth could avoid their reach.

Scratch's deep, powerful, commanding voice rang out. "Hold it right there, amigo." He didn't speak loudly, but everybody in the place heard what he said.

Bardwell sure did. The big man stiffened and slowly swung around. The glare on his face was as dark and ominous as a thundercloud.

"Are you talkin' to me, mister?" he demanded.

"You seem to be the only one in the place makin' a jackass of himself, so I reckon I am," Scratch said.

Bo hated to see it come to this. Bardwell towered over Scratch and probably was thirty years younger, too. But if Scratch hadn't stepped in, Bo would have had to. The blood of Texans flowed in their veins. Neither of them was going to stand by and do nothing while somebody was bothering a woman.

"Mister, you don't have to get mixed up in this," the woman said quickly. "This is between me and my customer."

Bardwell shook his shaggy head. "Not any more, it ain't. If this old rooster wants to horn in and start crowin', he's gonna have to pay the price." He took a step toward Scratch. "You know what happens to an old rooster, mister?"

"Why don't you tell me?" Scratch said coolly.

"He gets his neck wrung!"

The big man lunged at Scratch with surprising speed. Those ham-like hands reached for the silver-haired Texan's throat.

Scratch was pretty fast, too. He jerked to the side and lowered a shoulder, causing Bardwell's attempted grab to miss. He stepped closer to Bardwell. Scratch's right fist whipped up and out in a wicked blow that sank solidly into his opponent's midsection.

Unfortunately, Bardwell didn't even seem to feel it. He brought his right fist hammering down on top of Scratch's head. The big, cream-colored Stetson absorbed some of the blow's force, but it still landed plenty hard enough to drive Scratch to one knee. Bardwell reached down, grabbed Scratch's buckskin jacket, and hauled him up again. Scratch looked a little addled. He could hold his own in most fights and had been doing so for many, many years, but he had bitten off too big a chunk of hell this time.

Knowing that, Bo acted before his friend could get hurt too badly. He slipped his Colt from its holster, pointed it at Bardwell, and eared back the hammer.

That metallic sound was distinctive enough—and menacing enough—to make Bardwell freeze with one hand bunched in Scratch's coat and the other drawn back and clenched to deliver another thunderous blow.

"Let him go," Bo ordered.

Bardwell turned his head enough to give Bo a baleful stare. "Who're you?"

"His friend," Bo said. "Also the fella who's going to blow your kneecap apart with a forty-five slug in about two seconds if you don't let go of him and step back."

For a second Bo thought Bardwell was going to be stubborn enough that he'd have to go through with that threat. But then the hand holding up Scratch opened, and the Texan slumped against the counter. The woman reached across it to take hold of his arm and steady him while he got his feet under himself again.

"This was none of your business," Bardwell said, "but you made it that way. You'd best remember that."

"I'm not likely to forget," Bo said. "Have you paid the lady for whatever you ate?"

"I'm not gonna—"

Bo's voice cut across the angry protest. "Have you paid the lady?"

"He doesn't owe me anything," the woman said.

Bo nodded. "Then I'd suggest you mosey on out of here, friend."

"I ain't your friend," Bardwell said. "You'd better remember that."

"I can live with that . . . as long as you leave."

Bo stepped back to cover Bardwell as the giant stomped past him and out of the café. He moved to the door and watched as Bardwell moved off down Main Street. Bo didn't pouch his iron until he felt fairly sure Bardwell wasn't coming back.

He turned as he slid the gun into leather. Scratch had regained his wits and had his hat in his hands, pushing it back into shape where Bardwell's fist had partially flattened it.

Scratch's face was set in an accusing frown. "You didn't have to do that, Bo," he said. "I had things under control. I was about to give that big varmint his needin's."

"I know that," Bo said. "I just didn't want you to have all the fun by yourself."

The woman behind the counter said, "That's your idea of fun? If I didn't already know it from your accents, I'd know you were Texans from your sheer knuckleheadedness!"

"You're welcome," Scratch said. "We were glad to step in and help you, ma'am."

"You mean stick your interfering noses in where they weren't needed, don't you?" She gestured toward the stove and the coffeepot. "I was about to give Reese a faceful of hot coffee. He'd have behaved himself after that, I can promise you!"

She was in her thirties, Bo estimated, with work-roughened hands and enough lines in her face to show that life hadn't always treated her kindly. Thick auburn hair was pulled into a bun on the back of her head and pinned into place.

Bo thumbed his hat back and said, "Sorry if we added to the problem, ma'am. We were just trying to help."

Her expression softened a little. "Oh, I know that. And I suppose I appreciate it. It's just that this isn't the first time Reese has gotten a mite frisky. He's troublesome at times, but he's not really a bad sort. I've always been able to handle him. I just hope this doesn't make him turn really mean."

One of the customers drifting back to the plate of food he had left on the counter spoke up, saying, "Calling Reese Bardwell troublesome at times is being mighty generous, Sue Beth."

Another man said, "And if he's not really mean already, I don't want to be anywhere around when he is."

The woman nodded and said to Bo and Scratch, "See, that's what I mean. He's got a bad reputation around here, and some would say it's well deserved." She shook her head and wiped her hands on her apron. "I expect you want some lunch?"

"Yes, ma'am," Scratch said. "We'd be obliged."

"You will be, to the tune of a dollar each."

Scratch frowned. "That's a little steep, ain't it?"

"Deadwood is a mining town. Everything costs a little more here."

One of the diners put in, "And it's worth it, mister.

Sue Beth dishes up the best food since Aunt Lou Marchbanks quit the Grand Central and went to work cooking for the crew out at the Father De Smet mine."

"Go on with you, Hal," Sue Beth said. "You're just angling for an extra piece of pie."

"But without a kiss," the man said with a grin. "I wouldn't mind, you understand, but I imagine my wife would."

Sue Beth laughed, then pointed at a couple of empty stools in front of the counter and told Bo and Scratch, "You two sit down. I'll get you some coffee." As she fetched a pair of empty cups, she called through the pass-through to the cook, "I need two more lunches, Charlie."

Bo and Scratch sat down and took off their hats. Things were getting back to normal in the café now that the ruckus was over. As Sue Beth poured the coffee, Scratch said, "We ain't been properly introduced, ma'am. My name is Scratch Morton, and this here is my friend Bo Creel."

Sue Beth smiled. "Your mother actually named you Scratch, Mr. Morton?"

"Well, uh . . . no, ma'am. But it's been so long since I used my real name that I sort of disremember what it is. I can try to dredge it up if you want."

"No, that's all right." She looked at Bo. "And I suppose your name is short for Beauregard."

"No, ma'am," he told her. "It's just plain Bo, B-O. My pa liked the sound of it."

"I see. What brings you boys all the way up here to Dakota Territory from Texas?"

"Oh, we didn't come here straight from Texas,"

Scratch said. "We were in Colorado for a while, and then we decided to ride on up this way for a while."

"We tend to drift around a little," Bo added. "Never stay in one place for too long."

"Saddle tramps, in other words," Sue Beth said.

Bo shrugged. "Call it what you will. It seems to suit us, and has for a long time."

"Yeah, only this time we plumb forgot that you don't head north durin' the autumn," Scratch said. "We're like little birdies. We usually fly south for the winter."

"You'll get plenty of winter here if you wait a few weeks," Sue Beth said. "By the way, I'm Susan Elizabeth Pendleton. Sue Beth to my friends. You can call me Mrs. Pendleton."

"You're married?" Scratch asked. He couldn't quite keep the disappointment out of his voice.

"I was. My husband worked in one of the mines. He was killed by the smoke and poison gas when a fire broke out underground a couple of years ago."

"We're mighty sorry to hear that," Bo said.

Scratch nodded and said, "We sure are."

"Thank you."

To change the subject, Bo said, "I was wondering about something. The name of this place is the Red Top Café, but the roof's not red."

Sue Beth smiled and pointed to her auburn hair. "It's named after me, not the building. It was my husband Tom's idea."

"Oh. Well, it's a good one."

The face of a scrawny old-timer appeared at the pass-through. He pushed a couple of plates across it and said, "Here's those two lunches, Sue Beth."

"Thanks, Charlie," she told him as she turned and

picked up the meals. She set them in front of Bo and Scratch, who practically licked his chops. Bo didn't blame him. The thick slices of ham, the mounds of potatoes, and the biscuits dripping with butter and gravy looked and smelled delicious.

Before they could dig in, though, shouting erupted in the street outside. Bo and Scratch turned to look as one of the men at a table close to the door stood up and opened it so the customers in the café could hear better. The shouts had a frantic, frightened quality to them.

"What is it?" Sue Beth asked. "Trouble at one of the mines?"

Scratch said, "It sounds to me like preachin'. Somebody's hollerin' about the Devil."

Bo happened to be looking at Sue Beth Pendleton as Scratch spoke. All the color washed out of the woman's face, and she looked as scared as the people outside sounded.

"Not just one devil," Sue Beth said. "A whole gang of them. The Deadwood Devils must have struck again."

CHAPTER 3

"The Deadwood Devils," Bo repeated. "Doesn't sound like a very friendly bunch."

Sue Beth shook her head. "They're not. They're outlaws who have been causing trouble around here for the past few months. They've held up stagecoaches, hijacked gold shipments, and murdered at least a dozen men that we know of."

"Are you sure it's the same bunch doin' all that?" Scratch asked.

"We're sure," Sue Beth replied with a grim nod. "The Devils make sure we know. Any time they kill somebody, they carve a pitchfork on his forehead, right here."

She tapped a fingertip against the center of her forehead.

Bo frowned and said, "I've heard of people doing things like that, but it's usually vigilantes who are trying to warn lawbreakers what's going to happen to them."

"Same thing, in a way," Scratch said. "They want to keep folks scared."

"It's working," Sue Beth said as she wiped her hands on her apron again and walked down to the end of the counter. She moved aside a swinging gate there and stepped out. "I want to see what's happened now."

Scratch was on his feet. "We'll join you."

"But your lunches—"

"They'll keep," Bo said. He, Scratch, and Sue Beth headed for the door along with most of the other customers inside the café. In a frontier town like Deadwood, any news always attracted a lot of attention.

As they stepped out onto the boardwalk, Bo saw a crowd of people gathering in front of an impressive, two-story frame building across the street. A large sign stuck out from the front of the building above the boardwalk. It read BANK, and in smaller letters below that single word, STEBBINS, POST & CO. People seemed to be clustered around someone. Through a gap in the crowd, Bo caught a glimpse of a short man with a white beard and a mane of equally snowy hair.

Sue Beth saw the man, too, and exclaimed, "That's Chloride Coleman!"

"Who's he?" Scratch asked.

"An old-timer who drives for the Argosy Mining Company. I don't see his wagon anywhere on the street, though."

"Carries gold shipments, does he?" Bo asked.

"That's right."

"And delivers 'em to that bank across the street, I'll bet," Scratch said. "Reckon he got held up, Bo?"

"He must have, to cause this much commotion," Bo said. "You want to go see what we can find out?"

Scratch shrugged. "I'm a mite curious." He turned

to Sue Beth. "You reckon you could put our plates on the stove to stay warm, ma'am?"

"Why do you care about a robbery?" she asked. "It's no business of yours." Then she shook her head and went on, "Sorry, I forgot I was talking to Texans."

Scratch just grinned, and Bo said, "We'll be back in a few minutes."

They headed across the street to join the crowd that had formed around the old man on the boardwalk. Chloride Coleman wore faded and patched denim trousers, an equally hard-used flannel shirt, and a buckskin vest. An empty holster sagged on his right hip. He had several bloody scratches on the leathery skin of his face and hands and obviously had run into some trouble.

"—all three of 'em dead!" he was saying in a voice that cracked a little with age. "And I come mighty close to sayin' howdy to Saint Peter my own self!"

"You're certain it was the Devils of Deadwood Gulch who attacked you?" asked a tall, portly man in a tweed suit. He didn't have much hair on top of his head, but a pair of huge muttonchop whiskers framed his florid cheeks.

"Devils of Deadwood Gulch, Deadwood Devils, call 'em whatever you want to," Coleman replied. "It was that same bunch of murderin' skunks, no doubt about it! I seen 'em carvin' pitchforks on Turley, Berkner, and poor ol' Mitch Davis. The bodies are still out there on the trail, along with the wrecked wagon. You can go look for yourself if you want, Mr. Davenport."

The whiskered man shook his head. "No, I'll leave it to the undertaker and his helpers to collect the bodies. You can't blame me for being a bit puzzled, though, Chloride. As far as I know, you're the first victim of a robbery that the Devils have allowed to remain alive."

Coleman puffed up and started to sputter. "You're . . . you sayin' I was in on it? That I'm workin' with them no-good murderin' polecats?"

"No, no, not at all," Davenport said quickly in the face of the old-timer's wrath. "As I told you, I'm just puzzled. Why do you think they left you alive?"

"I done told you! That fella who done the carvin', he was like Satan his own self. He wanted me to come here and tell ever'body in town what happened. He wants ever'body to be scared of that bunch."

One of the bystanders said, "I sure as blazes am! It's not safe to travel any of the roads around here anymore."

"And how can the mines keep going if they can't get their ore and dust to the bank?" a woman in a sunbonnet asked. "If the mines go under, my husband will be out of a job!"

A wave of angry, agitated muttering rose from the crowd. Davenport lifted his hands and motioned for quiet. When the people had settled down a little, he said, "The mines aren't going under, and neither are the banks. At least, this one won't as long as I'm the manager of it!"

"But if somebody doesn't stop those outlaws—" a man began.

"Someone *will* stop them," Davenport insisted. "I'm sure of it. The Black Hills aren't as lawless as they were four years ago when Deadwood was founded. It's just a matter of time—"

"Just a matter of time until the Devils kill us all!" another man shouted. That set the crowd off again. Davenport motioned for an end to the hubbub, but the noisy crowd ignored him.

That lasted until a tall, hawk-faced man in a brown suit and Stetson strode up and said in a loud, clear, commanding voice, "All right, settle down, you people! There's no need for all this commotion."

Despite the fact that the day was chilly, Davenport pulled a handkerchief from his pocket and wiped it over his face as an uneasy quiet settled on the crowd. "Thank God you're here, Sheriff," he said to the newcomer. "The gold shipment from the Argosy Mine has been stolen."

Bo saw the badge on the hawk-faced man's vest now. The lawman said to Coleman, "You look like you've been through the wringer, Chloride. What happened?"

"Well, we was comin' down Deadwood Gulch," the old-timer began. Bo and Scratch listened attentively as Coleman went through the story of the robbery, ending with, "After they rode off, I checked on the guards, hopin' one of 'em might still be alive, but really, I knowed better. When I was sure they was all dead, I hotfooted it for town as fast as these ol' legs of mine'll carry me. I thought maybe I'd find that mule team, but I reckon the dang jugheads wandered off up one of the little side gulches."

The sheriff nodded. "I can send a search party to look for them, although the bosses out at the Argosy might want to do that since technically the mules belong to them. John Tadrack can fetch the bodies in and see to them."

"What about the outlaws, Sheriff?" Davenport asked. "Are you going to put together a posse to look for them?"

Instead of answering directly, the lawman looked at Coleman and asked, "How far out did this happen, Chloride?"

"'Bout four miles, give or take," Coleman answered.

The sheriff turned back to Davenport. "In the time it took Chloride to hoof it into town, those owlhoots are long gone, I'm afraid. I'll ride out there and see if I can pick up their trail, of course, but I wouldn't hold out much hope of that doing any good."

Davenport's face, which seemed to be flushed normally, darkened even more as blood rushed into it angrily. "Blast it, Sheriff, the community's in an uproar, and the very basis of the area's economy is threatened. You have to do something about it!"

The sheriff smiled thinly and said in a dry voice, "As I was coming up the street, didn't I hear you assuring these good folks that the Deadwood Devils will be found and stopped? Maybe you should just be patient and let me go on about the business of doing that."

Davenport looked like he was going to argue some more, Bo thought, but then the banker gave a grudging nod and said, "All right. But this situation is becoming intolerable."

The lawman didn't respond to that. He put a hand on Coleman's shoulder instead. "Come on down to the office with me, Chloride. I want you to tell me everything you remember about the men who held you up and killed those guards."

"Well, I'll try," Coleman said. "It ain't gonna

amount to much, though. I never got a good look at anybody's face."

"Maybe something else will help, like the clothes they wore or the horses they rode."

Coleman looked skeptical, but he allowed the sheriff to lead him away. With the old-timer gone, the crowd started to break into smaller groups that continued to discuss this latest outrage. Clearly, the citizens of Deadwood were upset and scared.

Bo and Scratch crossed the street again to the café. The Red Top's customers had gone back inside, and so had its namesake. Sue Beth was behind the counter again. She took the Texans' plates off the stove and put them in front of a pair of empty stools.

"This time you'd better go ahead and eat," she warned, "or I'm liable to be insulted." She got the coffeepot and warmed up their coffee. "Is Chloride all right? He's a likable old cuss."

"He was just scratched and shaken up," Bo said.

"From the sound of it, though, he came pretty close to crossin' the divide," Scratch added.

"Did the Devils hold up the Argosy gold wagon?"

Bo nodded. "That's right." He gave Sue Beth an abbreviated version of the story Coleman had told the sheriff.

"Seemed like there were some hard feelin's between the sheriff and that banker fella, Davenport," Scratch put in.

"Jerome Davenport knows that if things keep on like they have been, the bank may not be able to stay open," Sue Beth said. "It relies heavily on the gold deposits from the Argosy, the Homestake, the Father De Smet, and the other big mining operations in the area."

"Have shipments from all the mines been hit?" Bo asked.

Sue Beth thought about it, obviously going over in her mind the previous robberies by the gang. After a moment she nodded and said, "Now that the Argosy has lost a shipment, too, yes, all the big mines have been hit."

"How do the varmints know when gold is bein' shipped out?" Scratch wondered.

"It's not that difficult," Bo said. "With all these hills around, put some men with spyglasses on top of them and keep an eye on the mines. They'd be able to see when wagons were being loaded."

"Why don't they try some decoy shipments?"

Bo shook his head. "I don't know. Maybe they have." He looked at Sue Beth. "Have you heard anything about that?"

"No, but the mine owners and superintendents don't confide their plans in me," she said. "Now, are you going to dig into that food or just flap your gums over it all day?"

Scratch picked up his fork and grinned. "We're diggin' in, ma'am, don't you worry about that," he assured her.

Even though they weren't as hot as they had been earlier, the meals were still very good. Bo and Scratch ate hungrily and enjoyed every bite. Sue Beth's coffee was even better, strong and black just the way the Texans liked it. When they finally pushed their empty plates and cups away, Bo dug a couple of silver dollars out of his pocket and slid them across the counter to Sue Beth, who came along and scooped the coins up deftly, dropping them in a pocket in her apron.

"Thank you," she said. "I hope you'll come again."

"As long as you're servin' up food like that, Miz Pendleton, I reckon you can count on it," Scratch told her.

He and Bo left the café. Once they were outside, Scratch went on. "How much money do we have left now?"

"Enough to feed and stable our horses for a few nights."

"How about feedin' and stablin' *us*?"

Bo grunted. "You may have to make up your mind whether you want them to have something to eat and a place to stay, or if we do."

Scratch winced. "That bad, huh?"

Bo frowned in thought. "Yeah, but I may have an idea how to change that."

"I hope you ain't plannin' on us robbin' the bank. From the sound of it, there ain't much in there."

"No, we're not going to turn outlaw. I had something else in mind." Bo pointed to a building he had spotted down the street.

"What's in there?" Scratch wanted to know.

"The offices of the Argosy Mining Company."

CHAPTER 4

"Wait just a doggone minute," Scratch said as he followed Bo toward the mining company office. "What'd you have in mind?"

"Maybe the Argosy will offer a reward for anybody who can find those outlaws and recover the gold they lost," Bo suggested.

"You mean we're gonna be bounty hunters?" Scratch shook his head. "We've tried that before, Bo. It never works out too good."

"Always a first time for everything."

"Yeah . . . like gettin' our fool selves killed. I swear, Bo, sometimes it seems like you're gettin' even more reckless than I am in your old age. Folks look at you and think you're the sober, responsible one, but they just don't know."

Bo just smiled.

The offices of the Argosy Mining Company were housed in a two-story building even more substantial-looking than the bank. For one thing, it was constructed of brick, one of several brick buildings that now stood along Deadwood's Main Street and Sherman Street, the two principal thoroughfares. When the Texans had first visited the place, back in its mining camp days, Deadwood had consisted of tents, tarpaper shacks, and a few hastily thrown-together buildings of raw, splintery boards. The presence of brick buildings showed just how much it had changed, how respectable it had gotten.

But with the arrival of the Deadwood Devils, the same sort of wild lawlessness that had plagued the area back then had cropped up again. No wonder folks were upset. Nobody wanted to go back to the way things had been.

When Bo and Scratch went in, they found themselves in an outer office with a desk in front of a railing and two more desks behind it, along with a couple of doors. A man in a suit and a stiff collar sat at the desk with a number of papers in front of him. He looked up with an impatient glance at the Texans and said, "Yes? What can I do for you?"

"Is your boss around?" Bo asked.

The superior curl of the man's lip came as no surprise. "If you're looking for a job at the mine, you'll have to ride out there and speak to the superintendent," he said. "We don't hire any laborers here."

"We're not looking to swing a pickax, sonny," Bo said, keeping a tight rein on his temper. More and more, he and Scratch ran into these prissy, soft-handed types who would have been more at home back East somewhere, rather than out here on the frontier. But, as he had mentioned to Scratch as they were riding into Deadwood earlier, everybody had to be somewhere.

"Then what is your business with Mr. Nicholson?" the man wanted to know.

"He's the owner of the Argosy Mining Company?"

"He's the president," the clerk replied with barely suppressed annoyance. "And he's not accustomed to dealing with the likes of you."

Scratch grinned, but it wasn't a very pleasant expression as he leaned over the desk and placed his hands flat down. "You're kind of a snippy little cuss, ain't you?" he asked.

The clerk drew back and paled, although he already had such a pallor it was hard to be sure he lost even more color. He looked like he realized his arrogance might have gone too far.

But before he could say anything, the door to one of the inner offices behind him opened, and a man stepped out. He stopped short at the sight of Bo and Scratch and said in a loud, rumbling voice, "You two again!"

Bo and Scratch found themselves staring in surprise at the massive Reese Bardwell, who they had tangled with in the Red Top Café. Scratch straightened from his pose leaning over the frightened clerk's desk and said softly, "Well, this is an interestin' turn of events, ain't it, Bo?"

"Take it easy," Bo advised his old friend. "One ruckus a day with a fella ought to be enough."

Bardwell stalked forward. "What are you doin' here?" he demanded. "Did you follow me?"

"Mister, you're just about the last hombre we expected to see in here," Bo said. "We're looking for the boss." He glanced at the clerk. "Nicholson, right?"

"I'm Lawrence Nicholson," a new voice said. A man who had come out of the office behind Bardwell stepped around him. Bardwell was so big Bo and Scratch hadn't seen the other man until now. Dressed in a sober dark suit, he was around fifty, with a mild face, thinning gray hair, and deep-set dark eyes.

"Yes, sir, if you're the president of the company, you're the man we want to see," Bo said. "It's about that gold shipment of yours that got stolen today."

Bardwell clenched his huge fists and started forward. "You two had something to do with that?" he said. "I might've known it!"

Nicholson put a hand on Bardwell's arm to stop him. Bardwell was almost twice the other man's size, but he stopped when Nicholson touched him.

"Take it easy, Reese. I hardly think these gentlemen would just waltz right in here like this if they'd had anything to do with the robbery."

"That's right," Scratch said. "We ain't loco. And we ain't road agents, neither."

"Then why *are* you here?"

Bo said, "We thought you might be offering a reward for tracking down the gang that's been pulling these holdups."

Bardwell made a face like he had just bitten into a rotten apple. "Bounty hunters," he said.

Bo shook his head. "No, not really. We're just a couple of fellas who are down on our luck and short on funds. But we've done quite a bit of tracking in our time, and we thought we might have some luck.

That would help you out, Mr. Nicholson, and us, too, maybe."

"Only if you could also find the gold that the Argosy lost today," Nicholson said. "I'm as interested in that as I am in bringing the thieves to justice."

"Likely they ain't had a chance to spend any of it yet," Scratch pointed out. "If they've been hittin' as many shipments as we've heard about, they've probably got a whole passel of loot cached somewhere."

"It's the sheriff's job to track down those owlhoots," Bardwell snapped.

"Yes, well, Henry Manning hasn't done a very good job of that so far, has he?" Nicholson asked crisply. He put his hands in his trouser pockets and regarded Bo and Scratch intently. "I've got a good mind to take a chance on these men, Reese. You obviously know them, though, and if you're opposed to the idea, I'll bow to your judgment."

Scratch gestured toward Bardwell with his left hand and asked, "Just who is this big galoot, anyway, for you to be askin' his opinion?"

Nicholson smiled. "I got the impression you were already well acquainted with each other. Reese Bardwell is the chief engineer and superintendent of the Argosy mine."

Bo and Scratch couldn't stop the looks of surprise that appeared on their faces. After their encounter in the Red Top Café, Bo never would have pegged Bardwell as being smart enough to hold down such an important job. The big man looked barely intelligent enough to swing a sledgehammer or a pickax.

Bardwell seemed to enjoy their reaction. He sneered and said, "I'd be leery of hirin' them if I was you, Mr. Nicholson. They jumped me while I was having lunch in Mrs. Pendleton's café. That one in the fancy jacket attacked me, and the other one threatened me with a gun."

"That's terrible." Nicholson sighed and shook his head. "I'm sorry, gentlemen. But I can't go against the wishes of Mr. Bardwell in this matter. Maybe you can get the sheriff to sign you on as deputies. Sheriff Manning could use some competent help."

"You're sure?" Bo asked.

Nicholson shrugged again. "Sorry."

A triumphant grin spread across Bardwell's craggy face. The skinny clerk at the desk looked pleased, too. Bo felt a surge of anger but controlled it. Folks had a right to hire, or not hire, whoever they wanted to . . . even when they were wrong.

Bo's natural courtesy prompted him to touch a finger to the brim of his black hat. "I reckon we'll be going, then," he said.

"But, Bo—" Scratch began.

"Come on. There's nothing for us here."

Bardwell laughed harshly. "That's for damned sure."

When they were back on the street, Scratch said, "Now what?"

"Now we see if the livery stable owner is willing to let us sleep in the hayloft for a little bit extra if we keep our horses there," Bo said.

A few years earlier, sleeping space had been at a premium in Deadwood. The liveryman could have asked five dollars a night for the right to stretch out in the hay, and fortune-seekers eager to search for gold would have paid it gladly.

Now that things had settled down a little, the situation had changed. The elderly liveryman was agreeable to the arrangement Bo proposed. For an extra four bits a night, the Texans would have a place to sleep, even though they might have to share it with bugs and rats.

It wouldn't be the first time.

"We still got to eat," Scratch pointed out after he and Bo had left their mounts at the stable. "You reckon Miz Pendleton might let us have a few meals on the cuff?"

"She might," Bo said, "but I don't want to ask her. I never have liked being beholden to anybody."

"Me, neither," Scratch agreed. "Do we offer to wash dishes?"

Bo laughed. "It may come to that. Let's not give up just yet, though. There are other mining companies in Deadwood, and some of them have lost gold shipments, too. Maybe one of them would like to hire a couple of trackers."

"Worth a try," Scratch agreed.

They spent the afternoon going from office to office, but with no luck. Although the reception they got at the other companies wasn't as hostile as the one at the Argosy, no one was willing to hire them to try to track down the Deadwood Devils.

"That's the sheriff's job," they were told more than once.

The Texans were coming out of the office of the Black Hills Bonanza Mining Company when they almost ran into a smaller figure scurrying along the boardwalk. Bo put out a hand to steady the little white-bearded man, who he recognized as Chloride Coleman.

"Take it easy there, old-timer," Bo said, which drew an angry snort from Coleman.

"Who're you callin' old-timer? A few more years and your hair'll be just as white as mine, mister." Coleman jerked a thumb at Scratch. "His already is."

"My hair's silver," Scratch corrected. "Not white."

Coleman snorted again. "You still ain't that much younger'n me, and don't you forget it. Now step aside. I got business to tend to."

Bo inclined his head toward the door. "With the Black Hills Bonanza?"

"That's right." Coleman drew himself up to his full height, which was still a head shorter than the Texans'. "I got to see if they want to hire the best dang gold wagon driver in the whole blasted Dakota Territory."

"I thought you worked for the Argosy Mining Company," Bo said.

Coleman grimaced and for a moment looked like he was trying to chew a particularly tough piece of meat. Finally he said, "Not that it's any o' your business, mister, but word got back to Mr. Nicholson that that rascal Davenport over to the bank was askin' questions about how come the Devils didn't kill me like they have ever'body else they've held up. Must've got him nervous, 'cause he decided they could dispense with my wagon-drivin' services, as he put it." Coleman turned his head and disgustedly spat a stream of tobacco juice into the street.

"That's a shame," Scratch said. "We're outta work,

too, and been tryin' to hire on with one of the companies to track down those road agents."

"None of 'em hired you, did they?" Coleman guessed.

"Not yet," Bo said. "There's one more left, though."

"Which one's that?"

"The Golden Queen."

Coleman shook his head. "You don't want to work for that outfit. Take my word for it."

"Why not?" Scratch asked.

"For one thing, it's about to go under. It's been hit harder than any of the other companies. The fellas who work for the Golden Queen been gettin' by on promises instead o' wages for nigh on to a month now."

Bo rubbed his chin as he thought. "Maybe what we should do is try to find those outlaws first, and then find somebody who's willing to pay us for what we know."

"How do we eat in the meantime?" Scratch asked.

Bo sighed. "I don't like to say it, but maybe we could ask Mrs. Pendleton for some credit after all."

"Sue Beth Pendleton?" Coleman piped up. "That there is one handsome woman, lemme tell you. Serves up a mighty fine helpin' of vittles, too. Feisty, though. Mighty feisty. Darned shame about her husband Tom. He was a good fella."

Bo nodded. "Yeah, she told us about him getting killed. Something else I was thinking about, Mr. Coleman—"

"Call me Chloride," the old-timer interrupted. "Ever'body does. And come to think of it, you ain't told me your names. I know you're from Texas 'cause of the way you talk, but that's all I know about you."

"I'm Scratch Morton, and this here is Bo Creel," Scratch supplied.

Chloride nodded. "Pleased to meet you. Now, what was you sayin', Bo?"

Bo said, "I was just thinking that if we do decide to see if we can pick up the trail of those robbers, it might be helpful if you'd ride with us out to the place where they held you up. You could show us exactly where things happened."

Chloride scratched at his beard. "I dunno . . . I got some bad memories o' that place."

"It just happened today," Scratch pointed out.

"Well, they're still memories, ain't they? They ain't happenin' now!"

"We could cut you in on whatever reward we got out of it," Bo suggested, sensing that that might have some bearing on Chloride's reluctance to help them.

The avarice that instantly glittered in the old man's rheumy eyes told Bo his hunch was right. Chloride nodded and said, "I might could do that. If I got time, that is, once I get a new job."

"All right. We can find you around town?"

"Yeah, for a day or two, anyway, I expect. Where are you boys stayin'?"

"Hanson's Livery," Scratch said with a grin.

"The penthouse suite," Bo added.

Chloride laughed. "Beddin' down in the loft, eh? Well, I can't say I never did the same. So long!"

He went on in the Black Hills Bonanza office while the Texans headed along the street toward the office of the Golden Queen.

"You reckon there's any point in this, if the mine's as bad off as Chloride said?" Scratch asked.

"It might not be as bad as he thinks," Bo said. "Anyway, it won't hurt to go in there and ask."

When they reached the small, one-story clapboard building with the simple legend GOLDEN QUEEN MINING COMPANY painted on its front window, Scratch frowned and said, "Don't look too promisin'. This place ain't near as fancy as the Argosy or some of the other minin' companies."

"You can't always tell by looking," Bo said as he grasped the doorknob and turned.

They stepped inside, and Bo was somewhat surprised to see a young woman sitting at a desk, writing in a ledger. Blond curls fell loosely around her shoulders. Without looking up from what she was doing, she asked, "Yes?"

Bo took his hat off and said, "Pardon me, miss, we're looking for whoever's in charge of the Golden Queen Mining Company."

That made her lift her head so that Bo could see her face. It was a mighty attractive face, too, with a faintly exotic cast to it, highlighted by a small beauty mark on her cheek near the right corner of her mouth.

"That would be me," she said. "I *am* the Golden Queen Mining Company."

CHAPTER 5

Bo managed to keep the surprise off his face, although Scratch stared a little. "You own the company?" Bo asked.

"That's right," the young woman said. "I'm Martha Sutton. What can I do for you?"

"Well, I, uh, beg your pardon, miss, but we weren't expecting—"

"Weren't expecting to find a *girl* in charge of a mining company?" she broke in. "You're not the only one. Some other people in this town seem to have a problem with that, too. That's just too bad."

"I never said we had a problem with it," Bo went on quickly. "It's just a little surprising, that's all. My name's Bo Creel, and this is my friend Scratch Morton."

Scratch snatched his hat off and nodded politely. "Pleased to meet you, ma'am," he said.

The look of irritation on Martha Sutton's face eased a bit. She said, "Mr. Creel, Mr. Morton . . . I ask again, what can I do for you?"

"We're new in town, and we've been hearing about

the Deadwood Devils and how they've been holding up gold shipments from the mines around here," Bo explained. "Has that happened to your outfit?"

Martha set down the pencil she had been using and leaned back in her chair. "Not that it's any of your business, Mr. Creel, but yes, the Golden Queen has been robbed. Several times, in fact. The Devils have hit us probably more than any of the other mining operations around here."

"Us?" Bo repeated.

"My father founded the Golden Queen and ran it until about a month ago. That was when he died suddenly. His heart gave out, the doctor said, possibly from worrying about the holdups."

"We're sorry to hear that," Scratch said. "That'll happen sometimes when you've got a bum ticker."

"At any rate, that's why I'm running the company now," Martha said. "Our shipments have been hijacked several times since then, to the point that no one wants to drive for me anymore or hire on as guards because the others have been killed. The company is on the verge of collapse. Is that what you wanted to know?"

With all the bad luck that had befallen her, Bo couldn't blame Martha Sutton for being a little short-tempered. He said, "You've got us wrong, Miss Sutton. We'd like to help you."

"How are you going to do that?" she asked, wanting to know.

"If somebody could track down the Deadwood Devils and maybe even find all the loot they've stolen, I imagine it would make things look a lot more promising for the Golden Queen, wouldn't it?"

She regarded the Texans intently for a moment, then

said, "If you're angling for me to hire you and your friend as some sort of troubleshooters, Mr. Creel, I can't afford it. Right now I can't even pay the men working in the mine. I owe them a month's back wages, and it's all I can do to continue feeding them."

"If we were able to recover some of the gold you lost, how would you feel about cutting us in for a share?" Bo suggested.

Martha didn't reject the idea out of hand. Instead she considered it for a moment before finally nodding. "We could probably come to an arrangement like that," she said. "Ten percent of the value of whatever gold you recover."

Bo didn't like the idea of haggling with a woman, but he said, "I was thinking more along the lines of twenty percent."

"Ten's all I can afford," Martha said flatly.

"Well, in that case, ma'am, you got a deal," Scratch said before Bo could make a counteroffer. Bo glanced over at his old friend, who was grinning from ear to ear. Scratch never had been able to resist trying to please a pretty woman, even one who was young enough to be his daughter, or maybe even his granddaughter.

But to be honest, he probably would have agreed to the ten percent, too, Bo realized. If that was truly all Martha could afford, he wouldn't want to try to take advantage of her.

She stood up and came out from behind the desk, extending her hand to each of them in turn. She said, "I probably should have asked what your qualifications are to be hunting down gold thieves. Are you lawmen of some sort?"

"We've worked as deputies before," Bo explained. "Done some scouting for the army as well, so we have experience with tracking."

"Plus we've wound up in quite a few ruckuses with owlhoots that were none of our doin'," Scratch added. "We don't never go lookin' for trouble, but sometimes it seems like it looks for us."

"Well, if you find the Deadwood Devils, you can count on one thing," Martha said. "You'll find plenty of trouble, too. When are you going to start searching for them?"

Bo said, "It's too late in the day to pick up a trail today. First thing in the morning we'll ride out to the place where the Argosy gold wagon was held up today and see what we can find."

Martha made a face at the mention of the Argosy Mining Company, Bo noted.

"You and the folks at the Argosy don't get along?" he asked, making a shrewd guess.

"That's none of your business, Mr. Creel," she snapped. "You don't have to concern yourself with anything except finding the Devils and getting back as much of my gold as you can."

Bo nodded. "You're right, ma'am, we don't." He put his hat on. "Come on, Scratch."

They left Martha Sutton in the office. As they walked along the street, Scratch commented, "That's a pretty gal, but she's a mite prickly around the edges."

"I'd say she has reason to be, as much trouble as she's had. First those gold holdups, and then her pa dying, maybe because of them . . ." Bo shook his head in sympathy. "Meanwhile, we've got to eat tonight. I reckon I've got just enough money hidden away in my saddlebags to buy us a meal at the Red Top."

"You mean you been squirrelin' away dinero without tellin' me?"

"And it's a good thing, too," Bo said. "Otherwise we'd be going hungry tonight."

The fried steaks Sue Beth Pendleton and her cook Charlie dished up at the café were just as good as the ham at lunch had been. As the Texans were cleaning their plates and washing down the last of the food with coffee, Sue Beth paused on the other side of the counter and said, "I figured you boys would be back."

"With food this good, where else in town would we eat?" Scratch asked.

"And I figured you might ask me for credit," Sue Beth went on. "No offense, but you look a little down at the heels."

"We don't much believe in credit," Bo said. "We like to pay for what we get as we go along."

Sue Beth laughed. "If more people were like you, the world would probably be better off."

"We *are* runnin' a mite short, though," Scratch said. "But we got some work lined up that ought to help out."

"Well . . ." Sue Beth hesitated. "If you wind up needing a hand, you can always get a meal here. I don't believe in turning away a hungry man."

"It won't come to that," Bo said. "We'll be fine."

"Yeah," Scratch said. "We been makin' it for forty years now, so I reckon we'll get by a mite longer."

Sue Beth nodded. "I'm sure you will. But remember what I said." She smiled. "You remind me a little of my father, Mr. Morton. I couldn't let you starve."

"Well, I . . . uh . . ." Scratch fell silent for a moment before finally nodding his head and saying, "Thanks."

When the Texans left the café a short time later, Bo was smiling. He waited until they were outside and the door was closed behind them before he said, "That's the first time in a while I've seen you struck speechless."

"I don't know what you're talkin' about," Scratch said stiffly.

"The look on your face when Miz Pendleton told you that you remind her of her old pa . . . that was just priceless."

"She was payin' me a compliment," Scratch insisted.

"And telling you that you're really old," Bo said.

"Same age as you!"

"Difference is, I'm not denying it," Bo drawled.

Scratch muttered something under his breath, then said, "Dang it, let's just go to the livery stable, check on our horses, and turn in."

Bo nodded. "Sounds like a good idea to me."

When they got back to Hanson's Livery, though, they found someone waiting for them. Chloride Coleman was talking to a stocky Mexican who had taken over as the hostler on the night shift. Chloride raised a gnarled hand in greeting as he saw the Texans approaching.

"I figured you fellas'd show up here sooner or later, since you said you was stayin' here," he said. "I need to have a few words with you."

"Go ahead and palaver," Scratch told him.

Chloride licked his lips under the bushy white mustache. "Talkin' always goes better with a mite of lubrication, if you get my drift."

"If you want whiskey, you'll have to provide your own," Bo said. "We can't afford it."

"Oh, well." Chloride heaved a sigh. "You know what we was talkin' about earlier?"

"Which part?"

"The part about me helpin' you fellas track down the Deadwood Devils. You still interested in that?"

"Maybe," Bo allowed. "But I thought you were going to be too busy with your new job to give us a hand."

"Well, as it turns out, there ain't any openin's for drivers right now, so I got more time than I figured I would."

Based on what Martha Sutton had told them about the difficulty she had encountered in hiring drivers for the Golden Queen, Bo suspected the other mining companies in town were having the same trouble. Nobody wanted to risk his life serving as a target for the Deadwood Devils.

So the fact that Chloride couldn't get a job as a driver probably meant that word had gotten around town about Davenport's suspicions of him. Even though Bo instinctively believed the old-timer's story about the way the holdup had happened, the mine owners had to be worried that Chloride was tied in with the gang somehow. Otherwise under the circumstances they should have jumped at the chance to hire an experienced driver.

"We'd be pleased to have you ride out there with us in the morning, Chloride," Bo said. "You can help us take a look around and point out exactly where everything happened. But you know we can't pay you."

Chloride licked his lips again. "You could maybe cut me in on whatever reward you make out of the deal, though, couldn't you?"

Bo and Scratch looked at each other. Scratch shrugged his agreement. Bo said, "That's assuming we even make anything."

"Sure, sure, I understand that."

"Do you have a horse?"

"I got a mule. Ain't very comfortable for ridin', but it'll go all day."

"Is it here at the livery?"

Chloride shook his head. "No, I got a little shack up the gulch a ways. Some prospector must've had a claim there back in the old days, but he didn't find no color and abandoned the place." His bushy eyebrows rose as a thought obviously occurred to him. "Say, you boys could stay there if you want, and save a little money. You'd have to spread your bedrolls on the floor, but I wouldn't charge you nothin'."

Bo and Scratch shared a glance again. If they could get a refund from Hanson, they'd be able to eat for a few days longer without having to accept credit from Sue Beth Pendleton.

"That sounds like a good idea," Scratch said. He turned to the hostler. "What's your name, amigo?"

"Esteban Gonzalez, señor," the man replied.

"Well, Esteban, tell your boss we won't be needin' to stay here after all, and we'll be takin' our horses with us."

"He can take out for the feed he's already given them," Bo said, "but we'll expect the rest of our money back when we come by here in the morning."

Gonzalez looked doubtful. "I don't know, señores. Once Señor Hanson has money in his pocket, it is always very reluctant to come out again."

"Just tell him what we said," Bo requested. "We'll be by early."

The hostler sighed. "Sí, señor. I will tell him."

Bo and Scratch saddled their mounts and led them out of their stalls. "You can ride double with me, Chloride," Bo offered. He swung up into the saddle and helped the old-timer climb on behind him.

They rode out of Deadwood with Chloride giving them directions. Despite the town's façade of respectability during the day, at night it was obvious that this was still a mining town. The saloons were all busy as the Texans and their elderly companion rode past.

As they started up the gulch along Deadwood Creek, Bo said, "I've got an idea where you might be able to get a job as a driver, Chloride."

"Where's that? I tried ever'body in town."

"What about the Golden Queen?"

Chloride grunted. "Except that 'un! That's a hoodoo outfit, boys. Bad luck all around."

"Why do you say that?"

"Their wagons have been held up more'n any of the other mines, and besides, it's run by a gal! Women is bad luck. You been around long enough, you ought to know that."

"The only reason Miss Sutton's running the company is because her father died," Bo pointed out.

"Well, that proves my point right there, don't it? Ol' Mike Sutton just up and dropped dead one day. If that ain't a hoodoo, I don't know what is."

"Anything suspicious about his death?" Bo asked, apparently casually.

"Suspicious?" Chloride repeated. "Not that I ever heard anything about. Sutton was just walkin' along the street one day when he stopped and sorta grabbed his chest. He staggered along a couple more steps and then fell flat on his face. Doc said he was prob'ly dead when he hit the boardwalk. Heart gave out."

Bo nodded. "Yes, that's what Miss Sutton told us. Do you know where he'd been just before that happened?"

Chloride scratched his beard as he tried to remember. "Down at the bank, if I recollect right," he answered. "I think folks said he'd been talkin' to Jerome Davenport about extendin' him some money. The Devils had already hit a couple of his shipments, and he was already havin' trouble payin' the fellas who work for him."

"Davenport turned him down?"

Chloride leaned to the side and spat. "Davenport ain't got to worry about his heart ever givin' out. He ain't got one. I think there's a poke full of gold dust where it's supposed to be."

Scratch laughed. "Sounds like you ain't over fond of him."

"The varmint said he didn't suspect me of workin' with the Devils, but he sure made it sound like that's what he really thought."

"There's one really good way for you to prove that's not true," Bo said. "Help us catch them, and everybody in town will know you're not crooked, Chloride."

"Yeah, that's a pretty good idea, all right," the old-timer said. "Providin' that we don't get ourselves shot full of holes doin' it!"

CHAPTER 6

The old abandoned shack that Chloride had moved into was one step above a rat hole, but it wasn't a very big step. The walls were a shaky combination of scrap lumber, tin, and tarpaper. The cold wind penetrated through a number of cracks and gaps. But the roof was still fairly sturdy, Chloride claimed, and he hadn't fallen through the floor yet. He had a small stove for heat, an old barrel that served as a table and had a candle on it, and a narrow bunk. A rickety shed attached to the side of the shack provided shelter for the Texans' horses and Chloride's mule.

"See? All the comforts of home!" the old-timer declared proudly.

"Yeah, Bo and me woke up in a hog pen a while back, so this is better," Scratch said. "I guess."

They spread their bedrolls on the floor and went to sleep, since there was nothing else to do. It was a chilly night, a promise of much colder ones to come, but the Texans were fairly warm in their blankets. During their four decades of drifting, they had spent plenty of nights in places more uncomfortable than this one.

Despite that, they were both glad to get up the next morning and start moving around again. Stiff muscles protested at first but soon loosened up. Chloride had some coffee and a few stale biscuits. It wasn't much in the way of breakfast, but he was happy to share with the Texans.

After they had eaten, they saddled their horses and Chloride lifted an old saddle onto the bony back of his mule. On this cold, clear morning, smoke rose from dozens of chimneys in Deadwood, about half a mile down the gulch from the shack. They would have to come back this way when they set out to pick up the trail of the Deadwood Devils at the site of the latest robbery, but Bo and Scratch wanted to see about getting some of their money back from the livery owner.

As Esteban Gonzalez had predicted, Hanson was reluctant to turn loose any of the money he had collected from the Texans the day before. "When you make arrangements for accommodations, you're sorta bound by 'em," he claimed. "You wouldn't have wanted me to give you your money back last night and tell you you couldn't stay here after all, or your horses, either."

"We'd understand if there was a good reason," Scratch said.

"And we said you could take out whatever we owe for the grain you gave our horses," Bo added. "So you won't be losing any money on the deal."

Hanson gave a put-upon sigh and dug a hand into the pocket of his overalls. "I'll take out for feed and one night's lodgin' for the horses, since it was so late when you picked 'em up," he suggested. "That's fair, ain't it?"

It really hadn't been that late when they got their horses, but Bo nodded anyway and said, "Fine." He was ready to get started on the search for the Devils of Deadwood Gulch, and he knew Scratch was, too.

When they had settled with the liveryman, they rode out of town the same way they had ridden in, heading west along the gulch where Deadwood Creek flowed. Roughly paralleling it to the south lay Whitewood Gulch, formed by the creek of the same name. Four years earlier, miners had thronged to Whitewood Gulch as well and some of them had found gold there. Several successful mines had been established. Small camps had sprung up all over both gulches and the surrounding hills, but they had died out gradually as the town of Deadwood had grown in both size and importance until it was the main supply point for the entire area, as well as the center of banking and commerce for this part of the Black Hills.

The three riders passed by Chloride's shack and continued on up the gulch. The old-timer pointed out some small mining claims that were still being worked and said, "Most of the color's done gone from down here. The big mines are farther up. That's why it's a pretty good run into town when they want to bring their gold in. Lots of places betwixt here and there where the Devils can hide to ambush the shipments."

"Why don't the mines cooperate and go in together on their shipments?" Bo asked. "They could assemble a little wagon train and hire a couple of dozen guards."

Chloride nodded. "Yeah, that might work, but it'd

mean they'd have to get along, and they don't. Mining's been such a cutthroat business around here for so long, none of the owners trust each other. So they're tryin' to go it alone as long as they can."

"There's an old sayin' about cuttin' off your nose to spite your face," Scratch pointed out.

Chloride laughed. "Don't I know it! But that's the way it is in these parts."

So far during the ride, they hadn't met any wagons or even anyone on horseback. They could see smoke from chimneys and hear work going on at some of the claims they passed, but the trail seemed to be deserted. Bo commented on that.

"Folks are scared to ride out here," Chloride explained. "The Devils have killed more'n a dozen men so far. Nobody wants to be next."

"Yes, but have they ever jumped any solitary travelers?" Bo asked. "Or do they just rob stagecoaches and gold wagons?"

"Well . . . as far as I know, they've only gone after the coaches and the wagons. But maybe any lone pilgrims they massacred just ain't never been found. There are plenty of places in these hills where a body could disappear for good."

"They've never tried to hide their other victims, have they?"

Chloride shook his head. "Nope."

Scratch put in, "Seems to me like they want folks to find the poor varmints who run afoul of 'em. Otherwise what's the point of carvin' pitchforks in their foreheads?"

"Maybe so," Chloride said. "I don't know how some bunch of dang desperadoes thinks, because I ain't one of 'em! All I know is that folks are mighty leery about ridin' this trail these days because they don't want to wind up sportin' one of those bloody pitchforks!"

"Take it easy," Bo advised. "We believe your story about the robbery, remember? That's why we asked you to come with us. And you agreed to it. Aren't you worried about riding this trail, Chloride?"

The old-timer snorted in contempt. "It'll take more than them Devils to scare me off. I've seen and done plenty of things in my life, boys, and I ain't afraid to die."

"Neither am I," Scratch said, "but I wouldn't mind postponin' it as long as I can."

"Well, that's just common sense." Chloride leveled an arm and pointed. "We're comin' to the spot where those masked rannihans jumped the wagon yesterday. See the way somebody dragged that deadfall close to the trail up yonder? That's why the guards and I worried the Devils might be hidden behind it." He waved a hand toward the trees on the other side of the creek. "But they were lurkin' over there instead. Mighty clever of 'em."

"Where did the wagon turn over?" Bo asked. Deadwood's undertaker, John Tadrack, had been out here with his helpers and collected the bodies of the three slain guards, and somebody, probably from the Argosy Mine, had hauled off the wrecked and looted wagon, as well.

"Right there," Chloride answered, pointing again. "You can see some of the scrape marks in the dirt."

"Where did you land when you got thrown out?" Scratch wanted to know.

"Them bushes there to the left of the trail."

"Let's take a closer look," Bo said as he reined his horse to a halt.

The three men dismounted. Scratch handed his reins to Bo, then hunkered on his heels and closely studied the ground all around the spot where the wagon had crashed.

"If this is where the wagon turned over, this is where the Devils unloaded the gold from it as well, isn't it?" Bo asked the old driver.

Chloride nodded. "Yeah, that's right. I seen most of it from where I was hidin' there in the brush."

Scratch said, "The undertaker brought his wagon and helpers out here, and they all tramped around a heap. Same for whoever came after the gold wagon. There are too many tracks of men and horses both, Bo. I can't make no sense of 'em."

"What were you hopin' to find?" Chloride asked.

"Some distinctive prints," Bo explained. "Maybe one of the Devils was riding a horse with a shoe that's been nicked up so we'd recognize it if we saw it again. The same thing might be true of a man's boot print. But in this case there are too many tracks for that to do us any good. We don't have any way of knowing who they belong to."

Scratch straightened. "Maybe we ought to ride over to those trees where the bushwhackers hid. Might be something over there worth findin'."

"That's a good idea," Chloride said, "but hang on a minute first."

Without waiting to see if the Texans were going to agree to that request, Chloride scurried off into the brush where he had landed the day before, according to his story.

"You seein' a man about a dog in there, old-timer?" Scratch called after him. "We ain't got all day, you know."

"No, dagnab it, just wait a minute, will you?" Bo and Scratch stood there in the trail holding their horses' reins as they listened to Chloride rustling around in the bushes. After a moment, he let out an excited whoop. "I figured I might find 'em!"

"Find what?" Bo asked.

Chloride emerged from the brush carrying an old revolver in one hand and an even more ancient hat in the other. "I lost my hat and my gun when I got tossed off the wagon," he explained. "I was so shook up after watchin' what that boss Devil did to those poor dead fellas, I didn't think to look for 'em before I lit a shuck for town. That's one reason I agreed to come along with you boys today. I wanted to see if they were still here somewheres."

He checked the action on the cap-and-ball revolver and slid it into the empty holster he wore. Then he punched the old hat into shape—although to the Texans it seemed about as shapeless as before—and settled it on his head.

Chloride sighed in satisfaction and said, "That's better. I was feelin' plumb nekkid without my hat and my gun."

"That's somethin' nobody wants to see," Scratch said. "Come on."

They mounted up and rode along the trail until they were at the spot where the wagon had been when the road agents opened fire, between the deadfall on one side of the trail and the thick stand of trees on the other side of the creek. The stream flowed fast and cold over its rocky bed, but the water was shallow enough that the horses were able to splash across it without any trouble.

When they reached the trees, they swung down from their saddles again. Chloride held the reins of all three mounts this time while Bo and Scratch searched among the trees and examined the ground.

After a few minutes, Scratch reappeared with something in his hand. He held it out to show Chloride.

"Got a couple of hombres who smoke quirlies, and one who favors cheroots," the silver-haired Texan said as he displayed the remains of the smokes he had picked up.

Bo came out of the trees and added, "And at least one gent who prefers a pipe. I found where he knocked out the dottle."

"How about brass?" Scratch asked.

Bo nodded. "I saw quite a few cartridges. They didn't bother to pick up the empties when they left. Looked like standard forty-four-forty rounds, though."

"Yeah, same here. How about the horses?"

Bo nodded. "I can show you where they held them. Come on."

"That's more like it," Scratch muttered when he saw the welter of prints left by the horses while their owners were waiting for the Argosy gold wagon to come along. He knelt beside the tracks and studied them for long moments, filing away every detail, every nick and bent nail. Bo leaned over and peered at the hoofprints as well. His skill as a natural-born tracker wasn't quite as good as Scratch's, but he knew he would recognize some of those hoofprints if he saw them again.

"You reckon the Devils spend most of their time in Deadwood?" Scratch asked quietly.

"Sure," Bo said. "They probably have a hideout somewhere in the hills, but what good is a pile of stolen loot if all you do is squat in a cave somewhere all the time? Chloride said they were masked and that he never got a good look at their faces. Until now they've killed everybody they held up, so there weren't any witnesses left behind." Bo nodded confidently. "They're hiding in plain sight, I'll bet, right there in the middle of Deadwood."

Scratch grunted. "Probably pretendin' to be respectable citizens."

"I wouldn't doubt it a bit," Bo said. "Think you can follow their back trail from here?"

"Maybe. If we're right about them comin' from Deadwood, though, it won't do us much good. Chances are, they've got some rendezvous where they get together for their robberies, and from there the back trails'll scatter out all over hell and gone."

"Maybe the place where they rendezvous is the same place they cache their loot," Bo suggested.

A grin stretched across Scratch's face. "I didn't think about that. You might be right, Bo. It's sure worth checkin' out, anyway. Let's get Chloride and have a look."

"He may want to go back to Deadwood, since he's already shown us the site of the robbery."

"We can let him make up his mind about that."

They walked back through the trees and found the

old-timer where they had left him, still holding the two horses and the mule. "Any luck?" Chloride asked.

"We're going to try to follow their back trail," Bo explained. "Do you want to come with us, or would you rather go back to town?"

Chloride scratched his beard for a second, then said, "I'd just as soon go on with you fellas, if that's all right."

"Sure," Scratch said with a nod. He reached for the reins of his horse.

The sudden whipcrack of a rifle shot split the chilly morning air, and Chloride's hat leaped from his head into the air.

CHAPTER 7

Bo heard the slug sizzle between him and Scratch after it ripped through the old-timer's hat. His hand shot out, grabbed Chloride's arm, and swung him deeper into the trees.

"Hunt some cover!" Bo ordered.

More shots roared. Bo couldn't tell exactly where they were coming from, but at the moment that didn't really matter. The only important thing right now was finding shelter from the lead flying through the air around them.

Scratch snatched his hat off his head and slapped it across his horse's rump, causing the animal to take off running. Bo's horse and Chloride's mule followed. That put their mounts out of the line of fire.

But it also put the Texans' Winchesters out of reach, because the rifles were still in their saddle boots. They had their handguns and the extra ammunition they carried in their shell belts and pockets, but that was all.

Chloride had scrambled behind one of the tree trunks. Bo and Scratch hurried to find cover of their own as slugs whipped through the branches, chewed hunks of bark from the trees, and sprayed splinters.

Scratch called over to Bo, "You hit?"

"Nope. How about you?"

"No, they didn't wing me, either. Chloride?"

"I'm fine," the old-timer said. "But this is the second day in a row I been shot at, and I don't like it!"

A grim chuckle came from Bo. "Neither do we. What are we going to do about it?"

"Did you see where those bushwhackers are holed up?" Scratch asked.

"Not yet," Bo replied. "I was too busy getting out of the way of those bullets."

"Yeah, me, too."

"How about that deadfall on the other side of the trail?" Chloride suggested. "Just because they weren't there yesterday, that don't mean they ain't today!"

Bo considered the idea and said, "No, I don't think so. We've been within a couple of hundred yards of that big log for at least half an hour, searching the place where the wagon crashed and then here in these trees. Nobody could have snuck up behind it without us noticing them."

"Maybe some Apaches could have," Scratch said, "but those varmints shootin' at us ain't Apaches. And I reckon they couldn't have been hidin' there before we got here, because they didn't have no way of knowin' we were comin' out here today."

Bo thought about that for a moment as the firing continued. "That's not strictly true," he said. "We talked to quite a few people in town about how we wanted to try tracking down that gang of thieves. This would be the most likely place for us to start."

"Yeah," Scratch admitted, "but we only talked to folks at the various minin' companies."

"Word could have gotten around. Or maybe the Devils are connected to one of the companies."

"Hell's fire!" Chloride exclaimed. "That don't make no sense. All the big companies have been hit at least once. The robbers couldn't be workin' for any of 'em."

"Unless that's what whoever is behind the Devils wants everybody to think," Bo said. He looked over at Scratch, who frowned in thought for a moment before nodding.

"You might be on to something there, Bo," he said. "But we won't ever know if we get ourselves shot full of holes out here. Got any ideas about how we can turn the tables on them varmints?"

Bo took his hat off and edged his head out far enough from behind the tree trunk to get a look at the terrain across the creek. Now was the time to figure out where the bushwhackers were hidden.

That didn't take long. He spotted tendrils of gunsmoke curling from behind some rocks about halfway up the steeply sloping side of the gulch. The riflemen could have ridden along the top of the ridge, then worked their way unseen through the brush and the trees until they reached the rocks.

Bo told Scratch and Chloride what he had discovered. "Yeah, I see 'em now," Scratch said. "Sort of long range for a handgun, but we might be able to get a little lead up there."

"That old cap-and-ball of mine won't carry that far," Chloride said. "It'll blow a big hole through a fella at close range, but it ain't much good over twenty feet."

"Scratch, toss one of your Remingtons over to Chloride along with some ammunition," Bo suggested. "That way the two of you can keep them occupied."

"What're you gonna do?" Scratch asked as he looked over at his old friend.

Bo waved a hand toward Deadwood. "I thought I'd work my way downstream through the trees until the trail goes around the next bend. Then I can cross the creek and start back in this direction."

"Maybe get behind the varmints, eh?" Scratch nodded. "That might work. You know how to work one of these Remingtons, Chloride?"

The old-timer snorted. "There ain't a gun I can't fire."

"Well, just be careful with it," Scratch said as he gripped one of the revolvers by its long barrel and got ready to toss it over to Chloride. "I'm mighty fond of these hoglegs."

He made sure the hammer was resting on an empty chamber and sent the gun sailing through the air to land near Chloride's feet. Chloride scooped it up. Scratch tied a dozen rounds in his bandana and threw them over to the old-timer as well.

When Bo saw that his companions were ready, he said, "Space out your shots to make your bullets last longer. And if you could actually hit one or two of those bushwhackers, that would be good, too."

"You just tend to your part of the deal," Scratch said as he drew a bead on the rocks with his remaining gun. "We'll tend to ours."

The Remington roared as Scratch squeezed the

trigger. A second later, the gun Chloride was using blasted, too.

Bo darted out of cover and ran deeper into the grove of trees. The bushwhackers were still keeping up a steady fire. He heard several bullets thud into the trunks around him.

He didn't know if they could see what he was doing. If they spotted him, they would be ready for him when he worked his way back on the opposite side of the gulch. His only real chance was to take them by surprise, so he hoped they were just firing blindly into the trees on this side of the creek.

Bo used every bit of cover he could find to conceal what he was doing. He moved swiftly but carefully, and the site of the ambush soon fell behind him. Scratch and Chloride might have been able to slip away like this, too, but the three of them would have been left afoot if they had done that, and if the men who wanted them dead had come looking for them, they would be easy prey.

Besides, Bo wanted to get a look at the bush-whackers. He strongly suspected that the men were members of the Deadwood Devils. If he was lucky, he might even be able to take one of them prisoner.

The sound of the firing diminished somewhat, although the reports still echoed back and forth between the walls of the gulch. The men at some of the mines in the area probably heard the shooting, but if Chloride was right about how spooked everybody was, they probably wouldn't come to investigate. They would just think the Devils had struck again— and more than likely they would be right.

The trees thinned out before Bo reached the bend

in the trail. All he could do now was make a run for it and hope they didn't notice him. He broke out from cover and ran around the bend. No bullets whistled after him, and he took that as a good sign. After splashing across the creek, he stopped to lean against a slab-like boulder for a second and catch his breath. Not for the first time, he thought that he was getting too old for dust-ups like this.

He recovered quickly and started up the slope. From time to time he had to grab hold of a bush or a narrow tree trunk to help pull himself up. When he judged that he was about on the same level as the bushwhackers, he turned west and began making his way in their direction.

He still heard a lot of rifle shots, but the distinctive booming of Scratch's Remingtons had slowed. That probably meant Scratch and Chloride were running low on ammunition, Bo thought. He needed to make his move soon.

He was almost in position. The whip cracks of the rifles were close now. Bo drew his Colt and slid forward from tree to rock to tree. He could look across the creek now and see the place where his friends had taken cover.

As he crouched behind one of the pines, he peered around the trunk and saw four men kneeling behind rocks and firing across the stream with their Winchesters. Bo was a little surprised when he saw that all four wore bandanas tied around the lower halves of their faces and had their hats pulled down low. They were taking pains to conceal their identities even now. He had good shots at a couple of them, but the others would be trickier. He had hoped to get the drop on all the ambushers and force them to surrender, but that wasn't going to be possible.

No shots had come from across the creek for almost a minute now. That meant Scratch and Chloride had run out of bullets—or that they had both been wounded, maybe killed. Thinking about that possibility caused a grim, angry cast to steal over Bo's weathered face. He took a deep breath, gripped the Colt tightly, and swung out from behind the tree.

He didn't call out to the men and give them a chance to surrender. Bushwhackers didn't deserve that sort of consideration. Instead Bo leveled the Colt and fired, squeezing off three quick shots. The first one smashed the arm of the closest rifleman, making him drop his weapon, pitch to the side, and howl in pain as he clutched at the injury. Bo's second bullet struck a rock and whined off harmlessly. The third one ripped through the body of the other gunman he could see.

The other two masked men wheeled around, thrust their rifles past the rocks they were using as cover, and opened fire on the unexpected new threat. The slugs whipping around his head made Bo duck behind a tree again.

Across the creek, the two Remingtons again began to roar. Scratch and Chloride had been biding their time, waiting for Bo to get in position and launch a counterattack. Now they sent bullets ricocheting into the rocks where the bushwhackers were hidden. As Bo thumbed fresh cartridges into the Colt to replace the ones he had fired, he heard one of the men bellow an angry curse, then order, "Let's grab the others and get out of here!"

Bo didn't want them to get away. He knelt, leaned out from behind the tree, and sent a couple of rounds whistling past the rocks. A veritable storm of lead lashed back at him as one of the men started cranking off shots as fast as he could work his Winchester's lever. The barrage forced Bo to hunker down and try to make himself as small a target as possible.

When the shooting stopped a few moments later, he heard men forcing their way through the brush. A quick look told him the two men he had wounded were gone. The one with the busted arm might have been able to get on his feet and flee without any help. One of the other two men must have dragged the more badly wounded hombre away.

Bo knew he could go after them, but he had already pushed his luck considerably by taking on four-to-one odds and he knew that, too. Even though he had wounded two of the men, he couldn't be sure they were out of the fight. And even if they were, that would still leave him facing two would-be killers.

It chafed him to let them get away, but right now, that might be the smartest thing to do. Sure enough, a few minutes later he heard the rattle of hoofbeats from somewhere higher on the ridge. It sounded like four horses were hurrying off into the distance.

A tense silence that sounded odd after all the shooting had settled over the gulch. Bo waited it out for several minutes to be sure the bushwhackers really had fled and weren't doing a double-back or setting another trap. When he was convinced they were gone, he called across the creek.

"Scratch! Scratch, are you all right?"

The answer came back immediately from the

silver-haired Texan. "Yeah, me and Chloride are fine! How about you?"

"I'm all right," Bo told them. "Those hombres lit a shuck after I winged a couple of them!"

"Lay low for now!" Scratch called back. "We'll round up the horses!"

Bo reloaded and waited while Scratch and Chloride emerged from the trees on the other side of the creek and hurried upstream. The horses and Chloride's mule had headed that way when they ran off. Bo moved over to the rocks where the bushwhackers had hidden. He could see better from here. He kept an eye on the ridgeline, just in case the killers came back.

Evidently peace had descended again on the gulch, though. Nothing happened as Scratch and Chloride returned with the three mounts a few minutes later. Bo made his way down the slope and waded across the creek to join them. His feet were wet and cold, so Scratch and Chloride stood watch while he took his boots and socks off, wrung out the socks, and spread them on a rock to dry for a few minutes. He rubbed his feet to warm them up.

"Did you get a good look at any of the varmints?" Scratch asked.

"Afraid not. They had bandanas over their faces and their hats pulled down low. There was nothing special about their clothes, either."

"See?" Chloride said. "Just like I told folks in town! Some of 'em didn't believe me, but you seen the thievin' buzzards with your own eyes!"

"If they were part of the gang," Bo said.

Chloride snorted. "Who else'd ambush us to keep you from tryin' to track 'em down?" he asked. "Them

Devils are the only ones who'd have any reason to do that."

"He's right," Scratch said. "Question is, did they follow us out here from town, or did the big boss leave some of 'em here to keep watch and bushwhack anybody who came pokin' around?"

Bo shook his head. "I don't know, but I reckon we ought to try to pick up their trail and see where it leads." He started pulling on one of his socks. It was still damp, but he was too impatient to wait for it to dry fully.

Horses couldn't make it up the side of the gulch right here, even with their riders dismounted and leading them. The Texans and Chloride had to backtrack almost a mile before they came to a place where they could reach the top of the ridge. They retraced their path, looking down on the creek from high above now, until they reached the spot where the ambush had taken place.

"The ground's pretty rocky here," Scratch observed. "It won't be easy followin' them, but we'll give it a try."

With Scratch leading the way, they trailed the would-be killers into the rugged hills that bordered Deadwood Gulch. The going was slow. More gulches, many of them choked with brush, cut through the hills and formed obstacles. Finally Scratch reined in, sighed, and shook his head.

"I've lost the trail," he said. "We can back up and try to find it again, but it ain't likely to do us much good. There are too many rocks, too many creeks, and too many places where a fella can hide his tracks. My hunch is that they've done given us the slip, Bo."

"Mine, too," Bo agreed. "Let's head back to those trees where they ambushed the wagon yesterday and try to follow that trail."

They spent several hours doing that as the tracks of the outlaw gang wound into the rugged area between Deadwood Creek and Whitewood Creek. This trail was a little easier to follow because there had been more riders, but eventually it petered out, too, as the tracks branched in different directions as Scratch had predicted they would.

"Well, we didn't find their rendezvous after all," Scratch said as they sat on their mounts trying to figure out their next move. He glanced up at the sun. "Missed lunch, too."

"We might as well head back to Deadwood," Bo said.

"And do what?" Chloride asked. "How are we gonna earn any money if we can't find those no-good skunks?"

Chloride was including himself now as if they were partners, Bo noted. That was all right. He felt an instinctive liking for the crusty old-timer, and Chloride had handled himself all right during the battle with the bushwhackers. Besides, Chloride had a definite part to play in the plan that was forming in Bo's brain.

"There's more than one way to find the Deadwood Devils," Bo said as he smiled. "I think I know how we can make them come to us."

Scratch frowned and asked, "Does this idea of yours have anything to do with us gettin' shot at again, Bo?"

"It just might," Bo said.

CHAPTER 8

"Dadgummit, I ain't a-gonna do it!" Chloride insisted as they rode along Deadwood's Main Street. He had been arguing with Bo's plan all the way back to the settlement. "I already lived through one of those holdups when nobody else has. You reckon I want to push my luck by trying to do it again?" The old-timer shook his head stubbornly. "Besides, I done told you and told you, the Golden Queen is a hoodoo outfit. Just plain bad luck."

"And it's also the only mining operation that's desperate enough to hire you as a driver," Bo pointed out.

He had tried that reasoning on Chloride before, and this time it drew the same sort of disgusted snort as a response. "The gal can't pay no wages. She's flat broke."

"She's still feeding the men who work for her, and they have a place to stay," Bo said. "Besides, if the Golden Queen is producing much ore, it's probably piling up out there because there's nobody to bring it to town. If Miss Sutton could get a shipment or two in the bank, I'll bet her finances would look a lot better."

"Maybe," Chloride allowed. "The problem is gettin' it here."

"With you drivin' the wagon and me and Bo guardin' it, it'll get here," Scratch said. "You can bet that scroungy ol' hat of yours on that."

"Don't you go sayin' bad things about my hat! Me and this hat been through a heck of a lot together!"

"I believe it. It's probably as old as you are."

They had reached the office of the Golden Queen Mining Company, so Bo reined in and said, "We can argue about Chloride's hat later. Right now we need to go in and talk to Miss Sutton. Chloride, I'll ask you again to come with us. It'll be a lot easier getting the gold here if we have you along to drive the wagon. Otherwise one of us will have to handle that chore and there'll only be one of us left to keep an eye out for trouble."

Chloride scowled and tugged on his scraggly beard. "You're bound and determined to go through with this, ain't you?"

"We need jobs, even if they don't pay anything but room and board, and Miss Sutton needs help, if she'll unbend enough to accept it." Bo shrugged. "Seems like a good solution all the way around."

"Other than the probably gettin' killed part," Chloride shot back.

"Man takes a chance ever' time he gets out of bed in the mornin'," Scratch drawled. "Leastways with this one, there might be a nice payoff at the end."

Chloride jerked his head in a curt nod. "All right," he said. "We'll give it a try. But when you got a bullet in your belly and you're breathin' your last, just remember I told you it was a loco idea."

"Were you born with that sunny disposition," Scratch asked as he dismounted, "or did it just come to you?"

Bo led the way into the mining company office. It was late in the afternoon by now, but Martha Sutton was still there. In fact, she was on her feet and had an angry expression on her face as she looked at a man who stood in front of the desk.

"It's a good offer, Miss Sutton," the man was saying as the Texans and Chloride came in. He glanced over his shoulder at them but continued talking to Martha. "I'd advise you to take it. I don't know how long Mr. Nicholson will be in such a generous mood."

"I promise you, Mr. Ramsey, I'm not at a point where I need to rely on the generosity of Mr. Nicholson— or of you!" Martha shot back. "Tell your employer that I decline his . . . offer." Her voice dripped with scorn on the final word.

"You're certain?" Ramsey said.

"There's no doubt in my mind."

Ramsey shrugged and turned away. He was young, around twenty-five, with blond hair and a tall, lean body clothed in a gray tweed suit. He put on a narrow-brimmed hat that matched the suit and stepped past Bo, Scratch, and Chloride, regarding them now with definite curiosity. He didn't ask them who they were, though, just nodded and said, "Gentlemen." Then he paused in the doorway and added to Martha, "If you change your mind, Miss Sutton, I'm sure Mr. Nicholson will be happy to discuss the matter with you."

"I won't be changing my mind," Martha snapped.

Ramsey smiled and went out, closing the door behind him. With a weary sigh, Martha sank into the chair behind the desk and looked up at her new visitors with a mixture of anger and resignation.

"What do you three want?" she asked. Then she looked more closely at Chloride and added, "You're the Argosy driver who was held up yesterday, aren't you?"

Chloride said, "Yes'm, I am. But I ain't workin' for Argosy no more, as of yesterday, too."

Martha looked surprised. "Lawrence Nicholson fired you because you got held up? Or because you didn't give your life for the Argosy Mining Company like the guards did?"

"I dunno, miss, he just told me I wasn't workin' for him no more."

"So you're looking for a job like these two?" Martha said as she nodded toward Bo and Scratch.

Bo said, "Actually, Miss Sutton, Chloride gave us a hand today when we rode out to see if we could pick up the trail of the Deadwood Devils."

Martha sat up straighter and looked interested in spite of herself. "Did you have any luck?" she asked.

"If you call almost getting our hair parted with lead lucky," Bo replied with a faint smile. "Four men ambushed us while we were looking around the place where the Argosy wagon was held up yesterday."

"You don't look like you're hurt."

"That really *was* lucky," Bo said. Quickly, he explained what had happened when they were ambushed. "We tried to follow those men who shot at us," he concluded, "but we lost the trail. The same thing happened when we backtracked the outlaws who attacked the Argosy gold wagon yesterday. Following a trail in rugged country like this is pretty hard."

Martha looked at them solemnly. "When you said you were going to try to find the Deadwood Devils, you weren't joking, were you?"

"We generally don't, leastways not about the important things, miss," Scratch said.

"I appreciate your efforts, and I'm certainly sorry your lives were in danger . . . but I'm afraid I can't offer you any sort of compensation for what you've done."

"We're not asking for any," Bo said. "We haven't earned anything . . . yet."

Martha frowned. "I don't understand. Are you going to keep looking for the thieves?"

"Not exactly. I had another idea. You said you were having trouble finding anybody to bring your gold into town from the mine . . . ?"

"That's right. All my drivers have quit, and no one wants to hire on as guards . . ." Martha's eyebrows rose as she realized what Bo was suggesting. "Are you saying that the three of you want to volunteer?"

Chloride shuffled his feet. To keep the old-timer from saying anything about hoodoos, Bo replied quickly, "You need a driver and some guards, and we need jobs."

Impatiently, Martha said, "I've told you, I can't afford to pay wages."

"But you said you've been feeding the fellas who work for you, and I reckon they have places to stay out at the mine."

She shrugged. "That's true. You'd work for room and board?"

"And the promise of back wages once you've got plenty of gold in the bank and the company is back on solid footing," Bo said. He looked at his two companions. Scratch nodded and added, "That's right, ma'am." Chloride didn't say anything, but at least he didn't object.

Martha said, "It's true I might be able to feed three more mouths, and there's plenty of room in the bunkhouse out at the mine. But aren't you afraid of the Devils? They're liable to try to hold up the first shipment into town."

"To tell you the truth, Miss Sutton," Bo said, "we're sort of counting on that."

"You still want to find out who they are and where they've been hiding all the loot they've stolen, don't you?"

Scratch said, "We don't cotton to bein' shot at. Makes us take things real personal-like."

Bo nodded. "That's true."

"Well . . . I suppose we could give it a try. I don't like the idea of you putting your lives at risk, but if I don't get a shipment or two out pretty soon, the company can't keep going."

"Sounds like we've got a deal, then," Bo said with a smile.

Martha stood up and extended her hand across the desk. "My father always shook on it whenever he made a deal."

"Your father sounds like a good man," Bo said as he gripped her hand.

"He was. I don't want to let him down by losing the mine or being forced to sell out to someone like Lawrence Nicholson."

"That was one of Nicholson's men you were talking to when we came in, wasn't it?" Bo asked. "What was that about? Did the Argosy make an offer to buy your mine?"

"That's exactly what Phillip Ramsey did," Martha snapped. "And as for who that little weasel is, he's Nicholson's chief bookkeeper and secretary. Ramsey runs the office, Reese Bardwell runs the mine."

"We've met Bardwell," Bo said. "And there was somebody else in the Argosy office when we were there yesterday."

Martha waved a hand. "There are several clerks who work there, but Ramsey is in charge of them."

"The fella didn't look that weaselly to me," Scratch commented.

"Trust me, he is. I wouldn't trust him or Nicholson or Bardwell as far as I could throw them. My father never trusted them, either." Martha changed the subject by asking, "Are you going to ride out to the mine today? I can give you a letter explaining to my superintendent that I've hired you to bring in the gold shipments."

"It's a little late to be starting out there today," Bo said. "But if you could write that letter, we can pick it up first thing in the morning when we ride out."

Martha nodded. "I'll have it ready for you." She hesitated. "Do you have enough money to eat tonight? I might be able to find a little money . . ."

"That won't be necessary," Bo assured her, thinking about the coins they had gotten back from the liveryman, Hanson, early that morning. "We'll be fine."

"All right then," she said, obviously relieved. "I hope you men don't have reason to regret going to work for me."

Chloride was muttering something under his breath as they left the office. Bo didn't ask him to repeat it.

"I hope you ain't plannin' to eat at my place again tonight," the old-timer said when they were outside. "My cupboard's pert near bare."

"Actually," Bo said, "I was thinking we'd treat you to a meal at the Red Top. We got enough money back from Hanson for that."

Chloride licked his lips under the bushy mustache. "Really? Includin' maybe a piece of one o' those pies that widow lady bakes?"

"Including a piece of pie," Bo said with a nod.

"I'm much obliged. Maybe throwin' in with you fellas is gonna work out all right after all. Until the shootin' starts again, anyway."

They sat at an empty table in a rear corner of the Red Top this time. Sue Beth Pendleton came over, smiled at them, and said, "Where have you fellows been all day? I heard a rumor you and Mr. Morton intended to become bounty hunters and go after the Devils, Mr. Creel."

"We thought better of it and spent the day sightseeing instead, ma'am," Bo answered.

"That's right," Scratch put in. "Why go lookin' for trouble?"

After telling Martha Sutton about it, they had agreed not to say anything about the ambush out on the trail. The fewer people who knew about their clash with the Devils, the better. That way, if anybody brought it up, that would be a potential clue to who the members of the gang might be.

Sue Beth looked at Chloride and said, "Were you the one showing them the sights, Mr. Coleman?"

"Well, ma'am, I reckon I know the country hereabouts as good as anybody in these parts," the old-timer said.

"That's true," Sue Beth agreed, but judging by the shrewd look in the woman's eyes, Bo thought she might have some suspicions of her own. It would be hard to put anything past her for very long, he decided. She went on, "Are you here for supper?"

"Yes, ma'am, and we can even pay," Bo told her.

Sue Beth laughed. "I'll tell Charlie, and then I'll be back with coffee. It's fried chicken tonight, by the way. I hope that's all right."

"Yes, ma'am," Scratch said. "Nothin' better than some good fried chicken."

The meal lived up to its predecessors. Sue Beth kept their coffee cups filled, and when they had emptied their plates, she brought over saucers with a slice of apple pie on each of them. They didn't even have to ask for dessert.

Chloride finally leaned back and sighed. "I reckon that's the best meal I et in a month of Sundays. I'm obliged."

"Don't worry," Bo said. "You'll earn your keep before this is all over, I expect."

Chloride grew more sober and said, "Yeah." He didn't sound enthusiastic anymore.

Bo took a sip of the coffee remaining in his cup and asked, "What about that hombre Ramsey? You worked for the Argosy. You must know him."

Chloride shrugged. "I collected my wages from

him, but that's all. Don't reckon we ever said a dozen words to each other."

"Is he going to run back to Nicholson and tell him that he saw us in Miss Sutton's office?"

Chloride thought about it for a second and said, "Yeah, he might. He ain't exactly what I'd call a toady, but he works for Nicholson, after all, and the Golden Queen is one of the Argosy's competitors."

"How did Nicholson get along with Miss Sutton's father?"

"Nicholson and Mike Sutton weren't friends, you could sure say that much. Listen, the Argosy ain't the biggest, most profitable outfit around here. The Homestake and the Father De Smet are both bigger. But the Argosy's right there behind 'em, and the Golden Queen ain't much farther back."

Bo nodded slowly. "So if Nicholson was able to buy the Golden Queen, *his* operation would be the biggest around here."

Scratch said, "Bo, you been actin' like you think Nicholson might be tied in somehow with those road agents. That don't make any sense when you consider what happened yesterday."

"Yeah," Chloride agreed. "Mitch Davis, Berkner, and Turley all wound up dead, and I come mighty close to it. And all four of us worked for the Argosy."

"I know. The question is, would Nicholson be willing to let some of his men be killed if it helped him get what he wanted?"

"You mean the Golden Queen?" Scratch frowned. "I don't see it. The Devils have held up shipments from every mine in the area, plus they robbed some stagecoaches, too, didn't they, Chloride?"

The old-timer nodded. "Yep. Fact is, they hit two or three coaches on the run from here to Cheyenne before they ever held up any gold shipments. They took the express box ever' time and killed the driver and shot-gun guard."

"What about the passengers?" Bo asked.

Chloride shook his head. "There weren't any on those particular runs, which is mighty lucky for them 'cause any passengers likely would've been slaughtered, too."

"When the bodies of the dead drivers and guards were found, did they have the pitchforks cut into their foreheads?"

"Yeah, sure. I seen some of the bodies when John Tadrack brought 'em in. Grisly work, I'm tellin' you."

"Bein' an undertaker, or mutilatin' poor hombres once you've killed 'em?" Scratch asked.

"Both, as far as I'm concerned." With a slurp, Chloride drained the last of his coffee from the cup. "I reckon the gang decided they could make more money by hittin' the gold shipments, because the stagecoach robberies stopped after the other holdups started."

Bo nodded. "Yeah, I'm sure gold shipments are more profitable. But we'll see if we can put a stop to that."

They put on their hats and went over to the counter, where Bo took some coins from his pocket and paid Sue Beth for their meals. Scratch told her, "The food was mighty good, ma'am. We'll be back, whenever we're in town."

"Oh? You're leaving?" she asked.

"We've taken jobs out at the Golden Queen mine,"

Bo said. "Chloride's going to drive the gold wagon, and Scratch and I are going to guard the shipments."

Sue Beth's eyes widened. "You can't be serious! With the Deadwood Devils still on a rampage, you . . . you'll be risking your lives!"

"Somebody's got to do it. I figure the three of us are just the hombres to stand up to the Devils."

Sue Beth had already put the money Bo had paid her into the cash box under the counter. She opened it now, reached in, and took the coins out again. She slid them back across the counter and said, "Here. Take your money."

Bo frowned. "That paid for our food. Why are you trying to give it back?"

"Because I'm not going to charge men for what might be their last meals on this earth!"

CHAPTER 9

That night in Chloride's shack passed as quietly as the previous one. Early the next morning, they drank the last of the old-timer's coffee, then saddled up and rode down the gulch into Deadwood.

Bo still had enough money in his pocket to buy them breakfast at the Red Top, but after Sue Beth's disapproval of their plans the night before, he didn't know if they would be welcome there. Instead they stopped at the Empire Bakery on Lee Street, just across the bridge over Whitewood Creek, and bought a sack of bear sign to eat as they rode out to the Golden Queen Mine.

Despite the early hour, Martha Sutton was already in the mining company's office, and she had the letter she had mentioned the day before ready for them.

"My superintendent's name is Andrew Keefer," she told Bo as she handed him the folded and sealed paper. "Mr. Coleman probably knows him."

Chloride nodded. "By reputation, anyway. I don't reckon I've ever shook and howdied with him. Heard tell he's a tough hombre, but I never heard anybody say he wasn't a fair one."

"That's a good description of him," Martha said. "I'd add loyal, too. He worked for my father for several years, and after . . . after things got bad, he could have gone to work for the Homestake or one of the other big mines. But he hasn't. He's stayed right there at the Golden Queen and done everything in his power to keep it running, even though I owe him as many back wages as I do anyone. You shouldn't have any trouble with him, especially after he reads the letter."

Bo knew that when Martha talked about things getting bad, she really meant after her father had died. He stowed the letter in an inside coat pocket and asked, "How soon will we need to bring in a shipment?"

"There's probably already enough ore on hand to fill a wagon right now."

"Then we'll be back with it tomorrow, I reckon," Bo said with a smile.

They started to leave the office. Martha stopped them by saying, "Mr. Creel, Mr. Morton, Mr. Coleman . . . please be careful. I don't want your lives on my conscience."

"Don't worry, Miss Sutton," Bo said as he touched a finger to his hat brim. "It's our responsibility. We know what we're getting into."

After they had stepped outside and Scratch had closed the door, Chloride muttered, "A heap o' trouble, that's what we're likely gettin' into. You fellas believe in jumpin' right into the fire, don't you? Ride out to the mine today, get ourselves killed tomorrow tryin' to deliver that gold."

"We hired on to bring the gold into town," Bo said. "There's no point in waiting, is there?"

"No, I reckon not," the old-timer replied with a sigh.

They mounted up. As they rode out of town, they passed the Argosy Mining Company office. Lawrence Nicholson and Phillip Ramsey were just going inside. Both men paused to look at the Texans and their elderly companion. Nicholson gave them a curt nod. Ramsey merely watched them with a speculative expression on his narrow face.

As they started up Deadwood Gulch, Scratch dug the sack of bear sign out of his saddlebags and took one of the doughnuts from it. He passed the sack to Bo and Chloride in turn. Chloride smacked his lips with pleasure as he ate.

"That's mighty good bear sign. Helps lift a man's spirits," he declared.

"You mean you ain't worried about gettin' shot tomorrow?" Scratch asked.

"I didn't say that. But a man could die a mite happier with a belly full of this bear sign."

"Maybe we'd better save some for the trip back tomorrow," Bo suggested.

"That's a good idea," Chloride agreed.

The Golden Queen was about eight miles up Deadwood Gulch, he explained as they followed the trail alongside the creek. The mine wasn't actually located in the gulch, but rather up a side canyon that branched off to the southwest. A smaller stream flowed through the canyon and merged with Deadwood Creek.

"Where's the Argosy?" Bo asked.

"About a mile on up the gulch from where that canyon veers off," Chloride answered.

"What's Nicholson going to do for drivers and guards now? Has he been having the same sort of trouble getting men to work for him that Miss Sutton has?"

Chloride shook his head. "Not exactly. The Argosy can afford to pay more, so there are more fellas willin' to run the risk. Of course, it don't take very big wages to add up to more than the gal can pay right now, since she ain't payin' nothin'."

"She's promised to make up all those back wages," Scratch pointed out.

"Promisin' is easier than doin'," Chloride said.

Bo couldn't argue with that. The men who were still working for Martha Sutton were betting that eventually she would be able to pay them what she owed them. But like all bets, this one ran the risk of not paying off.

"And you got to remember," Chloride went on, "until a couple o' days ago, the Argosy shipments hadn't been hit. Reese Bardwell kept puttin' more guards on the wagons because of what's been happenin' to the other mines, so we all hoped the road agents would leave the Argosy alone. Shame it didn't work out that way."

"You'd probably still have a job if it had," Bo said.

"Maybe. To tell you the truth, though, Bardwell never much liked me, and Nicholson gen'rally does whatever that big galoot wants. They'd have found some excuse to get rid of me sooner or later."

Over the past four years, the hooves of countless horses and mules and the wheels of hundreds of wagons had worn a decent trail alongside the creek. The three riders had no trouble following it. They didn't push their mounts but instead ambled along, taking their time. When they passed the site of the ambush from the day before, Bo took a good look around, but he didn't see anything he hadn't already seen in the wake of the fight. There was nothing here to give them a lead to the Devils.

They rode on, and late in the morning they came to the mouth of the side canyon where the Golden Queen was located. As they reined in to rest the horses and Chloride's mule for a few minutes, Bo studied the steep, narrow, and rocky ridge that separated the side canyon from Deadwood Gulch itself.

"Somebody comin'," Scratch said, distracting Bo from his thoughts.

Bo looked up Deadwood Gulch and saw several riders approaching. The man in the lead was familiar, and as the group drew closer, Bo recognized him as Reese Bardwell, the Argosy's chief engineer and superintendent. Bardwell didn't look very comfortable on horseback. It took a pretty big horse to carry him, too, in this case a gray that looked more like a draft animal than a saddle mount.

"Who are the men with Bardwell?" Bo asked Chloride quietly.

The old-timer grimaced and shook his head. "They must be new guards. I don't recognize 'em. They don't look like hard-rock men."

Scratch grunted and said, "More like hard*cases*."

It was true. The three men with Bardwell wore range clothes and Stetsons, and each had a handgun belted on, as well as a Winchester in a saddle boot. Their eyes had the narrow look of constant vigilance that became second nature to men who lived by the gun.

The Texans and Chloride stayed where they were, standing next to their mounts, as Bardwell and the other men rode up. Bardwell reined in. His companions followed suit. The engineer had a dark scowl on his face as he demanded, "What are you three doin' out here?"

"That's our business," Bo said. "We could ask the same of you fellas."

Bardwell sneered. "Last I heard, *we* had honest jobs. You're just a couple of saddle tramps from Texas and an old man who can't be trusted."

Chloride's beard bristled belligerently as he exclaimed, "Why, you goldurn—"

Bo put out a hand to stop him as the old-timer took a step forward. "Take it easy, Chloride," he said. To Bardwell, he went on, "I reckon you haven't heard. We've got jobs. We're working for Miss Martha Sutton at the Golden Queen."

Bardwell frowned in surprise. "Marty? Why would she— Wait a minute. She didn't hire the three of you to get her gold to town, did she?"

"That's right," Bo said. Bardwell probably would have heard that news in Deadwood anyway, and Bo was interested in the man's reaction.

"I knew she was getting desperate, but I didn't know she had turned into a fool," Bardwell snapped.

"It's all over this part of the country about how Coleman's tied in with the Devils, and for all anybody knows, you two are part of the gang yourselves!"

Chloride shook a gnarled fist at him. "By jingo, if I was twenty years younger, I'd hand you your needin's, you overgrowed varmint! I never had no truck with outlaws, and that's more'n you can say!"

Bardwell's face darkened again as he said, "What're you talkin' about, you old pelican?"

"You know dang good an' well what I'm talkin' about! That no-good brother of yours!"

Fury mottled Bardwell's face. His hands clenched into massive fists for a second before he started to swing down from his horse. But before he could dismount, one of the men with him edged his horse up alongside and said, "Probably ought to forget it, boss. Mr. Nicholson's expecting you, and he won't like it if you're late."

Bardwell eased back into his saddle. "I suppose you're right," he rumbled. He pointed a thick, blunt finger at Chloride. "But you just watch your mouth, old man. Keep runnin' it and you're liable to be sorry."

Chloride just snorted in contempt.

Bardwell and the men with him rode past and headed on down the gulch toward the settlement. Bardwell glanced back one last time to glare at the Texans and Chloride. The other men didn't pay any more attention to them, which reinforced Bo's hunch that they were hired guns. Men like that didn't care about anything unless they were paid to.

Chloride swiped the back of a hand across his mouth. "Sorry about that, boys," he said. "Almost talked my way into a ruckus, didn't I?"

"We couldn't have stopped Bardwell if he'd gone after you," Bo pointed out. "Not with our fists, anyway. That means guns would have had to be involved, and then those other hombres would have taken a hand."

"Could've been bullets flyin' everywhere, Chloride," Scratch added.

"Yeah, yeah, I know," the old-timer said. "I'm a mite too touchy. Always have been. Bardwell just rubs me the wrong way, though."

"I understand the feeling," Bo said as he put his foot in the stirrup. He swung up and went on, "Let's get going."

They forded the creek and headed up the narrow, twisting side canyon toward the Golden Queen. As they rode, Bo asked, "What was that about Bardwell's brother?"

"There was a rumor goin' around the camp that he had a brother who was an owlhoot down Kansas way. Nobody would ask him about it to his face—"

"I reckon not," Scratch said. "That hombre's fists are big enough he could knock down a door with 'em."

"Anyway," Chloride continued, "some folks said that the law finally caught up to Bardwell's brother and hanged him, whilst others claimed him and his gang got away and disappeared. I don't know which is true, or if Bardwell even had an owlhoot brother to start with. I was just tryin' to stick a burr under his saddle."

Bo nodded. "I saw the look on his face when you brought up his brother. I'd say you succeeded, Chloride. And I'd say there must be something to the story, too, otherwise it wouldn't have bothered him so much."

"I reckon you're right. If it was a lie, he wouldn't have got so durned mad."

"That's sort of interestin'," Scratch mused.

"You mean the way a gang of outlaws shows up and starts raising hell in the same area where Bardwell's working as a mine superintendent?" Bo asked. "Yeah, interesting is the word for it, all right." He looked over at Chloride as they rode along the canyon. "How come you didn't say anything about Bardwell's brother before now?"

The old-timer grunted. "Nobody asked me, now did they?"

Bo had to chuckle. He said, "No, I reckon not."

They rode on, and a few minutes later Bo began to hear the steady, pounding thump of a donkey engine. "That's coming from the mine?" he asked Chloride.

"Yeah, they're probably usin' it to haul ore cars outta the shaft. All the mines in these parts started out as placer outfits, since the first prospectors panned for gold in the creeks just like the fellas did in the California rivers back in forty-nine. The bigger operators come in, bought up claims, and built flumes and long toms to wash more gravel from the stream beds. But at the same time, they were startin' to dig into the slopes, too, hopin' to find the quartz lodes those flecks o' gold in the creeks came from."

Bo nodded. "That's the usual pattern when there's a gold strike, all right."

"But the lodes here in the Black Hills ain't like the ones anywheres else," Chloride said. "Most places, if you find a pocket of gold-bearin' ore, you can make a pretty good guess which way it's gonna run. Not around here. A pocket or a ledge can run any which-a-way around here, which is why you got tunnels branchin' ever' which way underground. The placer gold's just about played out now. There's just enough left so that most of the outfits keep a sluice goin' to get as much dust as they can, but mostly they're after ore now."

"And it takes a big company to do that effectively," Bo said. "A lone miner with a shovel and a pickax can't dig out enough gold to make the effort worth his while."

"Yeah, it didn't take long for all the little fellas to get crowded out," Chloride agreed. "A lot of 'em wound up sellin' their claims for little or nothin', then stayin' on to work for wages from the big outfits."

"We saw the same thing happen in California and Nevada," Scratch said, "and when we moseyed up here to Deadwood a few years back, we could tell it was gonna be the same story all over again. That's why we didn't bother stayin' around and breakin' our backs lookin' for gold."

They rode around a bend and saw the mine buildings up ahead on their right. The bunkhouse, cook shack, and mess hall were on the fairly level ground at the bottom of the canyon, along with a sturdy log structure that housed the superintendent's quarters. The mill was built on the slope, at the head of the main shaft sunk into the ridge. A few smaller storage buildings were scattered around, and Bo spotted a squat building made of thick logs a hundred yards up the canyon. That would be where the supply of blasting powder was kept. A while back, he and Scratch had worked at a mine down in Mexico, a long way from here but a setup that had been remarkably similar in some ways.

Bo saw a corral with a dozen mules in it, and a couple of empty wagons were parked next to the enclosure. He pointed them out to Scratch and Chloride and said, "I guess we'll be using one of those to haul the gold."

"Can you handle a wagon like that, old-timer?" Scratch asked.

"There you go with that old-timer business again!" Chloride sputtered. "You ain't no spring chicken! And I can handle anything with four wheels and mules hitched to it!"

Bo grinned as he turned his horse toward the superintendent's house. "We'd better find Andrew Keefer and give him Miss Sutton's letter before he starts wondering who we are and gets nervous," he said.

However, it was too late for that. As they rode up to the house, the door opened and a stocky, balding man with bushy, rust-colored side-whiskers stepped out with a shotgun in his hands. He pointed the Greener at the newcomers and bellowed, "If you've come to rob us, you damned Devils, I'll blow you right out of your saddles!"

CHAPTER 10

Bo and Scratch were experienced enough to keep their hands well away from their guns in a situation like this. Bo could only hope that Chloride would do the same thing. The man on the porch was already spooked, and it wouldn't take much to make him pull the triggers on that scattergun.

"Take it easy, mister," Bo said in a calm, steady voice, just like he was trying to settle down a skittish horse. "We're not here to rob anybody, and we're sure not members of the Deadwood Devils. Are you Andrew Keefer?"

The question seemed to take the man by surprise, but it got through to him. He lowered the shotgun slightly as he frowned. "I'm Keefer," he admitted. "Who in blazes are you?"

Bo nodded toward his companions. "This is Scratch Morton and Chloride Coleman. My name's Bo Creel. Miss Sutton sent us out here from Deadwood to pick up a shipment of ore and take it back to the bank."

"Coleman," Keefer repeated as he studied the old-timer. "I know you. You drive for the Argosy."

"Drove," Chloride corrected. "I don't work for Nicholson no more."

"What happened?"

"You haven't heard about the Argosy gold wagon being held up a couple of days ago?" Bo asked.

"Nobody from out here has been to town and back the past few days," Keefer said. "No reason to go. Nobody's got any money to spend." The shotgun's twin barrels rose again. "How do I know you're who you say you are?"

"Miss Sutton sent a letter with us," Bo said. "If you'll let me reach inside my coat without your trigger finger getting too itchy, I'll get it for you."

Keefer nodded. "Go ahead. But be careful now," he warned.

Slowly, Bo reached inside his coat and drew Martha's letter from the pocket. He brought his horse closer to the porch and held out the paper. Keefer lowered the shotgun again and stepped up to take it. He moved back quickly, just in case this was some sort of trick, Bo suspected.

Keefer grunted as he looked at the wax seal, no doubt recognizing it. He tucked the scattergun under his arm, broke the seal, and unfolded the letter. His eyes scanned it quickly, and as he read, Bo saw him relax a little.

"It appears you're who you say you are," Keefer said as he folded the letter and stuck it in a pocket in his brown corduroy trousers. He also wore work boots, a gray wool shirt, and a brown vest. He was so short and stocky that he appeared to be almost as wide as he was tall, but there was an air of strength about him. He wasn't fat, but rather thick with muscle instead. Bo would have been willing to bet that Andrew Keefer had swung a pickax in many a mine shaft before he ever became a superintendent.

Keefer went on. "Come on inside. You can put your horses and that mule in the corral later."

The three men dismounted, tied their reins to porch posts, and followed Keefer into the sturdy log building. A fire crackled in the fireplace, combating the November chill that seeped in from outside. Keefer had a fire going in a cast-iron stove, too, with a coffeepot sitting on top of it.

"Coffee?" he asked. "That was probably a pretty cold ride from town."

"It was," Bo admitted. "Coffee sounds good."

This front room was an office, with a desk cluttered with maps, diagrams, ledger books, and assorted paperwork. There was an armchair in front of the desk and a sofa against the wall opposite the fireplace. When Keefer had filled tin cups for all of them, he went behind the desk and waved for his visitors to have a seat. Bo took the armchair, while Scratch and Chloride sat on the sofa.

"Tell me about what happened to the Argosy gold wagon," Keefer said.

Chloride told the story of the holdup, then Bo took up the tale of their efforts the previous day to follow the trail of the road agents, including the ambush attempt. Keefer listened with rapt attention, and when Bo was finished, he said, "It sounds to me like you fellows were mighty lucky not to wind up with pitchforks carved on your foreheads."

"I thought the same thing," Chloride said.

"I have to admit, I'm a little surprised the Argosy got hit," Keefer went on. "I was beginning to think the Devils wouldn't go after it. But I suppose it was just a matter of time."

"Maybe," Bo said, but he didn't elaborate. Instead, he continued. "We're hoping we'll have another crack at the varmints."

Keefer leaned forward in his chair and clasped his hands together on the desk. "Wait just a blessed minute," he said. "You're not telling me that you plan to use our gold wagon as bait for a trap, are you? I won't stand for that."

Bo shook his head. "No, sir. That's not what I meant. Scratch and Chloride and I will do our dead-level best to get Miss Sutton's gold to town, just like we signed on to do. But considering how many times the shipments from the Golden Queen have been hit already, it seems likely the Devils will come after us again. Maybe not on this run, but sooner or later they will."

"And when they do, we're gonna give 'em a hot lead welcome, you can count on that," Scratch added.

"I see what you mean," Keefer said, slowly nodding. "But what makes you think the three of you can stop the Devils from stealing the gold when nobody else has been able to?"

Scratch grinned and said, "We stopped ol' Santa Anna from runnin' roughshod over Texas, and the odds were against us and the rest of Sam Houston's boys. I reckon we can handle a bunch of no-account owlhoots."

Keefer grunted. "There's a difference. You Texas lads caught the Mexicans sleeping, as I recall. The

Devils of Deadwood Gulch will be ready for trouble. They'll be bringing it with them, in fact."

"We'll just have to get the jump on them somehow," Bo said. "In the meantime, Miss Sutton seemed to think you'd have enough gold on hand to make up a shipment right away."

Keefer nodded. "That's true. I have a few bags of dust in the safe, and we've milled enough ore to make up two loads. Better not try to get it all to town at once, though. I don't want to risk everything."

"That's good. One wagon at a time is plenty. Maybe you can get the shipment loaded this afternoon, and we can start for Deadwood first thing in the morning."

"Sounds fine to me," Keefer said. He stood up and extended his hand to each of them in turn. "There are a few empty bunks in the bunkhouse, and you'll eat in the mess hall with the rest of the men. Welcome to the Golden Queen. We're glad to have you with us, gentlemen . . ." He paused and added pointedly, "Even though it might not be for very long, if those blasted Devils have anything to say about it!"

Chloride was in his element here. He supervised the loading of the gold wagon during the afternoon. The raw ore had already been run through the stamp mill to break it up and then processed with mercury to free the gold from the quartz in which it was embedded. The resulting ore, even though it would be refined more later on, was mostly gold and was formed into rough bars by melting and casting it. Workers at the mine stacked those bars into crates, and then the crates were loaded into the wagon. The heavy canvas bags of gold dust from the placer operation were stowed away in a locked compartment under the wagon seat.

Keefer picked some of his most trustworthy men to stand guard over the wagon during the night. Everyone who worked at the Golden Queen was pretty reliable, he explained to the Texans and Chloride, otherwise they would have deserted Martha Sutton, but a wagon full of gold was a tempting thing even for the most honest man.

Bo agreed, and for that reason he and Scratch took turns checking on the wagon from time to time during the night. They got plenty of sleep, though—the mine's bunkhouse was as comfortable as the bunkhouses they had stayed in on numerous ranches—and were rested and ready to go the next morning after a hearty breakfast in the mess hall.

Chloride hitched up the team himself, checking every bit of harness. "Worn leather's fouled up many a man in times of trouble," he explained.

Bo and Scratch saddled their horses. Instead of riding in the wagon, they would be mounted so they could move quicker if the need arose. They were armed with their usual weapons, and they borrowed a couple of shotguns from the rack in Keefer's office and placed them in the wagon.

When the wagon was ready to roll, Keefer came outside to say so long. A number of the miners had emerged from the shaft and the mill to watch, too. Their livelihoods were riding on that wagon. If Bo, Scratch, and Chloride could get the gold safely into the bank in Deadwood, eventually some of the value from it would find its way back to the miners in the form of the wages they were owed. That was everybody's hope, anyway.

Chloride climbed onto the wagon seat and grasped the reins. Bo and Scratch swung up into their saddles. Resting a hand on one of the front wheels, Keefer said, "Good luck be with you, men." He added, "It's not too late to send a couple of fellows with you as extra guards."

Bo shook his head. "No offense, Mr. Keefer, but then we'd have to look out for them, too, as well as the gold. And from the looks of it, your crew here is a mite thin. You probably need every man you've got just to keep the operation going."

"That's true," Keefer said with a nod. "Some of the men quit when Miss Sutton starting having trouble paying them. Can't blame them, really, but it's left us shorthanded."

"We'll be back tomorrow," Bo said as he lifted his reins.

"Good Lord willin' and the creek don't rise," Scratch added with a smile.

"It's not the creek I'm worried about," Keefer said as he stepped back and raised a hand in farewell. Chloride slapped the lines against the backs of the team, and with the rattle of bit chains and the creaking of wheels, the wagon lurched into motion. Bo and Scratch returned Keefer's wave and rode after the vehicle. Their Winchesters rested across the saddles in front of them, rather than in the sheaths strapped to the horses. If they needed the rifles, chances were they would need them in a hurry.

Bo and Scratch split up and flanked the wagon. The trail was wide enough for this escort arrangement in many places, although at times they would have to ride one in front and one behind the wagon where the path narrowed down.

"I hope you fellas are plannin' on keepin' your eyes open," Chloride said as they left the Golden Queen behind them. "Our best chance of gettin' through alive is if you spot them Devils before they open fire on us."

"You ain't tellin' us anything we don't already know," Scratch said.

"If there's any shooting, don't whip up the team and try to outrun the trouble," Bo suggested. "You couldn't do it with an empty wagon, and you sure can't with one loaded down heavy like this one. You'll be better off stopping and taking cover under the wagon instead."

"What'll the two of you be doin' while I'm hunkerin' down?" Chloride wanted to know.

"That depends on the situation," Bo said.

"But you can figure we'll be tryin' to kill as many of those varmints as we can," Scratch added.

Chloride nodded and fell silent. Bo could tell from the tense look on his leathery face that the old-timer was worried. Under the circumstances, only a fool wouldn't be a mite nervous. There were dozens of places where some owlhoot with a pair of field glasses could be hidden, watching the Golden Queen to see when the wagon left. It was possible somebody was riding to carry word of the shipment to the rest of the gang right now.

To take Chloride's mind off the situation as they reached the end of the canyon and started down the gulch toward Deadwood, Bo asked him questions about his life and got the old-timer talking about all the places he had been and the things he had done. Chloride had been to see the elephant, no doubt about that. He had been part of the California Gold Rush and had chased after bonanzas in Nevada and Montana Territory. Much like the Texans, he'd had a host of other jobs over the years but had been too fiddle-footed to stay with any of them for very long.

There were hundreds, if not thousands, of men just like him scattered across the frontier, men who had never been able to settle down and live the sort of lives that most hombres did, men filled with a restlessness that denied them peace and stability and demanded freedom to roam. Sometimes the price of that freedom was loneliness, and when their time came to cross the divide, it would be on some freezing mountaintop or under a burning desert sun, with a bullet in their guts or a knife in their back or a sickness wasting them away from the inside out. They wouldn't die in bed, with their loving families gathered around them, and maybe there were times when they regretted that, but deep down they knew it was the way things had to be.

Bo and Scratch had lived that same sort of life, so they knew what Chloride was talking about and recognized the wistful tone that crept into the old-timer's voice now and then as he spun his yarns. The years rolled by in their bittersweet way for men such as them.

Even as those thoughts filled his mind, a large part of Bo's brain was alert for trouble, and his eyes, keen despite his age, never stopped moving. His gaze roamed over the thickly wooded walls of the gulch, watching for the sun's split-second reflection on metal, or movement where everything should be still, or any other indication that things were not as they should be.

Early that morning, as they were getting ready to go, their breath had fogged thickly in front of their faces in the cold air. By now the sun had risen high enough that the temperature had warmed a little, especially here in the middle of the gulch next to the creek. Up ahead on the left, a tall, rocky outcropping loomed up and cast a thick shadow over a brushy area at the base of the slope. The sun didn't penetrate there.

Bo's eyes narrowed as he spotted what looked like a tiny puff of smoke drifting over that brush. It wasn't smoke at all, he realized. It was somebody's breath fogging up because the air under that big slab of rock was a little colder, just cold enough to cause that telltale sign.

And there was no reason for anybody to be hiding in there unless they were up to no good.

Softly, Bo called across to his old friend. "Scratch. Up ahead on the left, under that big rock."

"I see it," Scratch replied, equally softly. "Chloride, get ready to move."

The old-timer stiffened on the seat. "What in blazes—" he began.

Then the brush trembled a little, and Bo caught a glimpse of a rifle barrel poking between branches. There was no time for anything but action. He yanked his horse to the side, shouted, "Chloride, get down!" and snapped the Winchester to his shoulder. Shots roared out as he worked the rifle's lever as fast as he could and sent a steady stream of lead into that brush.

CHAPTER 11

Bo went one way and Scratch went the other so the outlaws hidden in the bushes would have a harder time killing both of them. At the same time, Chloride yanked the team to a stop, grabbed one of the loaded shotguns from the floorboard, and slid off the seat. He ducked under the wagon and crouched there as bullets began to thud into the thick planks of the vehicle's sideboards and whine off the iron-rimmed wheels.

Bo sent his horse at a run toward some trees. He felt the heat of a bullet as it passed close by his face. Powder smoke floated over the brush now instead of the fogging of some owlhoot's breath. That had been a small thing, just enough to give away the gang's hiding place before they could spring their ambush.

As the horse reached the trees, Bo kicked his feet free of the stirrups and went out of the saddle. He landed running and managed to stay upright without crashing into one of the tree trunks. A slug sent bark flying into the air as Bo ducked into cover.

He glanced around, looking for Scratch, and saw

that the silver-haired Texan had splashed across the creek and gone to ground in a cluster of rocks that were big enough to offer some decent shelter. Scratch's rifle spoke from over there, blasting bullets toward the brush where the Devils were hidden.

Bo had no doubt that it was the Deadwood Devils in there. This holdup wasn't going the way the Devils were used to, though. Bo thrust his rifle around the tree trunk and opened fire, joining Scratch in peppering the gang's hiding place with lead. From under the wagon, the shotgun boomed and then Chloride's old cap-and-ball revolver began to roar as he got in on the action as well.

A grim smile touched Bo's lips. The outlaws were accustomed to their victims trying to flee. This time they were putting up a fight instead. The thicket waved back and forth as the Texans sent lead scything through the branches from two different angles. Even though the Devils outnumbered their enemies, judging by the shots coming from the brush, they had chosen their position for concealment, not to defend. By spotting them first and not running, the Texans had turned the tables neatly on the bushwhackers.

One of the outlaws lost his nerve and made a break for it. Bo spotted him as the man lunged out of the brush and tried to duck around the rocky shoulder. Letting instinct guide his aim, Bo snapped a shot at the fleeing man and was rewarded by a howl of pain and the sight of the outlaw staggering as he clutched at a bullet-shattered shoulder. The man made it around the rocks, but he was out of the fight.

A burst of renewed firing came from the brush and forced both of the Texans to duck. The outlaws used that to cover their retreat. Some of them kept shooting while the rest of the gang dashed for cover. Bo and Scratch had to keep their heads down and managed only a couple of shots to send the men hurrying on their way.

The gang's horses must have been hidden just around the bend in the trail. Bo heard hoofbeats pound as some of the men galloped down the gulch toward Deadwood. The ones left in the brush broke from cover and ran toward the bend, firing rifles and handguns as they went. Bo got a good enough look at them to see that they had their bandanas pulled up to mask their faces. A couple of the men staggered as the Texans' bullets found them, but they stayed on their feet and kept running, ducking out of sight around the bend in the trail. More hoofbeats sounded a moment later as the attackers reached their horses and lit a shuck away from there.

Chloride let out a whoop from under the wagon. "We done it!" he yelled. "We fought 'em off!"

"Stay where you are," Bo called as he saw the old-timer start to crawl out from under the wagon. "We want to make sure they're all gone before we show ourselves."

They waited until all the hoofbeats had faded away into the distance, then waited a while after that. Chloride grew impatient and muttered oaths, but the Texans stoically used the time to reload their rifles.

Finally, Bo emerged from the trees and whistled for his horse. As the animal trotted up, Chloride called, "Can I come out now, blast it?"

"Come ahead," Bo told him. "Just keep your gun

handy until Scratch and I have a chance to do a little scouting around."

Scratch left the rocks on the other side of the creek, called his horse, and rode back across the fast-flowing stream. He said, "I think I winged a couple of those varmints, Bo."

"Yeah, me, too," Bo said with a nod. "We're whittling them down."

"Not fast enough to suit me," Chloride said as he stood beside the wagon gripping his old revolver.

The Texans rode up to the bend in the trail and took a look. Nobody shot at them. "Stay here to keep an eye on Chloride and the gold," Scratch said. "I'll mosey a ways down the gulch."

Bo nodded his agreement and waited there while Scratch scouted their route. The silver-haired Texan soon was out of sight. Bo waited tensely for his friend to return . . . or for shots to break out.

His hands tightened a little on the Winchester when he heard a horse coming. Scratch rode into view a moment later and waved his rifle above his head to let Bo know that everything was all right. Bo turned in the saddle and waved to Chloride.

"Come on! The trail is clear!"

Chloride got the wagon moving again. Bo waited for him to catch up, and then they both went on down the trail to join up with Scratch.

"See anything of those owlhoots?" Bo asked.

Scratch shook his head. "Nary hide nor hair. That's twice we've fought 'em off. I reckon they must've had things their own way around here for so long they don't know what to make of it when somebody fights back. Seems like they spook pretty easy."

"They won't again," Bo predicted. "They know what they're up against now. They'll be better prepared next time."

On that cautionary note, Bo, Scratch, and Chloride proceeded on down the gulch toward Deadwood. The wagon couldn't move very fast. Noon came and went, and a short time after that, they stopped to rest the mule team and eat the food they had brought with them from the mine. The Golden Queen's cook had prepared them a lunch of thick slices of bread, bacon, and canned tomatoes.

The rest of the trip was surprisingly uneventful. Bo knew the Devils could have prepared another ambush, but evidently that morning's fight had shaken them enough to make them think twice about that. Around midafternoon, they spotted the smoke rising from Deadwood's chimneys, and a short time after that, the settlement itself came into view.

People on the boardwalks gawked as the wagon rolled down Main Street, flanked by the two Texans. The vehicle was obviously loaded with gold and bound for the bank. Someone must have run ahead to carry the word because when Chloride brought the wagon to a stop in front of the building, the bank manager, Jerome Davenport, had already stepped out onto the boardwalk to greet them.

Davenport hooked his thumbs in his vest and said, "I heard a rumor that you were working for the Golden Queen now, Coleman. Is that true? Do you really have a shipment of Miss Sutton's gold in that wagon?"

"What do you think?" Chloride replied as he wrapped the reins around the brake lever. "What do you reckon I did, loaded this here wagon with plain ol' rocks and brought them in?"

"It's gold," Bo said. "We'll be depositing it, and we'll want a receipt."

Davenport nodded curtly. "Of course. I must say, I'm surprised you were able to bring it into town without the Devils trying to hold you up."

"Nobody said that's what happened," Scratch drawled.

The banker frowned in thought as he tried to figure out what Scratch meant. Then Davenport's eyes widened in surprise as the realization came to him.

"You mean you *were* attacked by the Devils?" he demanded.

Bo dismounted. He looped his horse's reins around the hitch rail in front of the bank and said, "That's right. But as you can see for yourself, we're still alive and the gold is still in the wagon. Now, how about getting some of those clerks of yours to come out here and start unloading the shipment? The sooner that gold's safely locked up in the vault, the better."

"Of course, of course," Davenport muttered. "I just . . . You really mean to say that you fought them off?"

"See for yourself, dagnab it," Chloride said. "You're a banker. You ought to recognize gold when you see it."

A crowd had gathered around the wagon, and at the news that the Devils had tried to steal the gold, only to fail, several people hurried off to spread the word. As Bo glanced down the street, he saw several men calling out the news to their friends. Obviously, it was a big day in Deadwood. This was the first time the Devils had gone after something and not gotten it.

Davenport stepped back into the bank while Bo and Scratch stood by with their Winchesters tucked under their arms, intent on not letting the precious stuff out of their sight until it was locked in the vault. Chloride watched over it, too.

A slight commotion down the street drew Bo's attention. When he looked that way, he saw Martha Sutton hurrying toward the bank. She had her dress pulled up a little so she could move faster. Her blond curls bounced on her shoulders.

She was a little breathless when she came up to them and stopped. "You . . . you made it," she said. "You really got here with the gold."

Scratch tugged on the brim of his hat. "That's what we said we'd do, miss," he told her with a grin.

"I heard people talking about how the Devils tried to steal it. Is that true?"

"It's true, but we convinced them not to," Bo said with a smile of his own.

"You should've seen it," Chloride put in. "It was a real battle royal!"

Bo shook his head. "I wouldn't go quite that far. They tried to bushwhack us, and we discouraged them."

"There's no point in false modesty," a new voice said. Bo looked around to see Lawrence Nicholson standing there, a pearl-gray bowler hat on his head and his hands stuck in his trouser pockets. The owner of the Argosy Mining Company went on. "You've done something that no one else has been capable of, gentlemen. You not only survived an attack by the

Devils, but you also delivered the shipment of gold they wanted. A remarkable achievement, considering the events of the past few months. I'm beginning to think perhaps I was wrong not to hire you."

"We're happy workin' for Miss Sutton," Scratch said. "We intend to keep on doin' it."

Nicholson nodded. "I understand. I applaud such loyalty. I would point out, though, that the Argosy can afford to pay you more than the Golden Queen." He smiled at Martha. "No offense, my dear."

Despite that, she looked a mite offended anyway, Bo thought. But she just said, "I'd appreciate it if you wouldn't try to steal my employees away from me, Mr. Nicholson."

He laughed. "Of course. Congratulations on getting your shipment through." He nodded to Bo, Scratch, and Chloride. "And congratulations to you three on surviving your encounter with the Deadwood Devils."

As Nicholson moved on down the street, Chloride muttered, "You notice he didn't say nothin' about bein' wrong to fire *me*."

"He was thinkin' it," Scratch assured the old-timer.

Several of Davenport's clerks emerged from the bank to begin the task of unloading the gold. Bo followed the clerks inside and watched them place the crates full of gold bars into the vault while Scratch and Chloride stayed outside to keep an eye on the wagon. It didn't take long to get everything unloaded, including the bags of gold dust in the compartment under the seat. Davenport wrote out a receipt and gave it to Martha.

"There you are, Miss Sutton," he said. "I assume

you'll want some of the funds added to your drawing account?"

"That's right," she said. "I'm going to stock up on supplies for my workers and send them back out to the mine with the wagon."

While they were making those arrangements, Chloride eyed the saloons on the eastern end of the settlement, in the area sometimes known as the Badlands. The fire the year before had wiped out a number of those establishments, but they had been rebuilt. Chloride licked his lips and said, "I could sure use a drink to warm me up. The sun may be shinin', but it's still a pretty chilly day."

"I was thinking more about getting something to eat," Bo said with a nod toward the Red Top Café.

"That ain't a bad idea," Scratch agreed. "I got somethin' on my mind I need to ask Miz Pendleton about."

Bo looked over at his old friend. "You're not thinking about marriage again, are you? I know the idea crops up every time you meet a pretty widow—"

"Especially a pretty widow who can cook," Scratch said with a grin. "But naw, I reckon I know by now I ain't ever gonna settle down. I've got a question for the lady anyhow."

"All right, but don't be surprised if she slaps your face."

"It ain't that kind of question," Scratch said. "Chloride, you comin' along?"

The old-timer sighed. "I reckon so. Coffee don't cut the trail dust as well as a shot of red-eye, but it don't muddle the mind as much, neither."

Bo told Martha Sutton they would see her later, then the three men walked down the street to the café.

Sue Beth didn't look surprised to see them when they walked in. As they came up to the counter, she said, "I've been hearing all about your exploits. I guess I should have let you pay for those meals a couple of nights ago after all. I just thought that I'd never see you again."

Bo reached for his pocket. "I can pay you now—" he offered.

"Don't you dare!" Sue Beth said with a smile. "Next time, though, I'll have a little more faith in you." She paused. "I assume there *will* be a next time?"

"You mean, are we gonna bring in another shipment from the Golden Queen?" Scratch asked. He nodded. "I reckon we will, just as soon as we can manage it."

Sue Beth shook her head. "Amazing." She wiped her hands on her apron. "Well, what can I do for the conquering heroes?"

"It's a little early for supper," Bo said. "But how about some coffee and a piece of pie?"

"Apple or peach?"

Bo chose apple, while Scratch and Chloride both decided to have peach pie. As Sue Beth cut pieces of pie and put them on saucers, she said, "You're going to ruin your appetites, you know, eating pie this soon before supper."

Scratch said, "Considerin' the food you dish up, ma'am, there ain't no chance of that!" He sat down on one of the stools at the counter, and as Bo and

Chloride did likewise, Scratch went on. "You know, Miz Pendleton, Thanksgivin' is comin' up."

"Is it?" Sue Beth asked with a twinkle in her eye as she placed the saucers in front of the three men. "Out here on the frontier like this, it's hard to keep up with holidays."

"Yes'm, it is," Scratch said solemnly. "Where Bo and me come from, back in Texas, we always have a big feast on Thanksgivin' with turkey and all the trimmin's."

"I believe that tradition started with the Pilgrims, not in Texas . . . but go on, Mr. Morton."

"Well, ma'am, I was just wonderin' . . . if we can come up with a turkey, how would you feel about fixin' it for us?"

"A Thanksgiving feast, you mean?"

Scratch nodded. "Yes, ma'am."

Sue Beth took her time in answering, but Bo had a hunch she was just teasing Scratch. Finally, she smiled and said, "I think that can be arranged, Mr. Morton."

A relieved grin broke across Scratch's face. "I'll be much obliged, ma'am. You don't know how much. I can't remember how long it's been since Bo and me had ourselves a real Thanksgivin' feast."

"Well, this year you really have something to be thankful for, don't you? You brought that gold shipment in successfully . . . and you didn't get killed by the Deadwood Devils!"

CHAPTER 12

After they finished their pie and coffee, Chloride drove the wagon down to Hanson's Livery Stable. The Texans walked along behind, leading their mounts. When they got there, the wizened liveryman said, "Miss Sutton came by and told me you'd be leavin' the wagon and those mules here for the night. Ain't no charge. She's taken care of it already."

"I hope you gave her a fair price," Bo said.

Hanson bristled at those words. "Of course I did! I treat everybody fair."

Bo had his doubts about that, but he didn't figure it was worth arguing over. He gave Hanson instructions to have the mule team hitched to the wagon early the next morning for the return trip to the Golden Queen mine.

"Whatever you want," Hanson said.

They went to Martha's office next and found the young woman entering figures in a ledger. She looked up at them with a smile as she said, "Come in. I was just adding the shipment you brought in today to the balance sheets. I have to admit, it makes things look a lot better."

"And Mr. Keefer said there's that much again ready to ship," Bo told her. "We'll be heading back up to the mine first thing in the morning to get it. Be back in town day after tomorrow, if there aren't any problems. If that's what you want, that is. You're still the boss."

Martha set her pen back in its holder. "The sooner we get the gold here, the better as far as I'm concerned. When I get through here, I'll go over to Bullock and Star's store and give Mr. Star the order for the supplies I want you to take with you. He'll have it ready for you early tomorrow morning."

"Sounds good." Bo nodded and started to turn away.

"Wait a minute," Martha said. As the three men paused, she went on, "Tell me . . . how are things at the mine? Are the men still in good spirits? They . . . they haven't given up on me, have they?"

"No, ma'am," Scratch replied without hesitation. "As far as I could tell, everybody's workin' hard and pullin' for you to make a go of it."

Bo nodded. "I agree. They're a mite worried, of course, considering everything that's been going on—"

"How could they not be?" Martha said quietly.

"That's right. But like Scratch says, they're still on your side."

"Thank you," she said. "I'm going to do everything in my power to see to it that their loyalty is rewarded. Now, what are the three of you doing tonight?"

The question surprised Bo a little. "We figured we'd get some supper after a while, then head back out to Chloride's cabin, I reckon."

Martha shook her head and said, "Why don't you stay here in town? You can get rooms at the hotel for the night. I'll pay for them."

She was feeling mighty flush right now, Bo realized, and he didn't blame her. Having any sort of success again was probably a big relief to her. But as much as she still owed, she didn't need to be spending her money on hotel rooms for the three of them.

"We'll be fine at Chloride's," he said firmly before either of his companions could speak up. "You can find a better use for your money than that."

Martha looked a little disappointed. "Are you certain?"

"Yes, ma'am," Scratch said, following Bo's lead. "Shoot, I reckon old reprobates like us wouldn't feel comfortable stayin' in some fancy hotel."

"The Grand Central isn't exactly what you'd call fancy," Martha said with a smile, "but if you're sure, I suppose that's all right. Have a good evening, and I'll see you in the morning before you leave."

Bo smiled and nodded and ushered his companions outside.

"I notice you didn't ask *me* whether I wanted to spend the night in a fancy hotel," Chloride complained.

"With the kind of digs you've got, I didn't think you'd even consider it," Bo told him with a grin.

"Come on. Let's get some supper. Unless you're still full from that pie . . . ?"

"I could eat," Chloride said.

After they had eaten supper and traded some more pleasant conversation with Sue Beth when she could find the time in the busy café, Chloride once again brought up the idea of having a drink.

"You and Scratch go ahead," Bo said, trading a quick glance with Scratch to confirm that the silver-haired Texan would look after the old-timer. "I've got another errand I want to take care of."

"What errand's that?" Chloride wanted to know.

"Don't waste your breath askin'," Scratch advised. "I can tell by the look on Bo's face that he's got some idea percolatin' around in his head, but he don't like to talk about such things until he's sure he's got the whole shootin' match figured out."

"It's just something I want to check on, that's all," Bo said. "I'll find you later at the saloon, if you can tell me which one you're going to."

"The Bella Union's the best," Chloride said. "If we ain't there, try the Gem."

Bo nodded and said so long to the two of them.

While Scratch and Chloride headed down Main Street toward the Bella Union Saloon, Bo turned his steps the other way and headed for the sheriff's office.

He was glad to see a light burning in the window, telling him that someone was there. When he went in, he found Sheriff Henry Manning sitting behind the desk. The lean, hawk-faced lawman looked up and asked, "What can I do for you?"

"My name's Bo Creel, Sheriff. My partner Scratch Morton and I helped bring in that gold shipment from the Golden Queen mine today."

Manning nodded. "I heard about that, of course." He looked more interested now. "I also heard that you shot it out with the Deadwood Devils."

"That's right. I was wondering if you'd let me take a look through the wanted posters and reward dodgers you have on hand."

"You think you recognized one of the outlaws?" Manning asked with a frown.

"I didn't say that. I'd just like to check on something."

For a moment Bo thought the sheriff was going to refuse. Manning was curious, and he obviously didn't like his questions going unanswered. But then he shrugged and said, "All right. Things like that are a matter of public record, after all." He leaned over, opened a drawer in the desk, and took out a thick stack of papers that he placed on the desk. "Help yourself, Creel."

Bo nodded. "Much obliged."

"If you find anything that would help me bring those thieves and murderers to justice, it's your responsibility to tell me," Manning added.

"I'll sure do that, Sheriff," Bo promised. Of course, that left it open to his own interpretation of what he thought might be helpful, he told himself.

He took the reward posters and sat down in an armchair close to the potbellied stove, where a fire was burning merrily. It promised to be another cold night, and old bones felt the chill more than they used to. As he sat there warming himself, Bo began going through the papers, studying the pictures and descriptions of the wanted men printed on them.

Those posters told a story, too, a sordid tale of lawlessness, death, and desperation. Some of the men whose likenesses adorned the posters had been prodded to their crimes by bad luck. As the outlaw Cole Younger had put it a few years earlier, "We were victims of circumstances. We were drove to it."

Others, though, had been born bad. Bo had read in a newspaper once about how some doctor back East, or maybe in Europe, had claimed that pure evil didn't exist, that every lawbreaker had been forced into a life of crime by the way the world treated him. That was complete and utter horse droppings, and Bo knew it. He knew that some hombres were born evil and stayed that way their whole lives. He knew that because he'd had to blow holes in some of them to save his life or Scratch's or some other innocent person's.

When he stopped flipping through the reward dodgers to study a particular one, he couldn't tell by looking at the picture on it if the wanted man was one of the pure evil ones or some fella who'd had a run of bad luck. He was more interested in the name under the drawing of a craggy-faced man with a short, dark beard.

Tom Bardwell.

Wanted for bank robbery, train robbery, murder, and assault in Kansas. Also known as Black Tom or sometimes Four-Finger Tom because the little finger on his left hand was gone, lost in some unknown accident. There was a $2,000 reward on his head, and a

$500 reward, minimum, for anybody riding with him in the gang he led.

The date on the poster was two years earlier. It was a good thing Sheriff Manning didn't clean these out of his desk very often, Bo mused.

He didn't linger long on the poster before he set it aside with the others he had gone through already. To make it look good—because he could feel Manning's eyes on him—he continued studying the posters, pausing now and then over one that didn't mean anything to him. When he was finished, he picked up the whole stack, tapped it on his leg to square it up, and took them back to the desk.

"I appreciate it, Sheriff," he said as he set the stack of posters on the desk.

"Find what you were looking for?" Manning asked.

"Not really," Bo said, "but thanks for letting me look anyway."

Manning leaned back in his chair and regarded his visitor speculatively. "You know," he said, "a suspicious man might wonder if you were looking through those dodgers to make sure you and that partner of yours weren't on any of them."

That hadn't occurred to Bo. The thought brought a chuckle to his lips. "There's no paper out on us, Sheriff," he told Manning. "At least, not that I know of, and if there is, it's a mistake. We're peaceable, law-abiding hombres, Scratch and me."

"Who carry guns and look like you know how to use them."

"So do a lot of other men."

"Other men haven't been able to shoot it out with

the Deadwood Devils and stay alive. I think I'm going to be keeping my eyes on you and Morton, Creel."

"That's fine," Bo said. "We won't be in town for long, though. We're headed back to the Golden Queen mine tomorrow to pick up another shipment of gold."

"Good luck," Manning said. He added dryly, "You're liable to need it."

Bo left the sheriff's office and walked to the Bella Union. He found Scratch and Chloride at the bar in the large, ornate saloon. The fire that had raged through the eastern end of Deadwood the year before had almost reached this far, but it had stopped just short of the Bella Union, sparing the saloon.

"Get your *errand* done?" Chloride asked.

Bo nodded. "I did. Did you get your thirst taken care of?"

"I'm workin' on it." Chloride lifted the half-full mug of beer in front of him and drained the rest of the amber liquid in one long swallow. As he thumped the empty onto the hardwood, he wiped the back of his other hand across his whiskery mouth and then let out a loud belch. "There. I reckon that'll do the job."

Scratch finished off his own beer. "You ready to go?" he asked Bo.

"Yeah."

They had left their horses temporarily at the livery stable. Bo mounted up, then gave Chloride a hand climbing on behind him. The three of them rode up the gulch to the old-timer's cabin. An icy wind whistled along the creek.

"Got a hunch winter's comin' early this year," Chloride commented. "We're liable to see snow before Thanksgivin'."

"I hope not," Scratch said. "I got to find a wild turkey for Sue Beth to cook up for the feast."

"We'll keep our eyes open," Bo told him. "There are bound to be a few gobblers left around here."

The old cabin was dark and quiet when they reached their destination. Bo and Scratch kept their hands near their guns until Chloride had the candle lit, just in case anybody was lurking around who shouldn't be. The old-timer poked up the ashes in the stove and got a fire burning again to take some of the chill out of the air.

On a cold night like this, the best thing to do was curl up in some blankets and sleep. The Texans spread their bedrolls and turned in pretty quickly, followed shortly by Chloride. They would be up before dawn to get ready for the trip back up the gulch to the mine.

Long years of experience had gotten both Bo and Scratch in the habit of sleeping lightly. It didn't take much to wake them. The slightest unusual sound or any other warning of potential danger would do it.

In this case it was a smell. Bo didn't know how long he had been asleep when his eyes suddenly opened. Instantly he was fully awake. His life had depended on just such a swift reaction too many times for it to be otherwise. He lifted his head and sniffed the air.

The sharp tang he smelled was familiar, and as he recognized it, he threw the blankets off and reached for his boots. "Scratch!" he said in an urgent whisper.

"I smell it," the silver-haired Texan replied in the same tone. "Coal oil!"

"Yeah. Wake Chloride, but try to keep him quiet.

We don't want the varmints to know we're awake just yet."

There was only one explanation for the smell of coal oil being so strong inside the cabin. Somebody was splashing the stuff around outside, soaking the walls with it, getting ready to burn the cabin to the ground . . . with Bo, Scratch, and Chloride inside it. The citizens of Deadwood would probably think the candle or an overturned lantern had started the blaze, but in reality, it would be pure murder.

If the men outside got away with it. Bo didn't intend to let that happen.

Moving quietly, he pulled on his boots, buckled on his gunbelt, shrugged into his coat, and picked up his hat and Winchester. As he moved toward the door, he heard the soft whisper as Scratch tried to wake Chloride as quietly as possible, so they could take the would-be arsonists by surprise.

That didn't work. Chloride came up off his bunk sputtering and yelling. "What is it? Who's there? Injuns! Don't let 'em scalp you—"

Just as Bo reached the door, he heard a man's harsh voice outside, ordering, "Light it up!" Bo grabbed the door and jerked it open.

A sheet of fire roared up in his face.

CHAPTER 13

In the sudden burst of flame, Bo caught glimpses of several men in long coats, bandana masks, and pulled-down hats. The Devils of Deadwood Gulch had come to call, seeking revenge for having their plans ruined the past two days. Bo heard a gun roar, saw the muzzle flash, and felt the wind-rip of the bullet going past his ear.

"Keep your heads down!" he shouted to Scratch and Chloride. More shots blasted as he ducked back and kicked the door closed. Bo realized that the outlaws were giving him and his companions a choice: stay in here and burn, or flee through the door and be riddled with lead.

But there was a third option, Bo thought, and he liked their chances better with it.

He whirled toward Scratch and Chloride, who were grabbing up as much of their gear as they could carry. Flames were already licking up the front wall and one of the side walls, casting a garish light on the interior of the old cabin.

"Come on," Bo said. "Out the back!"

"But there ain't no back door!" Chloride protested.
"There's about to be!"

Bo lowered his shoulder, got as much of a running start as the close confines of the cabin would allow him, and rammed into the rear wall as hard as he could. The rotten old lumber, the tarpaper, and the flimsy tin was no match for his hurtling weight. With a splintering crash, he burst through the wall, lost his balance, and sprawled on the ground.

Scratch was there beside him a heartbeat later to reach down, grab Bo's arm, and hoist his friend back to his feet. Somewhere nearby, Chloride's old cap-and-ball pistol boomed.

Bo still had his Colt in his hand. In the nightmar-ish glare cast by the burning building, he snapped a shot at a masked figure he spotted near the cabin. The man bellowed, "They're back here! They got out!"

"Head for the trees!" Bo ordered. Pines grew thickly on the wall of the gulch, all the way down to the base of the slope. The Texans and Chloride re-treated toward them, backing away and sending bul-lets spraying around the cabin from Bo's Colt, Scratch's twin Remingtons, and Chloride's old horse pistol. The burning cabin itself gave them some cover because the Devils had to come around it to get a shot at them, and every time one of them stepped into sight, Bo or Scratch or Chloride sent a bullet his way.

They made it unscathed to the trees and got behind some of the thick trunks to continue the battle. Bo didn't expect the fight to last very long, and sure enough it didn't. The cabin was fully ablaze by now, but even over the crackling roar he heard the thud of hoofbeats as the outlaws took off into the night.

The cabin was close enough to Deadwood that somebody in the town was likely to spot the orange glow in the sky and know that something was burning. Nothing scared people on the frontier like fire. Deadwood had several volunteer fire companies already. Some of the citizens were sure to come hurrying up the gulch to see what was going on.

"Hold your fire, Chloride," Bo called to the old-timer. "They're not shooting at us anymore."

"Yeah, they're gone," Scratch agreed. "Took off for the tall and uncut when they saw we weren't gonna cooperate with them killin' us."

"The hydrophobia skunks!" Chloride raged. "They burned down my cabin! The dang no-good weasels!"

Bo thumbed fresh rounds into his Colt. "We got our guns and most of our gear out of there," he said. "Lost our bedrolls, but we can replace them. I see that a couple of poles on the fence around the shed and the horse pen are down, so I reckon our horses spooked and busted out when the fire started. They're probably still around somewhere."

"Bound to have lost our saddles, though," Scratch said. "We'll have to ride bareback into town."

Bo grunted as he holstered his gun. "Won't be the first time, will it?"

Scratch chuckled and said, "Not hardly. When I was a kid, I reckon I must've rode a thousand miles before I ever knew what a saddle was."

"Yeah, well, we ain't kids no more," Chloride pointed out. "None of us."

"No, but I'll bet Marty Sutton will advance us the money to buy new saddles and tack," Bo said.

"Folks comin'," Scratch said.

It was true. Bo saw the bobbing glow of lanterns coming up the gulch toward them. When he was able to make out one of the fire wagons from Deadwood, along with a crowd of men, he and Scratch and Chloride left the cover of the trees and walked toward the cabin. The roof had fallen in, and now the walls were collapsing as well. Showers of sparks climbed into the cold, black night sky. It would have been a pretty sight in a way, if not for the destruction it represented.

One of the men from town spotted them and shouted, "There they are!" A group hurried forward to meet them.

"What happened?" another man asked. "Are you fellas all right?"

"We're fine," Bo answered. "And as far as what happened . . . some of the Deadwood Devils came to pay us a visit."

"With a can of coal oil," Scratch added.

"Good Lord!" the townman muttered. "They tried to burn down the shack around you?"

Bo nodded. "That's right. We got out just in time and swapped some lead with them, but they got away."

"Three times!" one of the men exclaimed. "That's three times the Devils have gone up against you Texans, and you've come out alive every time!"

"Hey, what about me?" Chloride demanded. "I got away from 'em that first time, when they held up the Argosy gold wagon." He thumped his chest. "I reckon I'm the champeen Devil-buster around here!"

"You can have the title and welcome to it, old-timer," Scratch said with a laugh.

While Chloride was blustering again about being

called an old-timer, the captain of the fire company said, "Let's get some water on that debris, men. We don't want the fire spreading."

The volunteers went about the task with practiced efficiency, working the hand pump to send a spray of water from the tank on the wagon through the hose and onto what was left of the cabin. Smoldering wood sizzled and popped as the water hit it.

While they were doing that, Bo asked the captain, "Reckon we could get a ride back into town with you fellas? Our saddles burned up in the shed."

The man nodded. "Sure. Where are your horses?"

"Around here somewhere," Scratch said. He put a couple of fingers in his mouth and gave a piercing whistle. The Texans weren't surprised when their mounts came trotting up a minute later. The horses were well trained and had a knack for avoiding trouble when they could.

Once the fire was completely out, Bo, Scratch, and Chloride climbed onto the wagon with the rest of the men and rode back into town. The horses trotted along behind the wagon.

A crowd of curious bystanders was waiting in Deadwood. The news of what had happened spread rapidly, and one excitable gent called out, "Three cheers for the gallant Texans and their defeat of the Devils! Hip, hip, hooray!"

The rest of the crowd took up the cheer, which caused Bo and Scratch to exchange an uncomfortable glance. Scratch leaned closer to his friend and said quietly, "Some of those varmints may have took off their masks and snuck back into town already. They could be in this bunch right now."

"I know," Bo said. "And after spending months terrorizing the people around here, I don't imagine they're very happy about what's going on."

"That's liable to make 'em try even harder to kill us."

Bo nodded as he looked at the excited crowd and said, "I wouldn't be a bit surprised."

While Bo and Scratch were putting up their horses for the night at Hanson's Livery after all, Martha Sutton arrived with a shawl wrapped around her shoulders and a worried look on her face.

"Are the three of you all right?" she asked. "I heard that your cabin burned down, Mr. Coleman."

"Got burned down, you mean," Chloride said. "It was them durned Devils again."

"They seem to have declared war on the three of you."

"We've been in wars before," Bo said.

"Always came through all right," Scratch added.

"Then you're not hurt?" Martha asked.

Bo shook his head. "We're fine. We lost our saddles, tack, and bedrolls in the fire, but that's all."

"I'll replace those," Martha said with an emphatic nod. "It's my responsibility. The Devils wouldn't be after you if you weren't working for me. And you'll stay in those hotel rooms after all."

"We won't argue about that with you, ma'am," Bo told her. "I'm a little curious, though, about one thing . . . How did you know what happened to Chloride's cabin? It's late enough that you had probably turned in for the night, hadn't you?"

Martha looked a little uncomfortable and embarrassed, and for a second Bo wondered if he had gone and poked his nose into something that was none of his business. But then she said, "Phillip Ramsey came to my house and told me."

"Ramsey?" Scratch repeated in surprise. "That bookkeeper fella who works for Nicholson?"

Martha nodded. "He'd heard about it—I don't know where—but he didn't know if the three of you were all right. He thought I might want to know, since you work for me."

Scratch grunted and said, "I didn't much cotton to that young fella. Seemed a mite weasel-like to me."

"Phillip's not totally a bad sort. It's just that he works for the Argosy, and, well, Lawrence Nicholson and my father were rivals for a long time. Naturally, there's some hostility on both sides . . ."

But there was a part of Martha that wished the hostility didn't exist, Bo sensed. That didn't come as a complete surprise to him. Martha and Ramsey were about the same age, after all, and even though a gal and a young fella might be business rivals, that didn't always extend to the other parts of their lives.

To spare Martha any further embarrassment, Bo changed the subject by saying, "We'll head down to the hotel now and get some rest. Morning will come awful early, I expect."

Martha nodded. "Of course." She put a hand on Chloride's arm. "I'm very sorry about your cabin, Mr. Coleman. I'll do anything I can to help make it up to you."

That much attention from a pretty young woman did wonders for the old-timer's hurt feelings. Chloride shuffled his feet and said, "Aw, shucks, Miss Sutton, don't worry about it too much. It was just a ramshackle ol' cabin that didn't even belong to me, not really. I was just sorta squattin' in it."

"You lost some personal belongings, though. Just let me know what you need replaced, and I'll take care of it if I can."

Chloride nodded. "Yes'm, I'll do that. Right now, though, I'm fine."

She smiled at him and squeezed his arm, and Bo would have sworn that the old pelican was blushing furiously under all those whiskers.

Martha insisted on going with them to the hotel and making the arrangements for their rooms. Then the three men insisted on walking her back to her house, a neat frame structure in one of Deadwood's residential neighborhoods on the slope above downtown. It was the wee hours of the morning before they were all settled down and asleep in their hotel rooms, and as Bo had predicted, he seemed to have barely closed his eyes when the built-in instinct most frontiersmen possessed woke him. A check of his pocket watch told him it would be dawn in another hour.

Scratch stepped out into the hotel corridor at the same time Bo did. The Texans nodded to each other and went to the door of Chloride's room. Scratch put his ear to the panel and grinned.

"Sounds like he's still sawin' logs in there," he said. "We'll have to wake him up."

"Better be careful about it," Bo advised. "He may sleep with that old horse pistol under his pillow.

You saw what a ruckus he made when you woke him earlier."

"Yeah, he acted like he thought ol' Sittin' Bull and Crazy Horse were after him." Not wanting to disturb the other guests in the hotel, Scratch knocked quietly on the door and called, "Chloride! Hey, Chloride, wake up!"

Then he took a quick step to the side just in case the old-timer grabbed a gun and blasted a shot through the door without knowing what was going on.

Instead Chloride responded with a groggy, "Huh? What in blue blazes—"

"Time to get up, Chloride," Bo said through the door. "We've got things to do and places to be."

"Oh, yeah. Hang on."

Bo and Scratch listened for more snoring, in case Chloride went back to sleep, but a few minutes later the door opened and the old-timer emerged from the room, yawning. "All right, I'm ready to go," he said as he ran his fingers through his tangled beard.

They went to the livery stable first and found that Esteban, the Mexican hostler, was getting ready to hitch the mule team to the wagon by lantern light. Bo asked him when the saddle shop opened, and Esteban said, "Whenever you need it to, señor. The man who runs the shop lives above it, and since he is a bachelor, you will not have to worry about disturbing his family."

Bo nodded his thanks. "All right. We'll wait a little while before we go over there. I see the café is open already, so we'll have some breakfast first."

"Sí, Señora Pendleton is there early and late. She

works very hard." Esteban shrugged. "But what else is she to do, with no man in her life? It was very hard for her when her husband died."

"I'm sure it was," Bo said. He lifted a hand in farewell. "We'll be back after a while."

They went up the street and angled across to the Red Top. A couple of men were already at the counter drinking coffee. Sue Beth was nowhere in sight, but she emerged from the door into the kitchen a moment later.

"It'll be a while before the food's ready," she said as she greeted the newcomers with a smile, "but I can pour coffee for you."

"That'll be fine, ma'am," Scratch told her.

They settled down on stools at the counter while Sue Beth placed cups and saucers in front of them and then fetched the pot from the stove. "I heard about what happened last night," she said as she poured. "I'm sorry about your cabin, Chloride."

The old-timer shook his head. "It's my own dang fault, I reckon, for throwin' in with these two wild Texas boys and makin' the Devils mad at us."

"They don't like anyone defying them, do they?"

"Apparently not," Bo said. "They'd have to be pretty upset to burn down a fella's cabin with him in it."

Sue Beth frowned. "Are you certain it was the same bunch? There could be more than one gang of outlaws around here, you know."

"That's true," Bo admitted. "But these hombres wore the same sort of outfit that the Devils do. Anyway, another bunch of owlhoots would have tried to rob us. Those men last night just wanted us dead."

"I've been doin' some thinkin, too," Chloride put in. "Last night I heard one of the varmints give the order to light that coal oil they'd splashed around, and I'd swear it was the same fella I heard bossin' the others that day they hit the Argosy gold wagon." A little shudder ran through the old-timer. "The same one who carved the pitchforks into the foreheads of them dead guards."

"But you can't be sure of that, can you?" Sue Beth asked.

"I reckon not. But I got a feelin' in my bones that I'm right, and I've learned to trust these old bones."

Charlie the cook called through the opening behind the counter. "I got flapjacks and bacon ready!"

"I'll be right back," Sue Beth told her customers.

The food was as good as always. Bo, Scratch, and Chloride enjoyed their breakfast and washed the meal down with plenty of coffee. Having their bellies full helped them get over everything that had happened the night before.

When Bo went to pay for the food, Sue Beth shook her head and said, "Marty Sutton came by here a while ago and told me that if you stopped in for breakfast, I should just add the bill to her tab."

"Miss Sutton's already up and about?" Bo asked.

Sue Beth nodded. "That's right. She had some coffee, then said she was on her way to Bullock and Star's. She may still be there."

Bo put his hat on and ticked a finger against the brim. "We're much obliged. See you the next time we're in town."

"Hopefully that won't be too long."

"And maybe we'll have that turkey for Thanks-givin'," Scratch added.

Sue Beth laughed. "I'll be waiting."

The big mercantile down the street was owned and operated by Seth Bullock and Sol Star, Bo knew. He remembered both men from the previous visit he and Scratch had paid to Deadwood. At that time, Bullock and Star had only recently arrived from Montana and were selling their stock of goods out of a tent. Since then, they had built a big, prosperous-looking estab-lishment that took up most of a block.

Sol Star ran the place for the most part. His part-ner Seth Bullock had been the marshal of Deadwood for a while and done a fine job of it from what Bo had heard, bringing law and order to the raw mining camp and continuing to serve after Deadwood had become an actual town. Sol Star was something of a civic leader, too, having been elected as Deadwood's mayor several times. Star might still be mayor, for all Bo knew. All he cared about at the moment was the fact that the store was already open and Martha Sutton had gone over there, evidently to arrange for the supplies they were supposed to load on the wagon to take back to the mine.

Martha stepped out onto the store's porch as Bo, Scratch, and Chloride approached. She was bundled in a heavy coat this morning, her breath fogging in the air in front of her, but her blond curls hung free around her shoulders as usual. She smiled and said, "Good morning. Mr. Star and his clerks have the sup-plies ready, and they can load them as soon as you bring the wagon over."

Chloride nodded and said, "I'll go fetch it."

As the old-timer hurried off, Martha went on to Bo and Scratch. "I hope you don't mind, but Mr. Star had some good saddles, and I took the liberty of buying a couple of them, along with everything else you'll need."

Bo and Scratch glanced at each other. As veteran horsemen, they would have preferred to pick out their own saddles. Every rider had his own likes and dislikes, and they were usually different. But Martha's heart was in the right place, so Bo said, "I'm sure they'll be fine. We appreciate it, Miss Sutton."

"There hasn't been any more trouble since Mr. Coleman's cabin burned down, has there? I haven't heard about anything."

Scratch said, "The rest of the night was plumb peaceful."

"You think you'll be back tomorrow with the other load of gold?"

"We should be," Bo said.

"What will you do after that?"

Bo shrugged. "Keep poking around, I guess. We'd still like to find where the Devils stashed all the loot from those earlier robberies."

"If it's even still around here," Scratch added.

"But we'll stay in touch, and whenever Andrew Keefer and the men at the mine have another load ready to bring down the gulch, we'll handle that chore for you," Bo went on. "As long as you want us to, that is."

Martha laughed. "I think you can count on that, Mr. Creel," she said. "You and Mr. Morton are the only ones who've had any luck at all stopping the Devils. The way things were going, the mining business in this whole area was going to be ruined. Digging the gold out of the hills doesn't do any good if you can't get it into the bank."

Bo nodded and said, "That's true. And I reckon the way the Devils had everybody so scared was almost as bad as losing all that gold."

"Worse, maybe," Martha said. "If things had kept on, Deadwood might have been a ghost town in another year. Now, though, people have hope again. And they have you two to thank for that."

"And Chloride," Scratch added with a grin. "That old-timer gets a mite touchy when he's left out of anything."

"I heard that, dadblast it!" Chloride called out from the street in front of the store where he had just brought the wagon to a stop. "I ain't that much older'n you, you danged Texas roadrunner!"

CHAPTER 14

The trip back up the gulch and the side canyon to the Golden Queen mine was uneventful. Even the saddles that Martha had bought for the Texans turned out to be all right. Bo and Scratch were alert the entire way, watchful for even the tiniest hint of trouble, but nothing happened except the wagon reached the mine with its load of supplies intact. The supplies were very welcome, too, as provisions were starting to run a little low in the cook shack.

Andrew Keefer wanted to hear all about the journey to Deadwood. He was suitably impressed when the Texans and Chloride told him about fighting off the Devils, and he was livid with anger when he heard about how Chloride's cabin had been destroyed.

"I'm sure Miss Sutton will offer to make good your losses as best she can," the superintendent said.

"She already said she would," Chloride replied. "She's got bigger worries on her plate right now, though."

"Such as that next load of gold," Bo said. "Do you

still think there's enough on hand to justify another shipment right away, Mr. Keefer?"

"There certainly is," Keefer said with a nod. "No dust this time, but plenty of bars. I'll have the men start packing and loading it this afternoon, if you're willing to make the trip to Deadwood again so quickly."

"No point in waitin'," Scratch said. "For all we know, those owlhoots are a mite confused right now, and we ought to take advantage of that if we can."

Keefer agreed and issued the orders. By nightfall, the gold wagon was loaded and ready to go, and once again Keefer picked out some men to stand guard over it all night.

"The Devils have never robbed any of the mines themselves, have they?" Bo asked that evening as he, Scratch, and Chloride stood with the superintendent on the porch of the building that housed Keefer's office and living quarters.

"No," Keefer replied. "Only stagecoaches starting out, and then the gold shipments."

"And they've hijacked shipments from all the mines?"

"That's right, now that they hit that shipment from the Argosy. At least, they've struck at all the bigger mines. There are still a few smaller claims scattered through the hills that don't produce enough color to make it worthwhile to rob them."

"You're still thinkin', ain't you, Bo?" Scratch asked.

"Does he do that all the time?" Chloride asked.

Bo chuckled. "Just trying to figure out a few things, that's all. Something about the Devils doesn't quite add up to me."

"What's to figure out?" Keefer wanted to know.

"They're a bunch of no-good, greedy, murdering road agents! Seems pretty blasted simple to me."

"You're probably right," Bo told the superintendent. "Sometimes I make more out of things than they really are."

On that note, the men turned in for the night, and early the next morning they were up again, getting ready to roll out on the trip to Deadwood in the cold, pale dawn.

During the morning, clouds rolled in to obscure the weak, watery sunlight, and the temperature dropped even more. As Chloride sent the wagon rolling along the trail, he cast a wary eye toward the skies and warned, "Liable to be some snow 'fore we get to town." He brightened slightly. "On the other hand, maybe that means them varmints'll be more likely to leave us alone."

"If the Devils want to hit us again, I doubt if the weather will stop them," Bo said.

"I don't plan on lettin' my guard down," Scratch added.

"I never told you to do that," Chloride said. "I was just pointin' out that it might snow."

As a matter of fact, less than an hour later a few powdery flurries spat down from the gunmetal-gray heavens, and the old-timer gleefully pointed them out as evidence that he was right.

The flurries stopped a short time after that, and those were the only flakes that fell. Chloride insisted that since technically it had snowed, his prediction had been correct.

So was his comment about the outlaws not trying to hold them up, although it was impossible to know if the snow flurries had anything to do with the Devils' leaving them alone. Bo was inclined to doubt it, but it didn't matter. What was important was that late in the afternoon, the wagon rolled into Deadwood with its load of gold bars intact.

This shipment's arrival didn't create as big a commotion as the first one, possibly because the cold had a lot of people indoors close to their stoves, but a small crowd did gather in front of the bank to watch the crates of gold bars being unloaded. Once again Bo watched the clerks place the gold in the vault while Scratch and Chloride kept an eye on the crates that hadn't been unloaded yet.

That was still going on when Scratch stuck his head inside the bank's front door and called, "Bo, you better come take a look at this."

Bo heard the note of concern in his old friend's voice. That was enough to make him hurry out of the bank and join Scratch and Chloride next to the wagon. They looked down the street toward the eastern end of the settlement, where a troop of blue-uniformed cavalry was riding into Deadwood.

Four years earlier, with the news of the Seventh Cavalry's massacre on the hills above the Little Big Horn River still fresh in everyone's mind, the citizens of Deadwood had reacted with riotous celebration when a large detachment of cavalry under the command of General George Crook had ridden into town. In those days, people had been afraid constantly that the Indians were going to slaughter them in their beds some night.

Since then, the threat of an Indian attack had diminished dramatically. But the arrival of the cavalry in town still caused quite a stir. People forgot about how cold it was and came out of their businesses and homes to watch the troopers ride in.

It wasn't a big patrol, about thirty men led by a lieutenant and a grizzled sergeant. They rode to the middle of town and reined in, and by that time word of what was going on had reached the sheriff's office. Sheriff Henry Manning strode up, and as the young officer dismounted, Manning demanded, "Lieutenant, what's going on here? Are you and your men in pursuit of hostiles? I haven't heard anything about the Indians being on the warpath again."

The lieutenant didn't answer Manning's questions. Instead he asked one of his own. "Who are you, sir?"

"Henry Manning," the lawman snapped. "I'm the sheriff around here."

The officer came to attention and saluted. "Lieutenant Vance Holbrook reporting as ordered, sir. I'm to make myself and my men available to you."

Manning frowned at him, obviously baffled. "Available to me? What for?"

A new voice said, "I'll tell you what for, Sheriff." Lawrence Nicholson walked up. "A number of the mine owners got together and sent a letter to Washington several weeks ago requesting assistance with the plague of lawlessness that has erupted in the Black Hills in recent months. At first the Justice Department was just going to send in a United States marshal, but we prevailed upon the authorities to reconsider that decision and assign a troop of cavalry to Deadwood instead. The problem of the Deadwood Devils is too big for one man to handle."

Manning glared at Nicholson. His eyes were as cold and gray as the sky as he said, "Blast it, you had no right to do that. It's my place to request any outside help, if I determine that it's needed."

"It's also your place to stop those outlaws from ruining all the mines in the area, but you didn't seem to be accomplishing that, did you?" Nicholson shot back.

Bo watched with interest as Manning's face became darkly mottled with rage. "My primary responsibility is to keep the peace in town," the lawman said. "No one can deny that I've done that."

"Of course not, Sheriff. You've been exemplary at that part of your job. But the way things have been going, sooner or later you'll be keeping the peace in a ghost town after all the mines have shut down. The other owners and I aren't going to stand for that." Nicholson turned to the cavalry officer. "My name is Lawrence Nicholson, Lieutenant Holbrook. I own the Argosy Mining Company. I'll be glad to fill you in on everything that's happened around here and will help you carry out your orders any way I can."

"Thank you, sir," Holbrook said, "but I really ought to be working with the local authorities—"

"No, that's all right," Manning said in a choked voice as he visibly struggled to keep his temper reined in. "If you're here to catch the Deadwood Devils, Lieutenant, then by all means you should talk to Mr. Nicholson and the other mine owners. They can tell you what you need to know. You can operate independently as far as I'm concerned."

"There's no need to get your nose out of joint, Sheriff," Nicholson said.

"I'm just trying to give you what you want," Manning snapped. To Holbrook, he added, "Go to it, Lieutenant. You've got a free hand."

Holbrook nodded and said, "Thank you, sir."

"Come along to my office, Lieutenant," Nicholson invited. "I'll tell you all about it."

"Of course, sir." Holbrook turned to his non-com and went on. "Sergeant, locate a suitable place to camp and have the men fall out and set up their tents."

The sergeant, a stocky, middle-aged man with a drooping, gray-streaked mustache, said, "Beggin' your pardon, Lieutenant, but tents are gonna be sort of cold in weather like this."

"What would you have me do, put the company up at the hotel?" Holbrook snapped. "Carry out my orders, Sergeant."

The non-com nodded and said, "Yes, sir."

"Well, what do you think about that?" Scratch asked as he and Bo and Chloride watched the sergeant lead the troopers past the bank.

"It's pretty interesting," Bo said. "Makes me think twice about some of the ideas in my head. I'll have to ponder on it."

"You reckon them soldier boys'll be able to chase down the Devils?" Chloride asked.

Bo had his doubts about that, because he still believed at least some of the members of the gang were right here in Deadwood under their noses, masquerading as respectable citizens. Or at least semi-respectable citizens.

But all he said was, "We'll see. Right now, we need

to make sure that the rest of this gold gets unloaded and locked in the vault, and then I want to let Miss Sutton know that we made it all right."

Martha Sutton was already aware of that. She looked up from her desk with a smile when the three men came in. "I was just about to head down to the bank as soon as I finished up this paperwork," she said.

"No need for you to do that," Bo told her as he handed her the receipt Jerome Davenport had given him.

Martha looked at the paper with shining eyes. "This is wonderful," she said. "Now I can afford to pay at least some of the back wages I owe . . . including everything that I owe the three of you."

"We're in no hurry—" Scratch began.

Martha stood up and shook her head. "No, I'm going to settle up with you. I insist. If it wasn't for the three of you, I might have been forced to give up by now."

"What do you mean by give up?" Bo asked.

"Well . . . I suppose I would have sold the mine. Lawrence Nicholson has been offering to buy me out practically ever since my father died. There's been interest from some of the other companies, too."

"You might have been able to get enough money to live on for a long time," Bo pointed out.

"But not what the mine's worth," Martha insisted. "And giving up and selling out . . . well, my father never would have done it. I can be at least as stubborn as he would have been, can't I?"

Bo smiled. "I never met Mike Sutton, but I'd say you come by it honest, miss." He tugged on the brim of his hat. "We'll be going now. Tomorrow we'll take the wagon back up to the mine, and then Chloride plans to stay there until the next shipment is ready to bring down."

"If that's all right with you, miss," the old-timer added.

Martha nodded. "Of course." She looked at the Texans. "What about the two of you?"

"Reckon we'll have to play that by ear," Scratch said. "We'll be scoutin' around, though, tryin' to get a line on those road agents."

Chloride snorted. "You mean tryin' not to get in the way of them soldier boys."

"Soldiers?" Martha repeated. "What soldiers?"

"You haven't heard?" Bo asked, a little surprised that Martha didn't know about the cavalry's arrival. "A troop of cavalry rode in a little while ago. It seems that without anybody knowing about it, Nicholson and some of the other mine owners sent word to Washington asking for help cleaning things up around here. You weren't part of that?"

Martha smiled and shook her head. "Lawrence Nicholson and the other owners don't confide in me, Bo. They don't think a woman should be running a mining company in the first place, so naturally they don't include me in their plans. But I'm a little surprised the government would send in the army to catch some outlaws, even if it is just a cavalry patrol."

"The gold that comes out of the Black Hills means a lot to the government," Bo said. "They need it for all the coins they mint, and to keep another financial panic from brewing."

"I suppose that's true. Surely the cavalry will be able to find an outlaw gang."

"I dunno," Chloride said. "They didn't do such a good job of roundin' up all those Injuns that massacreed Custer and his boys. Fact is, a lot of the chiefs made it across the border into Canada 'fore Gen'ral Crook could catch up to 'em."

"Maybe Lieutenant Holbrook will have better luck," Bo said. "Come on."

The three men left the office. They had already seen to it that the horses and mules were put up for the night at the livery stable, out of the cold in nice warm stalls. Now they dealt with their own accommodations, stopping at the hotel to make sure they had rooms before heading to the Red Top Café for supper.

Sue Beth Pendleton greeted them with her usual friendly smile. "I heard you were back with another shipment from the Golden Queen," she said as the three men came up to the counter. "It's quite a big day for Deadwood. Another gold shipment gets through, and the cavalry shows up to chase down the Devils."

"Yeah, we'll see about that last part," Chloride said.

"You don't think the soldiers will be able to deal with those outlaws?"

"I ain't got a heap o' confidence, let's put it that way."

"Well, I hope you're wrong, Chloride," Sue Beth said. "Those killers and thieves have been a blight on these parts for long enough."

No one could argue with that.

"I suppose you're here for supper?" Sue Beth went on. "It's beef stew tonight, piping hot."

Chloride licked his lips, and Scratch said, "Sounds mighty good to me, ma'am."

"By the way, where's that turkey?"

Scratch heaved a sigh. "We didn't spy nary a gobbler while we were gone. But I ain't givin' up. It won't be Thanksgivin' for a few more days yet."

They sat at a table this time. Sue Beth brought over bowls of steaming stew and a plate full of thick slices of sourdough bread. After a day on the trail, Bo, Scratch, and Chloride attacked the food with gusto.

They were still eating when the café's front door opened, letting in some chilly air and the intimidating presence of the sergeant who had ridden in earlier with Lieutenant Holbrook. As the non-com closed the door behind him, he looked around the room. After a moment his gaze settled on Bo, Scratch, and Chloride, and to Bo's surprise, the sergeant came toward them with a heavy, determined stride.

He stopped next to their table and asked in a voice that held a hint of a Scandinavian accent, "Are you men Creel, Morton, and Coleman?"

"That's right," Bo said. "What can we do for you, Sergeant?"

The sergeant unsnapped the flap of his holster and rested his hand on the butt of his revolver as he said, "You can come with me, that's what you can do."

CHAPTER 15

The other customers in the café heard the sergeant's blunt declaration and saw his threatening gesture. A tense hush fell over the place as everyone waited to see if trouble was going to break out. Behind the counter, Sue Beth paled a little as she watched the confrontation.

Chloride opened his mouth to say something, and Bo had no doubt the old-timer's response would be an angry one. He silenced Chloride with a lifted hand. In a situation such as this, staying calm might be a better idea.

"Are we under arrest, Sergeant?" Bo asked.

"No, but the lieutenant told me to bring you, and he didn't make no bones about it. I won't be taking no for an answer."

"Why does he want to see us?"

The sergeant gave a curt shake of his head. "He didn't tell me, and it ain't my place to ask. Now, are you coming along peaceful-like?"

"Back to your camp?"

The sergeant grunted, and Bo heard a faint note of

contempt in the sound. "No, he's over at the hotel," the non-com said. *As if he'd be out in the cold like the rest of us,* he seemed to say after that, Bo thought, although the words went unspoken.

"We haven't finished our supper yet," Bo said. "Why don't you sit down and have a cup of coffee while you wait?"

"The lieutenant told me to find you and bring you—"

"Well, there's no way of telling how long it took you to find us, now is there?"

For a second, Bo thought the man was going to stick to his guns. But then the ramrod stiffness of the sergeant's back loosened a little, and he said in a more relaxed tone, "I looked several places for you before I got here. I don't suppose Lieutenant Holbrook would know exactly how many places I had to search to find you."

Scratch grinned, looked over at the counter, and said, "Sue Beth, could we get another cup of coffee over here?"

She looked relieved that there wasn't going to be trouble. "Right away," she said.

The sergeant snapped his holster flap, pulled out the empty chair at the table, and sank wearily into it. "We've been in the saddle all day for several days getting here," he said. "But that's the army for you. I can't complain."

"You can, it just won't do any good," Bo said with a smile. "We haven't been properly introduced. I'm Bo Creel, that's Scratch Morton, and the old-timer is Chloride Coleman."

"Sergeant Olaf Gustaffson," the non-com said before Chloride could complain about Bo's introduction.

"You've been wearin' the blue for a while, haven't you, Sarge?" Scratch asked.

"My first campaign was the Mexican War, if that tells you anything," Gustaffson replied.

"We missed that one," Bo said.

"We'd done fought the Mexicans already, at a little place called San Jacinto," Scratch added. "Figured it would be all right if we sat the next one out."

"Texans, eh?"

"I ain't," Chloride said. "I'm just ridin' with 'em these days."

Gustaffson grinned. "That's even worse. You've got a choice in the matter."

"There are some as might take offense at that," Scratch said. "We'll let it pass, though, figurin' that bein' a ignorant Scandahoovian you just don't know any better."

Sue Beth arrived at the table with cup and saucer and the coffeepot. She filled the sergeant's cup. Gustaffson said, "I'm much obliged to you, ma'am."

"You're welcome, Sergeant," she told him. "Thank you for not causing a scene."

Now that Gustaffson had unbent a little, Bo found himself instinctively liking the man. If Gustaffson had been in the army for more than thirty years as he indicated, he had probably been as many places and seen as many things as the Texans had. That meant there was a certain kinship between them, a bond that existed between veteran frontiersmen. It would be enjoyable to sit down sometime and talk to the sergeant about his military career.

But not right now. Bo was more interested in other things at the moment.

When Sue Beth had gone back to the counter, he asked, "Are you sure you don't know why the lieutenant wants to see us, Olaf?" In Bo's experience, non-coms usually knew more about what was really going on than anyone else in a uniform.

"Well . . ." Gustaffson hesitated. "I'm not sure, but when I got back to the hotel to report to the lieutenant that the camp was set up, I heard him and that Nicholson fella talking about how the three of you are the only ones who have taken on these so-called Devils and lived to tell the tale. I won't swear to it, but I've got a hunch Lieutenant Holbrook wants to draft you fellas into scouting for us."

"To help you find the Devils' hideout, you mean?"

Gustaffson nodded. "Wouldn't surprise me a bit."

"We've looked for it already," Scratch said. "Nary any luck so far."

"They've got to be around here somewhere, otherwise they couldn't keep holding up those gold shipments. And all the gold they've already stolen has to be somewhere, too."

Gustaffson had just put into words one of the things Bo had been thinking about. Even though he believed that some of the outlaws were spending most of their time here in town, the gang had to have a place where they cached their loot, and it was unlikely they would leave it unguarded. Some of them probably stayed at the hideout all the time, some stayed in town, and others moved back and forth carrying messages. If the cavalry could locate the hideout, they could recover the stolen gold and break the back of the gang. They might not ever be able to round up all the members, but at least the threat of the Deadwood Devils would be over.

"We'll help, if that's what the lieutenant wants," Bo said. "Otherwise we're going to risk getting in each other's way, because Scratch and I intend to keep looking for the gang."

"What about this old fella?" Gustaffson asked as he gestured toward Chloride.

"I can speak for myself," Chloride said. "And I'm goin' back up to the Golden Queen mine to wait for the next shipment o' gold to be ready. I ain't no dang outlaw-hunter like these two."

Gustaffson's eyes narrowed as he looked back at the Texans. "After a bounty, eh?"

"That's not exactly how he meant it," Bo said.

"But if there's a reward, we wouldn't mind claimin' it," Scratch added.

Gustaffson shook his head. "You'll have to talk to somebody else about that. The only money I ever see is my wages, and damned little of that." He swallowed the rest of his coffee and got to his feet. "You're done eating. Come on."

As they went out, the sergeant nodded to Sue Beth and added, "Mighty fine coffee, ma'am." He jerked a thumb at Bo, Scratch, and Chloride. "It's on these fellas."

Sue Beth smiled and told him, "I already added it to their tab, Sergeant."

"Good-lookin' *and* efficient," Scratch commented on the way out, loud enough for Sue Beth to hear him.

The four men huddled in their coats as they walked along the street to the Grand Central Hotel. The wind whipping through Deadwood's streets clawed at them like icy fingers. Bo was glad to get back inside and relished the warmth coming from the stoves scattered around the hotel's lobby and dining room.

Sergeant Gustaffson pointed to a doorway in the dining room. "Lieutenant Holbrook and that fella Nicholson are in a private room over there." He went to the closed door and knocked, and when there was a muffled response from within, he said, "It's me, Lieutenant. I've got those men you sent me to find."

Holbrook must have told him to bring them in, because Gustaffson opened the door and gestured for Bo, Scratch, and Chloride to go in.

The lieutenant and Lawrence Nicholson were seated at a table with glasses and a bottle of whiskey in front of them. With his hat off, Holbrook looked even younger, if that was possible. He had sandy hair and a somewhat angular face, and if he had been out of West Point for more than a year, Bo would be shocked.

Holbrook got to his feet and said, "Please, gentlemen, come in." He gave Gustaffson a curt nod. "That'll be all, Sergeant."

"Yes, sir," the non-com said. He had been dismissed, and now he had to go back to his tent and hope that it would keep a little of the frigid wind out. Bo didn't blame him for being reluctant to leave. All the troopers were in the same situation, though, and there wasn't a thing Bo or anyone else could do about it.

When Gustaffson was gone, Holbrook motioned toward the empty chairs at the table. "Have a seat. Would any of you like a drink?"

Chloride licked his lips. "I would."

"Reckon I could do with one, too," Scratch said.

Bo shook his head and made a gesture indicating that he would pass.

When they were all sitting down, Holbrook said, "Thank you for coming so promptly."

"Sergeant Gustaffson didn't leave us much choice in the matter," Bo said. "He's a good man."

Holbrook didn't seem to hear the compliment. "I'll get right to the point. Since you men are civilians, I can't order you to do anything."

"Not without placing the town under martial law," Nicholson put in, "which the lieutenant and I have agreed isn't necessary or advisable at this point."

"Why don't you just tell us what you want, Lieutenant?" Bo suggested. "Then we can tell you whether or not we'll go along with it."

"Fine. I'd like for you to serve as scouts and help me locate the headquarters of the outlaw band known variously as the Deadwood Devils and the Devils of Deadwood Gulch." Holbrook inclined his head toward the mine owner. "Mr. Nicholson here tells me that the three of you have had more experience with them than anyone else. Anyone still alive, that is."

"We've tangled with them a few times," Bo admitted. "We couldn't identify any of them, though, and we don't know where they hole up."

"Still, I need some experienced men to help me in my search. I've been charged with bringing them to justice, Mr. Creel, and I intend to do so, no matter what it takes." Holbrook paused. "I can offer you scout's wages—"

"Not me," Chloride said. "I already got a job. I drive for the Golden Queen Minin' Company, and I'm headed back up to the mine in the mornin'."

Nicholson smiled thinly. "Mr. Coleman here is a former employee of mine, Lieutenant, and I can tell you that it won't do any good to argue with him. He's every bit as stubborn as those mules he drives."

"I reckon you didn't mean it as such, but I'll take that as a compliment, Nicholson," Chloride replied.

Holbrook didn't seem bothered by the exchange. He looked at Bo and Scratch and asked, "What about you two? Are you interested in helping to put a stop to the plague of lawlessness in this area?"

"Darn right we are," Scratch said. "Bo?"

"I reckon we can come to an agreement, Lieutenant," Bo said. "Chloride is going to be taking the Golden Queen's wagon back up the gulch to the mine tomorrow. I suggest that you and your troop accompany him as an escort, and Scratch and I will come along, too."

"A military escort," Chloride said. "I sorta like the sound of that."

Holbrook frowned. "I'm not sure it would be proper to be seen as favoring one mine operation over another . . ."

Nicholson waved a hand and said, "Don't worry about that, Lieutenant. You'll need to be heading in that direction anyway to begin your search, so I don't see anything improper in riding that way at the same time as Mr. Coleman is returning in the wagon."

"Well . . . all right," Holbrook said with a nod. "If you're sure."

"It's settled, then." Nicholson sounded pleased. He reached for the bottle. "I think we should have a drink on it." He splashed whiskey into the empty glasses, then picked up his and went on. "To the end of the Deadwood Devils."

"To the end of the Deadwood Devils," Holbrook echoed. Scratch and Chloride didn't say anything. They just downed their drinks along with Nicholson and the lieutenant.

Bo wished it was that easy to get rid of the outlaws.

But he knew good and well it wouldn't be.

CHAPTER 16

The next morning dawned very cold but clear, the clouds that brought the snow flurries the day before having moved on. As the sun rose, the wagon with Chloride at the reins rolled out of Deadwood. It didn't carry any supplies this time, but in the compartment under the seat rode a canvas pouch containing a partial payroll for the miners at the Golden Queen. Martha couldn't yet afford to pay them everything she owed them, but it was a good start.

The presence of the payroll was another reason for the troopers to accompany the wagon. Bo seriously doubted that even as audacious a bunch of owlhoots as the Deadwood Devils would attack the wagon with a bunch of cavalry troopers riding behind it.

When they stopped at midday, Lieutenant Holbrook came over to Bo and Scratch and asked, "When will we reach the mine?"

"Probably around the middle of the afternoon," Bo replied. "We can make better time with an empty wagon than with one loaded down with gold."

Holbrook nodded. "Good. That will give us time to begin our search for the outlaws' hideout today."

"You don't want to spend the night at the mine and start looking in the morning?"

"And waste several hours?" Holbrook shook his head. "I think not."

Bo and Scratch glanced at each other. Like most young officers, Holbrook was eager to make his mark and get started on his climb up the ranks.

Scratch said, "That's fine, Lieutenant. Don't get your hopes up too high, though. This is a smart bunch. They ain't gonna be easy to find."

"Well, we won't find them if we don't look, will we?" Holbrook said crisply. He walked off before Bo or Scratch could say anything else.

Scratch rubbed his jaw and mused, "We've run across shavetails like that one before."

"Yeah, and they usually wind up in trouble," Bo said. "We may have our work cut out for us, partner."

"We usually do," Scratch said with a smile.

The little caravan arrived at the mine in the middle of the afternoon, as Bo predicted. Andrew Keefer was surprised to see the cavalry, and so were the other men. Holbrook shook hands with the mine superintendent and asked, "Any sign of those outlaws in the past two days?"

Keefer shook his head. "No, but that's to be expected. They don't bother the mines themselves. They just hold up anybody who tries to get any gold out over the trail to Deadwood."

"We'll soon put a stop to that," Holbrook promised

with a curt nod. He looked at Bo and Scratch. "We'll rest the horses for a quarter of an hour and then pull out. Do you have a plan as to where we'll begin the search?"

"I've been thinking on it," Bo said. He turned to Keefer. "Do you have a map of the area in your office?"

"Several of them. Do you want to have a look?"

"I wouldn't mind."

Scratch said, "You go ahead, Bo. I'll tend to the horses and make sure they get watered."

"You'll have to break the ice in the trough," Keefer warned. "It keeps freezing over."

Scratch nodded and led the mounts toward the corral. Sergeant Gustaffson was already making sure the enlisted men cared for their horses.

Bo went into the superintendent's office with Keefer. Lieutenant Holbrook followed. Bo would have preferred to study the maps without Holbrook being there, but he couldn't very well send the officer away. Even though he and Scratch were civilians, technically they were under Holbrook's command at the moment.

Keefer cleared off his desk, took several maps from a map case on the wall, and unrolled one of them on top of the desk. All three men gathered around it. It was a topographical map, and Bo had no trouble picking out Deadwood Gulch, Whitewood Gulch, and the numerous smaller canyons.

"Where are all the big mines?" Bo asked.

Keefer pointed them out with a blunt finger. "The Homestake . . . the Father De Smet . . . the Argosy . . . the Golden Queen right here, of course . . ." He named off half a dozen others and tapped their locations on the map.

"All the mines are located in the gulches instead of on top of the ridges," Bo said.

"Well, yes," Keefer agreed. "It's not necessarily easier to dig a shaft horizontally than it is to sink one vertically, but it's easier to get the ore out of the horizontal shafts. Plus the pockets of gold-bearing quartz tend to run horizontally, although they can take off at strange angles in some cases."

Bo leaned over the map and paid particular attention to the locations of the Argosy and the Golden Queen relative to each other. The Argosy was on the southern slope of Deadwood Gulch, while the Golden Queen was on the northern side of the smaller canyon. That meant there was nothing between the two mines except a ridge that was about a mile wide.

He filed that information away in his head and used a finger to trace one of the ridges. "What's up here?" he asked.

Keefer frowned. "You mean on top of that ridge?"

"I mean on top of all the ridges."

"Not much of anything, as far as I know. Trees and a lot of rocks."

"So there's no reason for any of the miners to go up there."

Keefer shook his head. "No. All our work is down in the gulches."

Lieutenant Holbrook said excitedly, "I know what you're thinking, Creel. You believe that the outlaws are hiding on top of one of these ridges."

"It's a possibility," Bo said. "The gulches are pretty

heavily traveled, or at least they were until the Devils started, well, raising hell."

"Most of the slopes around here are pretty steep," Keefer pointed out. "It would be hard getting horses up and down them. A lot of places it would be impossible."

"There wouldn't have to be a lot of places you could reach the top on horseback," Bo said. "Just one good one."

"Then that's where we'll start," Holbrook declared.

Bo tapped the map and asked Keefer, "Any chance we can take this with us?"

The superintendent nodded. "I've got others, so you're welcome to that one."

"Is there a place around here where we can get up on the ridge? I didn't see any between here and Deadwood Gulch."

"Keep going up the canyon," Keefer said. "The slope gets a little easier after about a mile."

"Excellent," Holbrook said with a nod. "Thank you, Mr. Keefer."

"My pleasure. I hope you find the scoundrels and deal harshly with them when you do."

"You can rest assured of that, sir," Holbrook said, "on both counts."

Bo still thought they should wait until morning to begin the search, but Holbrook wouldn't hear of it. He liked Bo's idea that the outlaw hideout was located somewhere on top of one of the ridges and wanted to put it to the test.

As the troops got ready to move out, Chloride

came up to Bo and Scratch and said quietly, "You fellas be careful out there. I've seen men like that lieutenant before. They think they know everything, and before you know it, they're neck-deep in trouble. Don't let him get you killed."

"We'll try not to," Scratch said.

Bo added, "I've got a hunch Sergeant Gustaffson knows what he's doing. He can steer the lieutenant in the right direction."

Chloride grunted. "If Holbrook will listen to him. I'm bettin' the odds are against that."

"Don't worry about us, old-timer," Scratch said with a grin. "We can take care of ourselves."

Chloride snatched his hat off his head and said, "There you go again with that old-timer business! I swear—" He stopped short and shrugged. "What the hell. I *am* older than you. Probably ain't many who can say that!" He clapped his hat back on his head and stuck out his hand. "Good luck, boys."

The Texans both shook with him, then mounted up. Gustaffson had the troopers ready to ride. Holbrook said, "Give the order, Sergeant."

Gustaffson bellowed the command and waved the men forward as Holbrook, Bo, and Scratch led the way. Some of the miners turned out to watch. They waved their caps over their heads as the cavalrymen trotted away, moving deeper into the canyon.

As Keefer had said, after the riders had gone about a mile, the slope of the canyon to their right fell away at a gentler angle. It was still covered with trees and rocks, but Bo thought that if the troopers dismounted, they might be able to lead their horses to the top. He pointed that out to Holbrook and suggested, "Let Scratch and me try it first."

"Very well," the lieutenant agreed. He signaled a halt.

The Texans rode to the base of the slope and swung down from their saddles. Holding tight to the reins, they started up. The horses balked a little at first but soon came on, climbing the slope with relative ease. Bo and Scratch tried to pick the route that would give the animals the least trouble.

When they made it to the top of the ridge, they found themselves with a spectacular view spread out before them. The late afternoon sun washed over the Black Hills in all their rugged glory. Down in the gulches, people got used to being closed in with dark slopes all around them and only a strip of sky above. Up here a man could breathe better, it seemed to Bo.

"Do we have to go back down there and fetch that stiff-necked lieutenant?" Scratch asked.

Bo chuckled. "I reckon we'd better. He and those troopers will come in handy when we find the Devils."

"You don't figure we could handle that bunch of owlhoots by ourselves?"

"Well, maybe. But I'd rather have the cavalry on our side, too." Bo handed Scratch his reins. "I'll go back down. You take a look around up here."

Going down the hill was almost as painful for stiff joints as climbing up it, but Bo was soon back on the floor of the canyon with Lieutenant Holbrook, Sergeant Gustaffson, and the rest of the patrol. Bo told them that the way up was manageable, then said, "Follow me."

The soldiers led their mounts by the reins like Bo

and Scratch had. It was slow going, since they had to proceed single file, but eventually all the troopers made it to the top of the ridge.

By that time the sun had sunk considerably lower. Bo said, "If we keep going, Lieutenant, we run the risk of falling off a cliff in the bad light. It would be better to make camp here."

He could tell that Holbrook wanted to squeeze out every minute of the day, but after a moment the young officer nodded. "All right," Holbrook said. "Sergeant, tell the men to make camp. There's enough level ground here to pitch the tents."

"Yes, sir."

It was true. The ridge was almost a mile wide, Bo knew from studying the map in Andrew Keefer's office, and while it was covered with thick stands of trees and a jumble of boulders, it was fairly level, unlike some of the ridges that came to an almost razor-like crest. This one twisted off to the southwest for several miles before rising into higher, even more rugged terrain.

As Gustaffson ordered the men to pitch their tents and build cook fires, Scratch advised, "It might be a good idea to keep those fires small, Sergeant. Hide 'em amongst the rocks, too."

Holbrook overheard the advice and said, "Why would we want to do that?"

"Build big fires and you're telling the world where you are," Bo said.

"You mean we'll be announcing our position to the enemy."

"That's what he just said," Scratch drawled.

"It's cold up here. The men need hot food, and they

need warmth from the fires as well. Sergeant, have the men build their fires as big as they can."

"Lieutenant—" Bo began.

"Really, Mr. Creel," Holbrook interrupted, "if these so-called Devils are as cunning as everyone seems to believe they are, don't you think they already *know* we're out here looking for them?"

As much as Bo hated to admit it, Holbrook had a point. Everybody in Deadwood had heard about how the cavalry was riding out today to look for the outlaws and their hideout. At the very least, the Devils had spies in the settlement. If Bo's hunch was correct, some of the gang even lived there. No doubt the word had already long since gone out to the members of the gang at the hideout.

Still, having the Devils know that they were *somewhere* in the Black Hills was a heap different from making their exact location obvious to anybody with eyes for miles around. Bo could only hope that Holbrook's stubbornness wouldn't come back to cause trouble for them.

As night fell and the Texans tended to their horses, Scratch looked at the campfires blazing brightly and murmured, "I'm startin' to wonder if this is such a good place to spend the night after all, Bo."

"Yeah, the same thought occurred to me," Bo said. "Those fires are pretty much an engraved invitation to an ambush. I think Olaf knows it, too. I saw him talking to the lieutenant a few minutes ago, and Holbrook didn't look happy about it. Looked like he chewed out the sarge and told him to mind his own business."

"Gustaffson ain't the type to disobey an order, either, even when he knows it's loco."

"No," Bo agreed, "he's not. But we're civilians, and if we want to slip off a ways and find a place to hole up for the night that's not right out in the open, Holbrook can't stop us."

Scratch nodded. "Maybe someplace where we can keep an eye on those soldier boys without them knowin' it."

"That's what I had in mind."

"Better tell Gustaffson, so if the shavetail comes lookin' for us, somebody'll know where to find us."

"Yeah, but we won't tell Holbrook. No need for him to know about it unless there's trouble."

"Right." Scratch patted his horse's shoulder. "You know, some folks say that devils like to roam around in the darkness. Tonight, I got a hunch they're right."

CHAPTER 17

The Texans made their camp in some trees about a quarter of a mile from the spot where the troopers had pitched their tents and built those big cook fires. Scratch arranged some rocks in a circle and kindled a tiny blaze just large enough to boil coffee and fry up some bacon. No one outside the trees would be able to see the flames. It was going to be a very cold night, Bo sensed, and a big fire would have felt mighty good, but every instinct in his body warned him against such a thing.

After they had eaten, Scratch put out the fire, but they lingered next to its ashes, sipping the last of the coffee. They could hear the troopers moving around, talking loudly, and laughing.

"Those fellas better hope the army never sends 'em to Arizona to fight the Apaches," Scratch commented. "If there were any 'Paches skulkin' around, some of those soldier boys would be dead by now."

"I expect you're right," Bo agreed. "Between the fires and the racket, the Devils probably know right where they are."

"Question is, what are they gonna do about it?"

Bo took a sip of his coffee. "Reckon we'll have to wait and see."

The Texans sat there in companionable silence for a few more minutes, then Scratch said, "It's time you tell me what you been ponderin' about these past few days, Bo. You got some ideas that the Devils ain't regular road agents, don't you?"

"The thought crossed my mind," Bo admitted. "As soon as Marty Sutton said something about the Argosy wanting to buy her out, I got to wondering about Nicholson."

"All the other big mines lost gold shipments before the Argosy did," Scratch said. "And the Golden Queen wasn't the only one."

"Yeah, but if the goal was to make Miss Sutton so desperate that she'd sell, what better way to disguise that than to hit all the other outfits, too, including your own."

Scratch thought it over and then nodded slowly in the gathering darkness. "That makes sense, I reckon. As much sense as you could expect from a snake-blooded varmint so ruthless he'd have some of his own men murdered and carved up just to keep suspicion from fallin' on him."

"That's not all," Bo said. "When we first rode up Deadwood Gulch with Chloride and I got a look at the terrain, I realized that it's not really very far as the crow flies from the Golden Queen to the Argosy. I confirmed that by looking at the map in Keefer's office this afternoon. You know how a pocket of gold-bearing quartz can run for a long way sometimes."

"Son of a gun! You think the Argosy miners are followin' a ledge that winds up smack-dab in the middle of the Golden Queen?"

"It's possible. And listen to this. Reese Bardwell, Nicholson's superintendent, has a brother named Tom who led a gang of outlaws down in Kansas."

"Yeah, I remember Chloride tellin' us about that rumor," Scratch said. "He didn't know if it was true or not, though. He was just tryin' to get under Bardwell's hide that day."

"It's not a rumor," Bo said. "I looked through the wanted posters in Sheriff Manning's office and found a reward dodger on Tom Bardwell. The poster was a couple of years old, so there was nothing to indicate that he'd ever been hanged, or even caught. I'd be willing to bet he hasn't been."

"So Nicholson hits on the idea of recruitin' his superintendent's outlaw brother to raid the gold shipments, with the idea that sooner or later he'll force Miss Sutton to sell out to him. That way he can keep minin' the ore that runs all the way through this ridge under us into the Golden Queen." Scratch smacked his right fist into his left palm. "That all fits together mighty nice, Bo!"

"Yeah," Bo said. "There's just one problem with it that ruins the whole thing."

"What's that? I'm danged if I see it."

"If Nicholson's really behind all the trouble, why would he go along with sending that letter to Washington asking that the army be sent in to deal with the Devils?"

For a long moment, Scratch didn't say anything. Then he muttered a curse and said, "Yeah, that don't make sense. Unless all the other big mine owners were gonna do it anyway and Nicholson had to go along with the idea to keep anybody from gettin' suspicious of him."

"Maybe," Bo said. "I can't help but think, though, that Nicholson's influential enough around here that he could have talked the other owners into waiting if he'd wanted to. When he was talking to the lieutenant, Nicholson looked and sounded like he really wanted Holbrook to be successful in putting a stop to the Devils."

"We've run across hombres before who were good at actin' all innocent-like when really they were no-good varmints."

"Shakespeare wrote, 'A man may smile and smile, and be a villain,'" Bo quoted.

"Ain't that what I just said? And what if it ain't Nicholson at all, but somebody else at the Argosy who's behind it?"

"Like Reese Bardwell," Bo said.

"He's the one who's got the owlhoot brother. He could be workin' behind Nicholson's back, tryin' to get his hands on the Golden Queen. Or maybe he's just out for a share of the loot."

Bo nodded. "Could be. Bardwell's a troublemaker, no doubt about that. I'm not sure he's a cold-blooded killer, though, brother or no brother."

"So where does that leave us?"

"Sitting in the cold and the dark," Bo said with a smile, "waiting to see if a bunch of outlaws are going to show up and try to kill us all."

* * *

The Texans took turns standing guard during the night, as they usually did in a potentially dangerous situation like this. Bo stood the first watch, and Scratch took over around midnight.

Bo wasn't sure how long he had been asleep when his friend touched his shoulder, but he was instantly awake. He sat up with the fog from his breath wreathing around his head and reached for the Winchester he had placed on the ground next to his bedroll.

"What is it?" Bo asked in a whisper that couldn't have been heard more than a few feet away.

"Horses smelled somethin'," Scratch replied, equally quietly.

"Mountain lion, maybe?"

"They ain't spooked. I'd say it's more horses."

Bo lifted his head to judge the cold wind that blew across the top of the ridge. It was from the northwest, and that meant their horses wouldn't be able to smell the cavalry mounts, which were picketed several hundred yards away to the east.

Here under the trees, it was too dark for the Texans to see each other, but they had ridden together for so long each of them knew what the other would be doing in these circumstances. Bo found his boots and pulled them on while Scratch ghosted through the trees to a point where he could see the camp.

Bo joined him a moment later. The big fires the troopers had built earlier had died down quite a bit, but they were still visible. Bo saw dark shapes cross between him and the orange glows as the guards Holbrook had posted walked their picket lines.

"You hear any horses earlier?" Bo breathed.

"Nope. But that don't mean anything. The Devils

could've dismounted a ways along the ridge and started sneakin' up on foot."

Bo knew Scratch was right. Cold-blooded killers could be slipping into position to open fire on the camp right now. As far as anybody knew, the Deadwood Devils numbered around a dozen men, maybe a few more. That wasn't enough to take on a troop of thirty or more well-armed cavalrymen, even if the soldiers *were* under the command of a greenhorn like Vance Holbrook.

But if the outlaws could take the camp by surprise and kill some of the troopers in the first volley, that would go a long way toward evening up the odds. Bo and Scratch couldn't let that happen.

"Let's make some noise," Bo said as he lifted his rifle. He had levered a round into the Winchester's chamber before he ever turned in for the night.

"What if the Devils ain't around?" Scratch whispered.

"Then we'll apologize later for disturbing Lieutenant Holbrook's sleep." Bo had the rifle at his shoulder now. He pointed the barrel at the sky and cranked off three shots as fast as he could work the lever. Beside him, Scratch did the same thing. The thunderous racket of the shots rolled across the top of the ridge toward the camp.

Then the Texans hit the dirt, just in case some of the startled troopers jumped up and started blazing away in the direction of the shots without knowing what they were shooting at.

Somewhere in the darkness a man's harsh voice yelled, "Hit 'em!" and tongues of orange muzzle flame licked out from a different clump of trees near the camp. Bo knew that was where the bushwhackers were hidden. He propped himself up on his elbows, lined his sights on those trees, and started firing. Again, Scratch followed suit.

The pickets weren't sure exactly where to shoot, but they knew they were under attack. They opened fire, the shots from their Springfields snapping out. Since all the soldiers could do was aim at muzzle flashes, some of their shots were directed toward the trees where the ambushers were hidden, while others whipped through the branches and thudded into the trunks in the grove where Bo and Scratch lay. The Texans had known when they opened fire that they ran a risk of being shot by their own allies, but there wasn't anything they could do about that except stay low.

The troopers who had been sleeping scrambled out of their blankets, lunged from their tents carrying their rifles, and took cover behind the rocks scattered around the camp. Even over the roar of guns, Bo heard Sgt. Olaf Gustaffson bellowing orders. This wasn't Gustaffson's first fight. He would know what to do.

Bo wasn't surprised when the firing from the other clump of trees abruptly stopped. He spotted several dark shapes racing through the shadows, and so did Scratch. The silver-haired Texan exclaimed, "They're lightin' a shuck!" Scratch tracked one of the running figures with his Winchester and squeezed off another shot.

The fleeing outlaw tumbled off his feet. Bo threw lead after the others but couldn't tell if he hit any of them. Over at the camp, Gustaffson yelled, "Cease fire! Cease fire!"

"Countermand that order!" Lieutenant Holbrook shouted, his voice a little higher than normal from excitement and probably fear. "Continue firing! Over there in those trees!"

"Better duck, partner," Bo warned.

Both Texans hunkered as low to the ground as possible while a storm of lead tore through the trees above them. During a brief pause in the firing, they rolled away from each other and crawled behind a couple of pines, putting thick trunks between themselves and the camp.

After a few moments, the shooting trailed off again. Bo heard Gustaffson saying, "Lieutenant, I think that's where Creel and Morton were!"

"My God!" Holbrook yelped. "Why didn't someone say so?"

Because you didn't give them a chance to, Bo thought. But now that the guns were silent, he took advantage of the chance to cup his hands around his mouth and call out, "Hold your fire! It's us!"

"You reckon the Devils left behind any sharpshooters?" Scratch asked as the Texans got to their feet.

"I hope not," Bo said.

He hoped their horses had been picketed far enough into the trees that the animals had remained safe during all the shooting, too. He hadn't heard either of the horses scream, so maybe they hadn't been hit.

Bo and Scratch reloaded, then held the rifles ready as they trotted toward the camp. Bo noticed that the fires had been doused completely, plunging the whole area into darkness. Probably Gustaffson's idea, he told himself.

"Hold it!" a voice said as they approached. Bo recognized it.

"It's just us, Sergeant," he said.

Gustaffson stood up from behind the rock where he had been kneeling. "Come ahead," he told them. "Either of you fellas hurt?"

"No," Bo said, and Scratch added, "Nope." Bo heard a man groan somewhere nearby and went on. "Sounds like somebody else is, though."

"Yeah, we've got casualties," Gustaffson said, his voice grim now. "Including the lieutenant."

That surprised Bo. "I heard him just a few minutes ago."

"He ain't dead, just wounded. He's being tended to now. Come on, I'll take you to him." To the troopers scattered behind the rocks, Gustaffson said, "The rest of you men stay where you are, and for God's sake, stay alert. If you see anybody move out there, chances are it ain't a friend."

The sergeant led Bo and Scratch to the largest of the tents, where a makeshift field hospital had been set up. By lantern light, one of the troopers was cleaning a bloody gash on Lieutenant Holbrook's upper left arm where a bullet had creased him. Holbrook looked pale and queasy, and he turned his head away from his wounded arm as if he was afraid the sight of the blood would make him sick.

"How's he doing, Wilson?" Gustaffson asked the trooper. The man was older than the usual cavalry private. His weathered face and iron-gray hair put him at least in his forties.

"He'll be fine, as long as he doesn't get blood poisoning," Trooper Wilson replied. "And I'm doing everything I can to prevent that. The lieutenant was lucky."

Luckier than the two soldiers lying on the ground with blankets pulled up over their faces, Bo thought. Blood soaked through those blankets in places. Those troopers hadn't made it.

A couple of other men, one with a bloody bandage around his right thigh and another who had been shot through the hand, were in better shape, certainly better than the two fatalities. Holbrook's wound appeared to be the least serious of the lot.

The lieutenant winced as Wilson used a carbolic-soaked rag to clean the gash. "Where were you two men?" he demanded of the Texans. "You're supposed to be helping us! Instead you let those outlaws attack us!"

"If we hadn't fired those warning shots, the first shots you heard would have been the ones that killed all your pickets," Bo said bluntly. "And then the Devils would have riddled all the tents before your men could even crawl out of their blankets. They had plenty of light to aim by, after all, with those fires still burning."

Holbrook flushed angrily, which at least got a little color back into his face. "This was our first night out here," he said. "I didn't think the Devils would attack us yet—"

"I don't reckon they saw any reason to waste time,"

Scratch said. "They didn't like the idea of havin' a cavalry patrol out here huntin' 'em."

"They'll soon learn they can't get away with ambushing the United States Cavalry," Holbrook snapped. "Sergeant, did we suffer any other casualties?"

"A few nicks," Gustaffson answered. "Nothing the men can't tend to themselves."

"Very well." Holbrook flinched again, this time as Trooper Wilson bound a dressing in place around his arm, and went on. "Organize a burial detail. We'll lay Troopers Rutherford and Bennett to rest first thing in the morning. Assign one of the uninjured men to accompany Mitchell and Stoneham back to Deadwood."

The man who had been shot through the hand spoke up, saying, "Beggin' your pardon, Lieutenant, but I don't have to go back. I can ride just fine, so I should stay with the patrol."

"You may be able to ride," Holbrook said, "but you can't handle a rifle one-handed, Stoneham. You're going back."

"I'll see to it, Lieutenant," Gustaffson said before the young soldier could protest again.

Holbrook nodded. "Excellent. The rest of us will continue searching for the enemy."

"What about you, sir? You're injured, too."

Holbrook's face hardened. "I said, the rest of us will continue searching for the enemy. That's exactly what I meant, Sergeant. Tell the men we'll be leaving as soon as it's light enough to follow a trail." He frowned at Bo and Scratch. "That is, if our *scouts* think they'll be able to pick up the trail of the men who ambushed us."

Bo could tell that Scratch was about to make some angry response, and he couldn't blame his old friend for feeling that way. The lieutenant was making it sound like they were somehow responsible for what had happened, when the truth was it had been Holbrook who had ordered those big fires built. Chances were, things would have been a lot worse if the Texans hadn't done what they did.

But Holbrook was in no mood to listen to that, Bo knew. To keep Scratch's hot temper from annoying the officer any further, Bo said quickly, "We'll be ready, Lieutenant. The Devils may have overplayed their hand this time. Could be they'll lead us right to their hideout."

CHAPTER 18

When Bo got around to checking his watch, he saw that it was only an hour or so until dawn. No point in trying to go back to sleep now, he decided, and Scratch felt the same way, so they walked back to the trees where they had been camped earlier and fetched their horses to the main camp. The animals were unharmed, as Bo had hoped.

It was unlikely the Devils would come calling again tonight, and if they did, all the troopers were alert and on edge after the attack. They wouldn't be surprised a second time.

As a cold gray light appeared in the sky, Bo saw that more clouds had moved in. The wind picked up, blowing harder. Scratch gazed at the thick overcast and said, "Looks like we might be in for a blue norther."

"I don't think they call them that up here in Dakota Territory," Bo said.

"Well, whatever they call it, could be some rough weather on the way." Scratch looked over at Bo. "Say, what's the date?"

Bo pondered that for a moment, then said, "The twenty-fourth, I think."

"Son of a gun. Tomorrow's Thanksgivin'. No turkey feast for us, I reckon." Scratch shook his head. "Although with that wet-behind-the-ears lieutenant in charge, I reckon I'll be plenty thankful if we're still alive tomorrow."

Bo couldn't argue with that.

He and Scratch rode over to the trees where the Devils had hidden to launch their ambush, and they had a look around. There wasn't much to see, just some empty shell casings littering the ground. Any wounded outlaws had been taken with the rest of the gang. The Texans dismounted and walked the same direction the outlaws had fled the night before. Scratch pointed out some broken branches and rocks that had been turned over.

"They were in too big a hurry to cover their tracks," he said. "If we're lucky, maybe they were that careless all the way back to their hideout."

Bo grunted. He didn't think that was too likely.

They found the spot where the outlaws had left their horses. Hoofprints led away from there, following the ridge to the southwest. Of course, there really wasn't anywhere else for the gang to go. The walls of the gulches on both sides of the ridge were too steep for the horses to handle in all but a few places.

By the time the Texans returned to camp, the two troopers who were killed in the ambush had been buried, and Gustaffson was getting the men ready to ride. Lieutenant Holbrook came up to meet Bo and Scratch. He wore his left arm in a black silk sling that Trooper Wilson had rigged.

"Did you find the trail?" Holbrook demanded.

Bo nodded. "It won't be much trouble to follow."

"Good! I'd like to catch up to those outlaws and deal with them today, if possible. There's no need to give them another chance to ambush us tonight."

"Now *that* I agree with, Lieutenant. Are you sure you'll be able to handle the ride?"

"What should I do?" Holbrook snapped. "Go back to Deadwood with my tail between my legs and leave the patrol under the command of Sergeant Gustaffson and a couple of civilians?"

"Well—" Scratch began.

"We just don't want you to get blood poisoning, like Trooper Wilson warned you about," Bo cut in.

"I'm fine." Holbrook made a curt gesture with his right hand. "Let's get on the trail of those thieves and killers."

The sky had lightened a little more, but the clouds were so thick Bo figured the heavens would remain gloomy and overcast the rest of the day.

Sergeant Gustaffson must have felt the same way. As the patrol proceeded along the ridge, the non-com brought his horse up beside Bo's and said, "That sky looks so threatening I expect old Odin to part the clouds at any minute and glare down at us with his one good eye as he pronounces judgment on us. He'll have all the rest of those grim, gray gods with him."

"What are you talkin' about?" Scratch asked from Bo's other side.

Gustaffson laughed and shook his head. "Nothing. Folks in the part of the world where my family comes from tend to be a mite down in the mouth most of the time. I reckon you would be, too, if it was always cold and dark where you lived."

"Maybe," Scratch said. "I like Mexico, myself. Warm sun and good food and pretty little señoritas . . . It's plumb peaceful down there."

"Yeah, that's not what you thought the last time we were there and all those hombres tried to kill us," Bo pointed out.

"Well, everywhere has its drawbacks, I suppose."

Something else occurred to Bo. Quietly, he said to Gustaffson, "Trooper Wilson did a good job taking care of those wounded men. Almost like he had medical training."

Gustaffson looked around to make sure no one was riding very close to them before he said, "Yeah, Wilson's good enough at patching up wounds that it's almost like he was a surgeon back during the War Between the States. I'll bet some of those doctors who wore Confederate gray changed their names and came west after the war. A cavalry troop would be mighty lucky to have a fella like that join up with them."

"As long as some of the men who still hate Rebels didn't know about it," Bo said.

Gustaffson nodded. "Yeah. As long as that was true."

Satisfied now, Bo let the subject drop. But it was good to know that they had a man with the knowledge and skill to treat the wounded with them.

Because there was no doubt in Bo's mind that more blood would be spilled before this was over.

* * *

By late morning, the patrol reached a spot where several ridges came together. Craggy cliffs rose above them. A number of canyons cut into those cliffs, the walls leaning toward each other like the jaws of a trap about to snap shut.

Lieutenant Holbrook reined in and signaled for the patrol to halt. He turned to Bo and Scratch and said, "I suppose now it'll become more difficult to follow the trail, since there are several ways they could have gone."

"Yeah, they may have even split up," Scratch said.

"That wouldn't surprise me a bit," Bo added.

The silver-haired Texan swung down from his saddle. "Let me take a look around," Scratch said.

For several minutes Scratch walked back and forth, studying the ground. Large stretches of it were too rocky to take a print, but there were other ways of following a trail. Finally, Scratch rejoined Bo and the lieutenant and said, "It looks like they stayed together and rode into that center canyon."

He pointed out the opening in the cliffs he was talking about. It was twenty feet wide and ran straight for perhaps fifty yards before it took a sharp turn.

"Are you sure?" Holbrook asked. "I don't see any tracks at all."

"Horses can't travel over rocky ground without turnin' over some of the rocks, and their shoes leave little nicks and scratches on the rocks, too," Scratch explained. "And there are places where there's enough dirt to pick up part of a hoofprint. I can see enough sign to tell that a bunch of riders came through here in the past twelve hours, and there ain't nothin' pointin' to any of those other canyons." Scratch nodded.

"That's the way they went, all right. You can count on it."

"And if Scratch says it, you can believe it," Bo put in. "He's a fine tracker. Always has been."

"All right," Holbrook said. "That means we go after them."

"Hold on a minute," Bo said. "I'm not sure that's a good idea."

Holbrook frowned at him. "What do you mean? We came out here to track down the Deadwood Devils, didn't we? Who else could it have been that attacked us last night?"

"I'm not saying it wasn't the Devils," Bo replied. "I'm saying it might not be a good idea to follow them into that canyon. Can't you see that it's a perfect setting for another ambush?"

Scratch added, "They haven't gone to any trouble to cover their trail, Lieutenant. It's sorta like they want us to follow 'em."

"Nonsense," Holbrook said. "They were just in a hurry to get away once it became obvious that their ambush wasn't going to work."

"I don't know," Bo said. "Maybe they thought it would be easier just to lure you into a trap."

Sergeant Gustaffson had listened to the conversation with great interest. Now he spoke up, saying, "Beggin' your pardon, Lieutenant, but what these fellas are saying makes sense. If those outlaws really wanted to get away, they could have split up here and gone half a dozen different directions. Instead they stayed together and rode into that canyon."

"Which is probably where their hideout is located," Holbrook said with irritation and impatience in his voice. "You men don't seem to understand. This is our chance to catch them all together and wipe them out. The best time to attack is when the enemy is concentrated in one spot. You'd understand that if you'd been trained in tactics like I have."

Scratch and Gustaffson both looked like they were about to lose their tempers. Bo was more than a mite annoyed himself at Holbrook's smug certainty that he was right. Keeping a tight rein on his own anger, Bo said, "Maybe you'd better let Scratch and me do a little scouting before you go charging in there, Lieutenant. That's why you brought us along, isn't it?"

Holbrook shrugged. "I suppose so. I don't want to waste this opportunity, though. I'll give you a few minutes to reconnoiter in that canyon, but then I'm leading my men in pursuit of the enemy."

"Just wait until we get back," Bo suggested.

"And if you hear shots, don't come chargin' in there," Scratch added. "We'll get back to you if we can. If we can't, then you'll know it was a trap and we've sprung it."

"Go ahead," Holbrook said. Bo noted that the lieutenant didn't actually promise to go along with what they had asked, and that left him with an uneasy feeling as Scratch mounted up and the two of them rode toward the dark cleft.

"I knew no good would come from gettin' mixed up with some greenhorn glory hound," Scratch muttered as they approached the canyon mouth.

"Maybe he'll wait," Bo said.

"You really think so?"

"Well, it depends on whether or not he listens to Olaf."

"He ain't showed no signs of it so far," Scratch pointed out.

"Yeah, I know," Bo said, and he couldn't keep a note of worry out of his voice.

The Texans drew their Winchesters and rested them across the saddles as they reached the mouth of the canyon. The wind that whistled down the cleft was bone chilling. Steep, rocky walls rose fifty or sixty feet on both sides of them, and the dark, overcast day meant that a thick gloom clogged the canyon as they proceeded into it. They rode side by side, Bo on the right and Scratch on the left, and each of them watched the rimrock on his side, alert for any sign of an ambush. There were no sounds except the slow, steady hoofbeats of their horses.

They reached the first bend and rode around it. Now they could see another hundred yards or so ahead of them. The canyon floor was empty except for some boulders and stunted bushes here and there along the base of the walls.

"This cut's liable to zigzag along for a mile or more, without ever runnin' straight for more'n a hundred yards at a time," Scratch said. "And then it might run smack-dab into a dead end."

Bo knew his friend was right. Some geological upheaval in the dim, distant past had created this canyon, possibly at the same time the rest of the Black Hills had risen. He had read about such things in books, and he had seen the results many times with his own eyes.

That cataclysm had left a number of large rocks broken and perched on the rims of both sides of the canyon. Bo eyed them warily as he and Scratch rode past.

"It wouldn't take much to start an avalanche along here," he said quietly. "Get a log and lever one or two of those boulders over the edge, and it would pick up plenty more on the way down."

"Yeah, this place gives me the fantods," Scratch agreed. "But the Devils came this way. I'm still seein' sign."

"Yeah, me, too. Maybe the lieutenant's right. Maybe their hideout really is up here."

Scratch grunted. "If that shavetail was ever right about anything, it was a pure-dee accident. I got a hunch that havin' that old sarge around is the only reason the young fella's still alive."

Scratch might be right about that, Bo thought. Unfortunately, Olaf Gustaffson was just a sergeant. When it came down to the nub, Gustaffson had to obey the orders of his superior officer. Holbrook was so bound and determined to catch the Devils and grab some fame and glory—and maybe a promotion—in the process, he might not let Gustaffson continue to influence his decisions.

The canyon continued to twist back and forth, almost as sinuous as a diamondback rattler wriggling its way across the ground. The walls became more sheer and rose even higher by the time Bo and Scratch had penetrated half a mile into the canyon. The shadows thickened even though the sun was high overhead now. That was because the clouds were so thick and threatening. At least they were past the area where the threat of a rockslide loomed, Bo thought.

They reined in for a moment, and Bo asked, "You

reckon we ought to go back and fetch the lieutenant and the rest of the patrol?"

"Everything looks clear so far," Scratch admitted. "Maybe it'd be a better idea if we split up. You can go back and fetch the soldier boys, and I'll keep headin' deeper into—"

"Wait a minute," Bo interrupted. "You hear that?"

Scratch's eyes narrowed in concentration as he listened. Then they widened and he let out a curse. "Horses comin' up the canyon!" he exclaimed. "The dang shavetail got tired o' waitin'!"

It was true. The faint rataplan of hoofbeats on the rocky ground echoed up the canyon toward the Texans, growing slightly louder with the passing of each second.

Bo started to wheel his horse. "I'd better get back there with them—" he began.

He stopped short as he heard a new sound. It was an ominous, deep-throated rumble, and both Texans instantly knew what it meant.

"Avalanche!" Scratch yelled.

CHAPTER 19

They jerked their horses around and sent the animals galloping back down the canyon. It was clear what had happened: the outlaws had been hidden up on the rimrock, possibly on both sides of the canyon, and had let Bo and Scratch ride past without springing the trap. The Devils were after a bigger payoff than just two Texans.

Then, when Lieutenant Holbrook had led his men up the canyon as well, the outlaws had struck. Scratch had said all along that they weren't going to any trouble to hide their trail, and now it was obvious why. They had this plan ready to fall back on if their ambush of the night before failed, and Holbrook's impulsive actions had played right into their hands.

"Dang fool couldn't wait!" Scratch shouted over the pounding hoofbeats. Bo nodded grimly. The avalanche's roar was louder now. Bo knew that any men and horses caught in its path wouldn't stand much of a chance. It was probably too late already to help any of the troopers, but he and Scratch had to try.

They raced around the bends in the canyon at breakneck speed. The terrible rumbling began to subside. Avalanches were horribly destructive but usually didn't last all that long. This one seemed to be coming to an end.

As the Texans guided their horses through another twist, they spotted clouds of dust billowing up in front of them. Along with the noise, that was another sign of an avalanche. All those tumbling rocks kicked up a lot of dust.

Bo reined in, and Scratch followed suit. Plunging into that blinding cloud wouldn't do any good. They wouldn't be able to see where they were going.

Scratch bit back a curse. "We're gonna have to wait for some of that dust to blow away," he said.

"Yeah, but it shouldn't take long," Bo said. "Not with the way the wind's blowing through this canyon."

It was true. The cloud of dust began to drift down the canyon. As it did, the sudden, sharp rap of gunshots made the Texans stiffen in their saddles.

"The Devils are tryin' to finish off the troopers who survived the rockslide!" Scratch said.

"Come on!" Bo called as he urged his horse into motion again. "We'll give them a hand!"

Now that they knew at least some of the cavalrymen had survived the avalanche but were still in danger from the outlaws, there was no time to waste. Bo and Scratch galloped down the canyon and came in sight of a huge pile of rocks that filled the cleft from one side to the other. Muzzle flashes stabbed into the gloom from some of the rocks at the edge of the slide and were answered by more orange tongues of flame from the rimrock.

Bo and Scratch left the saddles while their horses were still running and landed with their rifles in hand. They snatched their hats off their heads, slapped at the horses and yelled, and sent the animals galloping back up the canyon, out of the line of fire.

The Texans ran behind some rocks just beyond the bend and opened fire on the bushwhackers along the rimrock. A haze of dust still hung in the air, stinging eyes and noses and making it harder to see. But that was true for the men up on the canyon walls, too. They had to be having trouble picking out targets down below.

A man suddenly staggered into view on the rimrock, clutching at his belly. A bullet had found him, and he was mortally wounded. With a terrified scream, he toppled off the sheer cliff and plunged to the canyon floor, landing on the massive pile of rocks with a grisly thud that silenced him in mid-shriek.

That was one of the varmints down, anyway, Bo thought.

But there were still plenty more up there, and they continued to pour lead down into the canyon.

"This ain't doin' any good, Bo!" Scratch called.

"I know! We need to get up there somehow."

"There ain't no way!"

Bo looked at the rough canyon walls and said, "Not for a man on horseback, but a fella might be able to climb!"

Scratch looked at him like he'd gone loco. "A mountain goat, maybe, but not a man!"

"I'm going to give it a try anyway. Stay here and do what you can to help those troopers!"

Without giving Scratch a chance to argue any

more, Bo lunged out from behind the boulder where he had taken cover and raced around the bend in the trail. A bullet whined over his shoulder as he did so. The Devils up on the rimrock probably thought he was giving up and fleeing while he had the chance.

He hoped he would be able to give them a nice hot lead surprise before too much longer.

When Bo was safely around the bend, he paused and took off his belt, then used it to rig a sling for the Winchester so he could carry it over his shoulder. His eyes searched the canyon walls for footholds and handholds he could use in his climb. It wouldn't be easy, and he knew he ought to be twenty years younger to be trying such a fool stunt, but if something didn't happen to change the odds a little, the Devils could perch up there on the rimrock and take all day to wipe out the patrol if they needed to.

Bo settled on his route and went over to the wall. He took his hat and coat off and dropped them on the ground. The cold wind cut through his shirt and vest, but the coat would be a hindrance while he was climbing. He slung the rifle over his shoulder and reached up to grip the first handhold he had spotted.

Bo's muscles protested as he lifted himself, but they would just have to get used to it. He wedged his foot against a rocky knob and shoved himself higher. Now he could reach the next handhold and grip it firmly to haul himself up.

Around the bend, the gunfire continued without slacking off. The troopers were putting up a good fight. Bo hoped that meant quite a few of them had survived the avalanche. If Sergeant Gustaffson was among them, they might have a chance to hold off the outlaws long enough for Bo to reach the rimrock and lend them a hand.

The wall rose about fifty feet above the canyon floor. Some stretches were almost sheer, but other parts were easier going. Bo climbed doggedly, never looking down but keeping his eyes on the wall above him. He didn't even let himself think about how there was nothing underneath him but empty air.

There was one especially bad moment when a rock he was gripping shifted a little under his hand, threatening to throw him off balance, but the rock didn't pull loose and he was able to press himself against the wall until the frenzied thudding of his heart slowed slightly. He had two good footholds at the moment, so he tested the rock again. This time it held, and he was able to use it to pull himself higher.

He had no idea how long he had been climbing, so it took him a little by surprise when he suddenly reached the rimrock and rolled over the edge. With solid ground under him again, he lay there for a moment catching his breath. Then he rolled over and pushed himself up onto one knee.

The Devils were all on the other side of the canyon. They gathered among the rocks where they had started the avalanche, using the remaining boulders for cover. They were still firing down into the canyon and didn't seem to have noticed Bo reaching the top on the other side.

In the weak light of the overcast afternoon, he could see several of the outlaws. They weren't wearing their usual bandana masks, but he couldn't make out enough details of their faces to recognize any of them. The rimrock rose a little on this side of the canyon, enough to give him some cover if he stretched out behind it. As he did so, he picked his targets and worked out in his mind the order in which he would take them.

Some fast, accurate shooting on his part was really the only chance those troopers down there had.

Lying on his belly, Bo propped himself on his elbows and snugged the butt of the Winchester against his shoulder. The rifle already had a bullet in the firing chamber. He took a deep breath, settled his sights on the first man he was going to try to take down, and squeezed the trigger.

Before the whipcrack of the shot could even start to echo through the canyon and join the echoes of all the other shots, Bo had worked the Winchester's lever and shifted his sights. A second shot blasted out. He didn't take the time to see if his bullets found their targets. Instead he jacked the lever and fired again and again and again, so that the shots formed a continuous roar.

Bo didn't stop shooting. He had reloaded the rifle before starting his climb, so he'd had a full sixteen rounds in it, one in the chamber and fifteen in the magazine. He fired all sixteen shots in that many seconds, maybe a little less. From this angle, even the outlaws he couldn't see were in danger from the storm of lead because the bullets were bouncing around among those rocks on the other wall.

Bo counted off the shots, and when the Winchester was empty he quickly scooted backward, knowing that the Devils would return his fire. Dirt and pebbles leaped into the air as bullets chewed into the edge of the rimrock. Bo stayed as low as he could. He heard slugs whining through the air just above his head. Where he was, though, they couldn't reach him.

Of course, he couldn't stick his head up, either, not without getting a bullet through the brain.

While he was lying there, he thumbed fresh cartridges through the Winchester's loading gate. A sudden outburst of firing from the opposite wall of the canyon made him glance in that direction. For a second he thought some of the Devils had moved down there to get better shots at him, but then he saw a familiar figure kneeling behind a rock on that side and directing his fire toward the outlaws.

Scratch!

The silver-haired Texan ducked lower behind the rock as his rifle ran dry. Bo shouted over to him. "What in blazes are you doing up there?"

Scratch flashed a grin back at him. "I was always a better climber than you!" he called. "Figured if you could do it, I could, too, and we could lay into the varmints from two directions at once!"

Actually, it wasn't a bad idea, Bo thought, although Scratch was in more danger because he was on the same side of the canyon as the Devils.

But it appeared they had the outlaws on the run again. The shooting had died down, and when Bo risked a look, he spotted several of the figures in their long coats dashing away from the edge of the canyon. He opened fire on them again, hoping to bring down one or two more, but they were out of sight too quickly for that.

"Varmints are lightin' a shuck!" Scratch called as hoofbeats sounded.

"I know. Did you see how many of them got away?"

"Half a dozen, I reckon. Maybe one or two more."

They had to have wiped out at least half the gang, Bo thought. But that left a number of them still on the loose, free to raise more hell. Also, there was no way of knowing how many confederates the Devils might have who were still back in Deadwood.

Right now, though, since the shooting had stopped, the immediate problem was helping the survivors of the avalanche. That meant climbing back down into the canyon.

"I'll keep an eye out in case they double back," Bo called across to Scrach. "You can climb down first."

Scratch reached down to the ground and lifted a coil of rope. "I brought my lariat with me," he responded. "I'll tie it on to something and get down that way. Won't take long."

"Good idea," Bo told him. He held his rifle ready and scanned the opposite ridge while Scratch made the rope fast to a rock and went down it hand-over-hand, using his feet to hold himself away from the canyon wall.

When Scratch was down, Bo went back to the spot where he had climbed up. Since he knew all the handholds and footholds now, the descent went slightly faster, but he still had to take it slow and be careful. He didn't want to fall and break a leg or worse now that the fight with the Devils was over.

By the time Bo reached the canyon floor, Scratch had already gone to see what the situation was at the site of the avalanche. Bo joined his old friend and found Scratch talking to Sgt. Olaf Gustaffson. Relief went through Bo at the sight of the non-com, who had a bloody scratch on his head but otherwise appeared to be all right. Several of the troopers were nearby, searching through the rockslide.

Gustaffson gave Bo a curt nod. "Glad to see you're all right, Creel. And thanks for giving us a hand like that. If you hadn't come back to help us, those outlaws would've sat up there like buzzards and picked us all off sooner or later."

"I'm glad you made it, too, Sergeant," Bo said. "Where's the lieutenant?"

Gustaffson grimaced and nodded toward the huge pile of rocks in the center of the canyon. "Under there somewhere. His horse went down while we were making a run for it. I turned back to try to pick him up, but before I could get there, a bunch of rocks swept right over him." Gustaffson sighed. "I didn't like him, but Lord, I wouldn't wish something like that on anybody."

"You and those other men are the only ones who made it?"

"Yeah. Less than a third of the patrol. And it was pure luck that we survived. The edge of the slide didn't miss us by more than ten feet. Some of the smaller rocks pelted us." Gustaffson gestured toward the cut on his head. "That's how I got this. The other men are beaten up, too. But we're alive, and that's more than you can say for anybody who got caught under that. I told the men to look for more survivors, but between you and me, they're not going to find any."

Bo had to agree with that grim assessment. He asked, "You have your horses?"

"Yeah, our mounts got clear with us."

"Then you can get back to Deadwood. With the canyon blocked off, you may have to go a long way around, but you should be able to make it."

"What about the two of you?" Gustaffson asked.

Bo and Scratch exchanged a glance. "I reckon we're still goin' after the Devils," Scratch said.

Bo nodded. "That's right. They have even more to pay for now."

"Our orders were to find those outlaws and deal with them," Gustaffson said with a scowl.

"The lieutenant's dead, and so are most of your troop."

"That doesn't change the orders," Gustaffson said. "I'm in command now, and I say we're going after them. Some of them were killed, too. The odds ought to be close to even."

The sergeant had a point. Over the past week, the Deadwood Devils had been dealt considerable damage. If the remainder of the cavalry patrol could catch up to the gang now, they might be able to put the Devils out of commission permanently.

"All right," Bo said, "but if we're going after them, we can't waste any time. Your men might be able to recover some of the bodies and give them proper burials if they stay here, but they probably wouldn't be able to catch up to the Devils."

Gustaffson heaved a sigh and nodded. "I know. And as much as I hate to leave the bodies, we don't have any choice in the matter. I'll tell the men to abandon the search and mount up."

While Gustaffson was doing that, Bo and Scratch retrieved their horses. Five minutes later, they rode up the canyon at the head of a small column that included Sergeant Gustaffson and seven of the cavalry troopers. Ten men in all, counting the Texans. The Devils couldn't number much more than that after all the men they had lost in recent days.

Quietly, Scratch said to Bo, "We may have another problem that ain't been talked about yet. What if this canyon's a dead end? We can't go back the other way. It'd take a week to dig out enough of that rock slide for the horses to get through."

Bo nodded. "I know. We'll just have to hope there's a way out at the other end."

They followed the canyon on its twisting path into the hills. Bo kept an eye out for a place where the walls were gentle enough for horses to make it. Eventually the canyon petered out in a long slope where an avalanche had taken place sometime in the past. The ground was loose rock, and Bo could tell by looking that it would be easy to trigger another slide. But they had no choice except to try to get out of the canyon this way.

"Have your men dismount," he told Gustaffson. "We'll take it slow and easy, one at a time, leading the horses. Everybody back off while I go first."

Bo picked his way up the slope, talking quietly and calmly to his horse as he did so to keep the animal from spooking. The climb was actually an easy one, only about a hundred yards and not very steep, but it took several nerve-racking minutes anyway before Bo finally reached the top. He had recovered his hat and coat earlier, so now he took off the black Stetson and waved it over his head to let Scratch know he had made it safely to the top. Scratch started up next.

It took most of the rest of the afternoon, but Gustaffson and the other survivors from the patrol were able to climb out of the canyon without any mishaps. When they were all up, Bo said, "We'll backtrack now and pick up the Devils' trail at the place where they started that avalanche."

Gustaffson looked at the sky. "We're going to run out of light," he said. "I don't like the look of those clouds, either. I think they've got snow in them."

Scratch chuckled. "You sound like old Chloride, Sarge. But I got a hunch you're right."

Bo said, "You won't have any trouble following the canyon from up here, Olaf. Scratch and I will go ahead and try to pick up the trail. We'll leave markers for you to follow us."

Gustaffson looked like he was going to argue, but then he shrugged and said, "I hate to split up such a small force, but you two seem to know what you're doing. We won't be far behind you."

The Texans lifted a hand in farewell and then galloped ahead of the patrol. In the fading light, it wasn't long before the troopers were out of sight behind them.

It was only a few minutes later when Bo felt the first snowflake plant a cold kiss on his face.

CHAPTER 20

The snow was light and intermittent at first, but it began to fall thicker and faster as Bo and Scratch reached the spot where the avalanche had taken place. Scratch dismounted long enough to retrieve his lasso, which he coiled and fastened to his saddle again. While he was doing that, Bo located the place where the Devils had left their horses during the ambush. The temperature was below freezing and the snow was starting to stick, resulting in a dusting of white on the piles of horse droppings.

"We won't be able to follow their trail once the snow starts to pile up," Scratch said.

"I know. It's going to be dark soon, too."

Scratch sighed. "You reckon we ought to just wait here for Gustaffson and those troopers and make camp for the night?"

Bo thought about it for a moment and then shook his head. "No, let's give it a try," he said. "One thing about the snow, it'll make it easier for Olaf and the others to follow us. They'll be able to see our tracks."

"Yeah, I reckon. But where are we goin'?"

"I've been thinking . . . Lieutenant Holbrook might've been onto something. The Devils' hideout wasn't up this canyon, but it could be hidden in one of the others. That would be a good place. It's isolated, and there aren't any mines up here this high."

"You figure we should check the other canyons?"

"It's a place to start," Bo said.

They rode through the snow, which whipped up in swirls around them. Cutting across the ridge, they came to another of the rugged canyons. The thin layer of snow on the ground was enough to muffle their horses' hoofbeats, and Bo was thankful for that. If he was right about the hideout being up here, he didn't want to ride right into the place without any warning, and he sure didn't want the Devils to know they were coming.

The gray light in the sky was almost gone when they reached the head of the canyon without finding any sign of the outlaws. Bo was about to say that they would stop and look for a place to camp when he suddenly stiffened in the saddle. A faint, familiar scent had drifted to his nostrils.

"Scratch, do you smell that?"

The silver-haired Texan sniffed the air and nodded. "Wood smoke," Scratch said. "Somebody's got a fire goin'."

"In weather like this, they'd have to. Let's see if we can follow the smell."

They set out across the rugged terrain, and after several hundred yards they came to another canyon that stretched across the landscape like a black, hungry mouth. Bo and Scratch reined in and dismounted.

They tied their reins to a scrubby tree and stole ahead on foot, carrying their rifles. When they came to the edge of the canyon, they knelt in the snow and looked over the edge of the rimrock. The smell of smoke was stronger now. Bo saw a faint glow off to his right and silently pointed it out to Scratch.

"That's lamplight comin' through the cracks around a shutter," Scratch breathed in Bo's ear. "The varmints got themselves a cabin down there!"

"Probably an old prospector's cabin that was abandoned," Bo said. "Like the one where Chloride was staying."

"Maybe we ought to burn it down around 'em, like they tried to do to us!"

After all the death and havoc the Devils had wreaked, it was a tempting suggestion, but that would be cold-blooded murder, and besides, they didn't know for certain that their enemies were in there, Bo thought.

"We'd better make sure it's them," he said. "Let's see if we can find a way down there."

He suspected there was a trail of some sort leading down into the canyon, since the gang had approached the place from this direction. The Texans cat-footed along the rim in the gathering gloom. They came to a pair of boulders spaced apart like a marker, and sure enough, Bo made out the faint beginnings of a trail between the big rocks. The trail turned into a ledge that zigzagged down the canyon wall.

Bo and Scratch were about to start along the ledge when they heard a voice and stopped short. Somewhere nearby, a man was cursing monotonously. His ire was directed at the fact that he was stuck up here in such miserable weather. When no one replied to him, Bo figured out that the man was talking to himself.

The Devils had posted a guard on this back door into their headquarters. That didn't come as a surprise. It was a sensible precaution. Quickly, Bo motioned to Scratch, explaining in gestures what he was going to do. Scratch nodded his understanding.

Bo started down the ledge, which was just wide enough for one man on horseback. He would have to be careful. There was literally no room for error. In a struggle, it would be easy to fall off the ledge and plummet the thirty or forty feet to the floor of the canyon.

Bo spotted a little cleft in the rock up ahead to his left. That was where the muttered curses came from. He took a deep breath and walked right past it.

The muttering stopped abruptly. The guard stepped out behind Bo, rammed a rifle barrel into his back, and said, "Hey! Where the hell do you think—"

That was as far as he got before Scratch came up behind him and slammed a rifle butt into the back of his head. At the same time, Bo whirled and grabbed the barrel of the guard's rifle, wrenching it up so that if the outlaw managed to pull the trigger, the bullet wouldn't tear through him.

Scratch had struck too swiftly and efficiently for that to happen. The guard folded up without ever knowing what hit him. Bo's other hand shot out and grabbed the man's coat to keep him from toppling off the ledge. Scratch got the unconscious man under the arms and dragged him back up to the rimrock.

Once they got there, Bo checked the sentry for a

heartbeat but didn't find one. "I hope he was one of the Devils," he told Scratch, "because he's dead."

"Reckon I hit him a little too hard and busted his skull," Scratch said without sounding particularly worried about it.

"He stuck a gun in my back, so there's a good chance he was one of the hombres we're after. We'll leave him here and get on down there, maybe see if we can find out what they're planning."

They could see the cabin now, squatting on the canyon floor at the base of the wall like some malignant toad. Built on to the side of it were a shed and a corral for the horses. Bo's plan was to sneak up on the place and try to spy a glance through one of the crudely shuttered windows, maybe eavesdrop on what the outlaws were saying.

They were only about halfway down the ledge, though, almost directly above the ramshackle structure, when the cabin door suddenly opened, spilling light out onto the snowy ground. More than a dozen men in heavy coats and pulled-down hats walked out carrying rifles. There were more of them than Bo expected. Maybe all the gang hadn't taken part in the ambush at the other canyon.

One man lingered in the doorway, and the last of the others paused to talk to him while the rest went to the corral to saddle their horses. Bo and Scratch flattened out on the ledge so they wouldn't be as likely to be seen and listened to the conversation taking place in front of the cabin below them.

"When Lowell comes down from guard duty in the morning, you and him start packin' up all that gold. I want it ready to go when the boys and me get back from Deadwood."

The voice was familiar. Bo had heard it that night in Chloride's cabin, when it gave the order to light the coal oil. Chloride had been convinced this man was the leader of the Deadwood Devils, the one who had carved pitchforks into the foreheads of the dead guards on the wrecked Argosy gold wagon.

The man standing in the doorway said, "Sure, Tom, I understand."

Tom . . . Reese Bardwell's outlaw brother was named Tom. As Bo looked down at the men below him, he would have been willing to bet that one of them had only four fingers on one hand.

"Good," the leader went on. "I'm done with this. Once we hit the bank in Deadwood and clean it out, we'll be back to pick up you and Lowell and the rest of the gold, and then we're puttin' these damned Black Hills behind us. I don't care what the boss says."

So Bardwell—if that's who the leader of the Devils was—was working for someone else. That went along with Bo's theory, too. He didn't know who the boss was or if there was anything behind the Devils' reign of terror beyond sheer profit, but at least some of his hunches had been confirmed.

"It's a shame those blasted Texans had to come along," the man in the doorway said. "This was a sweet setup until then."

"Yeah, not knowin' whether they're dead or not is the one thing that bothers me," the leader agreed. He laughed harshly. "But havin' all that gold will help me get over it."

The man lifted a gloved hand in farewell and headed for the corral, where one of the other outlaws had saddled his horse for him. They all mounted up and rode away, their horses' hooves thudding on the snowy ground as they started back down the canyon. They could follow it to the ridge that ran between Deadwood Gulch and the canyon where the Golden Queen mine was located. In weather like this, especially, it would take them most of the night to reach Deadwood.

But once they got there, no one would expect the raid on the bank they had planned. It was the finishing stroke in this violent game. The Devils would sweep into town on a cold, snowy morning and clean out the bank. Sheriff Henry Manning would probably try to stop them, but the lawman wouldn't be any match for a dozen hardened owlhoots.

But if Gustaffson and the rest of the cavalrymen, along with Bo and Scratch, could get there first, they could have one heck of a surprise waiting for the Deadwood Devils.

Once the outlaws were out of sight, Bo motioned for Scratch to head back up the ledge. When they reached the rimrock, Scratch said, "There ain't no doubt about it now. Those were the Devils."

"Yeah," Bo agreed, "and that dead guard is the one the boss was talking about called Lowell. The other one will probably find his body in the morning when he doesn't come in from guard duty, but by then it'll be too late for him to warn the others. They'll be in Deadwood already . . . and so will we."

"We're goin' after 'em to put a stop to that bank robbery?"

"Yeah, but we have to find Olaf and the other troopers first. Let's hope they were able to follow our trail."

It was dark as midnight now, even though it wasn't long after sundown. The snow still fell. When the wind gusted particularly hard, it seemed to be falling sideways.

"Gettin' hard to see," Scratch said as he and Bo rode back the way they had come from. "I hope those soldier boys don't ride right off a cliff into a canyon."

That was a legitimate worry, Bo thought. If the storm got much worse, they might not be able to travel, even if they did manage to rendezvous with the survivors from the cavalry patrol.

A few minutes later, dark figures loomed up in front of them, made indistinct by the snow. Bo and Scratch reined in and lifted their rifles. The other riders did the same, and one of them called out the traditional military challenge.

"Who goes there?"

Bo relaxed as he recognized Sergeant Gustaffson's voice. "It's us, Olaf," he called. "Bo Creel and Scratch Morton."

The cavalrymen prodded their horses forward. "Thank God," Gustaffson said fervently. "With this snow, we were riding around blindly. I was able to follow your tracks for a while, but between the darkness and the wind, we were lost."

"There's only so much room up here on this ridge," Bo said, "so I was hoping we'd run into each other. We have news."

"You found the Devils' hideout?"

"That's right, but there's only one man there

right now. They left him to guard the loot from their previous robberies."

"Where'd the rest of them go?" Gustaffson asked.

"They're headed for Deadwood," Bo explained. "They're going to rob the bank there first thing in the morning and then take off for the tall and uncut."

Gustaffson let out a surprised curse. "We've got to stop 'em! Nobody in Deadwood will expect the Devils to ride right into town like that. It'll be a massacre."

Bo nodded and said, "It could be. But not if we can get there first."

Gustaffson lifted his reins and turned his horse. "What are we waiting for? Let's go!"

With Bo and Scratch in the lead, the little group started toward Deadwood. The Texans were relying on instinct to guide them now more than anything else. Decades of wandering had given them a built-in sense of direction, but even so, they had to wonder if they were going the right way. It was going to take a lot of luck for them to get back to Deadwood at all in this storm, let alone get there before the outlaws reached the settlement.

The wind blew harder and the snow fell thicker. Every bone in Bo's body was frozen and aching from the cold, and he knew Scratch felt the same way. This late autumn storm was becoming a blizzard, and there wasn't a blasted thing they could do about it. All the men hunched deeper in their coats, and the horses plodded on.

Bo's horse suddenly stopped and wouldn't go on. Trusting the animal's instincts, Bo cried out over the howling wind, "Hold it! Everybody stop!"

Scratch, Gustaffson, and the troopers came to a halt. "What is it, Bo?" Scratch asked.

"I don't know! Everybody hold on for a minute!"

Keeping a tight grip on the reins, he swung down from the saddle and walked forward, taking each step slowly and carefully. After a couple of strides, when his booted foot came down it didn't find anything except empty air. Quickly, Bo backed up a step.

He handed his reins to Scratch, then reached into his coat to fish out a match. He cupped the lucifer in his hands and struck it with a flick of his thumbnail, but the wind snatched out the flame immediately. Muttering to himself, Bo got another match and tried again.

It took three tries before he was able to get a match to stay lit long enough for him to see anything. But that time the feeble glow revealed a snowy brink with black nothingness beyond it.

"We almost rode off a cliff," Bo reported to the others. He felt his heart sink as he continued. "We can't go on! It's too dangerous! We'll wind up falling into a canyon or a ravine!"

"What should we do?" Gustaffson asked, lifting his voice to be heard over the icy wind.

"Find a place to camp, maybe where we can build a fire and thaw out a little!"

"But what about the Devils and that bank robbery?"

Bo hated to say it, but the weather left them with no choice.

"I reckon the people of Deadwood are on their own."

CHAPTER 21

Finding a suitable place to camp wasn't easy. Bo led the way on foot now, with Scratch's lasso tied around his chest under his arms in case he fell. He made his way carefully, sliding his feet along the ground through the snow. The flakes stung his face, and he knew that he and the other men risked frostbite on any exposed skin.

After an unknowable time, Bo bumped into something hard and unyielding. He tipped his head back and saw something dark looming over him. Resting his gloved hands on the surface, he explored it until he was convinced it was a huge slab of rock. If they could get on the side of the rock where it blocked the wind, they might be able to build a fire and thaw out a little.

Bo worked his way along the rock. For all he knew, it was a cliff that ran for miles. But luck was with him, and after only a few yards he felt the surface curving under his hands. He followed it, and gradually the wind died down as the rock blocked the icy gusts. Bo kept moving until he couldn't feel the wind at all. He tugged on the rope to signal Scratch that the rest of the group should follow him.

Moments later, Scratch and the troopers arrived. Bo was already feeling around, searching for something that would burn. He found some brush and broke off a few of the bare branches. Huddling next to the rock, he arranged the branches. Scratch gave him a sheet of newspaper. The Texans always carried a few old newspapers in their saddlebags to use for kindling. Bo tore the sheet into strips, piled them under the branches, and struck a match. Blocked by the rock, the wind didn't blow out the flame. A welcome glow rose, bringing with it a little heat, as the kindling caught. After a moment the branches began to burn as well.

Bo worked patiently with the fire until he had a nice little blaze going. The men crowded around it and held out half-frozen hands. The face of the rock slab leaned out a little, which helped to trap and reflect the heat onto the men.

"My teeth were chatterin' so bad, I thought they were gonna wear themselves down to little nubs," Scratch said. "Feel a mite better now."

"We lost a lot of our supplies in that avalanche," Gustaffson said, "but I think we have some coffee and jerky left."

"Sounds good," Bo said.

Half an hour later, after drinking some hot coffee and gnawing on strips of jerky, the men felt considerably better. They hunkered around the fire, which Bo kept going by judiciously feeding branches into the flames.

Now that they weren't in immediate danger of

falling off a cliff or freezing to death, Gustaffson scowled and said, "I sure wish we could've made it back to Deadwood in time to stop that robbery."

"So do I," Bo said, "but I've been thinking. The Devils left the loot from their other robberies in that cabin Scratch and I found. I heard their leader say that they're going back there to collect the rest of the gold before they leave this part of the country. We're between them and that loot."

"Son of a gun!" Scratch said. "You're right, Bo. Maybe we can ambush them for a change."

"That's what I was thinking."

Gustaffson nodded. "It's a good idea. By then they'll think they're free and clear. They won't be expecting us to be waiting for them. I say we do it."

"We'll have to wait for morning, so we can see where we are. There's no telling where we wandered during that storm. We'll need to find the canyon where the hideout is."

"Shouldn't be too far off," Scratch said. "It seemed like we slogged a long way, but I don't reckon we really covered all that much ground."

"That's what I think, too," Bo agreed. "For now, we need to get some rest. Scratch, you and I will take turns standing guard."

Gustaffson said, "Some of us could do that."

Bo shook his head. He thought it was highly unlikely any of the outlaws would be coming back this way tonight, but it didn't pay to take chances. Somebody had to keep the fire going, too. He didn't figure it was a good idea to trust their safety to a bunch of young, inexperienced cavalrymen.

"That's all right, we're used to it," Bo said. "You and your men get some sleep if you can, Sergeant."

He could tell that Gustaffson knew what he was thinking. The non-com nodded and said, "All right, but if you need somebody to lend a hand, wake me up. I don't mind."

"I might do that," Bo said.

The troopers rolled up in their blankets. So did Scratch, as Bo stood the first watch. As he knelt next to the fire and fed branches and twigs into it, he was careful not to look directly into the flames. That ruined a man's night vision quicker than anything. Instead he peered off into the snowy night.

The leader of the Devils had mentioned their boss, and Bo couldn't help but wonder who that was. Lawrence Nicholson? Reese Bardwell? Someone else he hadn't even thought of? Who else in Deadwood had a reason to strike at the mines using the Devils?

Anybody who wanted to collect a fortune in gold, of course. That was the simplest and most likely answer. But something stirred in the back of Bo's mind, something he had seen or heard that might mean something, even though he couldn't figure out what it was.

After a while he put those thoughts out of his mind without coming up with any answers. It was too cold to think, he told himself with a faint smile. His brain just didn't want to work in this weather. Instead he concentrated on keeping the fire going and listening for the sounds of anyone approaching the camp. It was hard to hear with the wind blowing like that, of course, but depending on what direction somebody was coming from, it might also carry the sound of hoofbeats to him.

That didn't happen. There was just the wind and the snow and the cold, and as Bo hunkered there next to the fire, he felt like he and his companions were the last living souls in a vast, icy wasteland.

The wind died down sometime during the night, and the snow stopped, too. The sky was still overcast the next morning, but it lightened enough with dawn to reveal that the storm had dumped about a foot of snow on the Black Hills. Certainly not a great amount for this area, where the drifts could be twenty feet deep at times, but it was early in the season for such a snowfall.

There was something Bo had forgotten, too, but Scratch reminded him of it. When Scratch nudged Bo's shoulder to wake him, he said, "Happy Thanksgivin'."

Bo sat up and yawned. "You're right. It *is* Thanksgiving, isn't it?"

"Yeah, and I'd sure be givin' thanks right now if I was back in Deadwood gnawin' on a drumstick from a big ol' turkey Sue Beth cooked."

"Deadwood," Bo muttered. The Devils would be there by now. They might even be robbing the bank at this very moment. It wouldn't matter to them that the bank wasn't open on a holiday like this. They would kick down the door anyway and probably blow the vault open with dynamite. The citizens of Deadwood probably wouldn't have much to be thankful for this morning.

The men had a skimpy breakfast of coffee and jerky, then Bo, Scratch, and Gustaffson held another council of war. "We need to backtrack," Gustaffson suggested. "That ought to take us to the hideout."

"That won't be as easy as it sounds," Bo pointed out. "The wind blotted out all our tracks, and the snow's covered up some of the landmarks. We know the right general direction, though, so we can head that way."

"And at least we'll be able to see well enough we won't have to worry about fallin' off a cliff," Scratch added.

They gave the horses a little grain from the supply carried by the troopers in their saddlebags and melted some snow in the coffeepot so the animals could drink. Then it was time to saddle up and see if they could find a good place to ambush the gang when the Devils came back this way to retrieve the rest of their loot.

If they hadn't been facing a deadly shootout with a gang of killers and thieves, it would have been easier to appreciate the snow-covered beauty of the rugged terrain around them. The dark, pine-covered hills provided a vivid contrast to the sweeping vistas of snow. Growing up in Texas, Bo and Scratch had seldom seen sights like this, and even though in their years of wandering they had looked out over many snow-covered landscapes, they were still impressed by the spectacular scenery.

"Don't get me wrong," Scratch said. "I'd still rather be in Mexico or some other warm place right now, but this ain't bad, Bo."

"No, it's not," Bo agreed. "You can see why the

Sioux believe these hills are a sacred place. It's sort of a shame folks ever found gold up here."

"The hills will still be here when the gold is gone," Gustaffson put in. "They may even be here when all the people are gone. We'll never know."

Scratch looked over at the sergeant. "Sorta philosophical for an old three-striper, ain't you, Sarge?"

Gustaffson scowled. "You figure I never think about anything except the army?"

"No offense meant," Scratch said with a grin.

Bo interrupted the exchange by pointing and asking, "Do those twin pines on that knob look familiar?"

"I think so," Scratch replied. "Did we see 'em when we were tryin' to follow the gang yesterday?"

"That's what I'm thinking." Bo turned slowly from side to side in the saddle, studying the countryside around them. He pointed again, this time to the left. "I think the canyon where the hideout is should be over that way."

"Let's take a look," Scratch suggested.

About a quarter of an hour later, Bo spotted a thin tendril of smoke climbing into the sky ahead of them. Scratch saw it at the same time and said, "I'll bet that's comin' from the chimney of that old cabin."

"I won't take that bet," Bo said. "I think you're right. That gives us something to aim for."

The ten men headed for the smoke. As they drew closer, Scratch said, "The fella they left behind to get the gold ready to go probably found that dead hombre by now."

Bo nodded. "Yeah, when Lowell didn't show up from guard duty this morning, I'm sure the other man went looking for him. So he knows by now that something's wrong."

"It'd be a good idea to get our hands on him so he can't warn the rest of the bunch."

"That's just what I was thinking," Bo said.

Gustaffson asked, "How would it be if we forted up in that cabin you told me about? We could hide the horses and make it look like everything was normal, and the Devils would come riding right up to it. They'll want the rest of that gold."

Bo thought about it and nodded. "That's not a bad idea. We don't want to put everybody inside the cabin, though. Unless we got all of the outlaws on the first try, they could bottle us up in there. It would be better if we had a couple of men in the cabin and the rest up here on the ridge. There are plenty of rocks to provide cover."

"That sounds like it could work," Gustaffson said. "God rest the lieutenant's soul, but I don't reckon he knew near as much about tactics as he thought he did."

Scratch said, "The only way you live through as many fights as Bo and me have is to learn a few things along the way. Either that, or be the luckiest hombres on the face of the earth."

"A little of both isn't bad," Bo added with a smile.

They reined in and dismounted a hundred yards from the edge of the canyon. The Texans and Gustaffson went forward on foot while the rest of the troopers stayed with the horses. The body of Lowell, the unlucky guard, was gone, indicating that the other man left behind had found it, although it was possible that wolves could have dragged it off. There was no sign of that, however.

"The fella's gonna know something's wrong," Scratch said. "He'll be ready for trouble. Might be keepin' an eye on the trail through a chink in the wall right now."

"That's why we're not going down that ledge," Bo said. "You feel like climbing down a rope again?"

Scratch grinned. "Sure. We'll come up behind the cabin?"

"That's what I had in mind."

"What do you need me to do?" Gustaffson asked.

"Wait for Scratch and me to give you the all-clear," Bo said. When Gustaffson scowled, Bo went on. "I know you want to be in the middle of this, Olaf, but it's a two-man job, at most."

"All right," Gustaffson replied grudgingly. "I suppose there'll be plenty of fighting later."

"I think you can count on that," Bo said.

They fetched Scratch's rope from his horse and tied one end of it around the trunk of a scrub pine growing fairly close to the edge of the canyon. When Scratch dropped the rest of the lariat over the edge, it fell to within a few feet of the canyon floor. He looked at Bo and asked, "You ready?"

"Yeah. Who's going first?"

In answer to that, Scratch grasped the rope, sat down on the edge, and turned to lower himself over the brink. He dropped out of sight as he went down the rope hand over hand.

"Keep an eye on that lasso," Bo told Gustaffson. "We don't want it starting to fray where it goes over the edge."

"I'll watch it," the non-com promised.

Bo looked over the edge and watched Scratch make the descent. As soon as the silver-haired Texan's feet were back on the ground, Bo swung himself over the brink and started down. He had never been overly fond of heights and wondered why in blazes he had to be climbing up and down rock walls and ropes all of a sudden like some sort of ape. He didn't like heights, and he didn't like boats, either. Solid ground, that was what he wanted under his feet.

It didn't take long to lower himself to the canyon floor. Scratch waited behind a rock with both of his Remingtons drawn. Bo pulled in a deep breath to steady his nerves and drew his Colt from its holster.

"Let's go," he said quietly.

They trotted across the snowy ground toward the cabin. They were behind the old shack and there were no windows on this side, but the outlaw inside might still catch a glimpse of them through gaps between the logs.

Half a dozen horses were in the corral next to the cabin. Two of them would belong to Lowell and the other man, and the others were probably spare mounts. The Texans were about twenty feet from the cabin when Bo noticed that one of the horses was already saddled, and a couple of others had heavy-looking packs slung over their backs. Instantly, Bo knew what that meant.

Spooked by Lowell's death, the outlaw who'd been left behind was running out on the Devils, and he was double-crossing them and taking as much of the loot as he could carry, too.

That thought had just gone through Bo's mind

when the man stepped around the front corner of the cabin, staggering a little under the weight of the pack full of gold bars he was carrying. He started toward the corral gate but stopped short at the sight of the Texans.

"Hold it!" Bo shouted.

The outlaw ignored the command. Instead he dropped the pack at his feet and sent his hand stabbing toward the gun on his hip.

CHAPTER 22

That wasn't a smart thing to do.

The outlaw had barely cleared leather when Bo and Scratch both fired. The Texans hadn't hesitated because they had any doubts about what needed to be done. This man was part of a gang that had murdered, stolen, and terrorized an entire region. Plain and simple, he deserved to die.

But he deserved to die with a gun in his hand.

Two slugs from Scratch's Remingtons and a round from Bo's Colt punched into the man's chest. The impact lifted him and threw him backward. His revolver went spinning out of his fingers unfired. It thudded to the ground at the same time he did. One leg jerked and kicked and his back arched as blood spouted from the holes in his chest. The blood diminished to trickles as the outlaw sagged and went still. Death had finished claiming him.

"Well, we were probably gonna have to kill him anyway," Scratch said into the silence that descended on the canyon as the echoes of the shots died away.

"Yeah," Bo said. "He made sure of it."

The gunfire had spooked the horses in the corral. They milled around nervously. Bo went on. "We can let them calm down, then we'll need to get that gold off of them. We don't want the others riding up and suspecting that something's wrong."

Scratch picked up the dead outlaw's gun and tucked it inside his coat, behind his belt. "I'll bet Olaf's lookin' down from up yonder and worryin' about those shots. Better let him know that everything's all right."

Bo nodded and moved out into the middle of the canyon where Gustaffson couldn't help but see him. He took his hat off and waved it over his head, then motioned for the sergeant and the rest of the troopers to come on down the trail that followed the ledge.

Scratch looked inside the cabin and reported, "The other dead hombre's in there. Looks like this one dragged him down here and left him inside so the wolves wouldn't get him. He wasn't gonna try to bury him, though. He was just gonna take as much loot as he could carry and get out of here."

"That's the way I figure it, too," Bo agreed. "We've got time to bury both of them, though. The rest of the Devils won't be back until later in the day, and the ground shouldn't be frozen yet."

"Seems like a heap of wasted effort for a couple of no-good owlhoots," Scratch said.

"If we drag them over into the trees, that'll attract scavengers," Bo pointed out. "If the rest of the Devils were to see buzzards circling, that might tip them off that something was wrong. And I don't particularly like the idea of sitting inside that cabin all day with a couple of dead outlaws."

Scratch gave a grim chuckle. "I see what you mean. Anyway, we can get Olaf to order some of them greenhorn troopers to dig the grave."

"Yeah, that's what I was thinking," Bo said with a bleak smile of his own.

Gustaffson and the other survivors from the patrol were on their way down into the canyon now, riding single file down the ledge. Bo and Scratch went to meet the sergeant when the group reached the canyon floor.

"We heard the shots," Gustaffson said as he dismounted. "I suppose that means we don't have to worry about the outlaw who was left here."

"Only about burying him and the guard we took care of last night," Bo said.

Gustaffson nodded. "I'll handle that." He turned his head and called to a couple of the troopers. "You'll form a burial detail. I suppose you'll want the graves out of sight, Bo?"

"Yeah, over in the trees would be good," Bo said, waving toward some pines that grew along the canyon wall.

"What happened?" Gustaffson asked.

The story didn't take long to tell. When the Texans were finished, Bo said, "We'll take the gold back in the cabin. The men can warm up inside. You'll need to post some sentries down the canyon, though, just in case the Devils turned back for some reason before they got to Deadwood and show up back here sooner than we expect."

"Good idea," Gustaffson agreed. "We'll take shifts, so that everybody will get a chance to thaw out."

Bo nodded. "Later, we'll leave a couple of men in

the cabin and the rest will spread out. Some up on the rimrock, maybe a few over in the trees. We'll have the gang caught in a cross fire."

"Are you sure you were never in the army?"

Scratch laughed. "Only the Texian army, and we was both just wet-behind-the-ears youngsters then."

Everyone got to work. Several of the troopers carried the dead outlaws into the trees and started digging a grave big enough to hold both bodies. Some of the men looked a little queasy about handling the corpses, but the others seemed to have been hardened to sudden death by seeing so many of their comrades crushed in that avalanche.

Gustaffson sent two men down the canyon to watch for the Devils, as Bo had suggested. The Texans, with Gustaffson's help, unloaded the packs filled with gold bars from the horses and lugged them back into the cabin. The owlhoot who had been running out on the gang had loaded less than half the gold that was stacked inside.

Gustaffson let out a whistle at the sight of it. "That gold's worth more money than I'll ever see in my whole life, even if I live to be a hundred."

"Yeah, it's quite a sight," Scratch agreed. "You ain't gettin' tempted, are you, Olaf?"

"Me?" Gustaffson let out a short bark of laughter. "I've worked hard all my life. I wouldn't know what to do with myself if I was a rich man. If all I had to do was lie around and take it easy, it probably wouldn't be a month before I was so restless I couldn't stand it."

Bo nodded. "I know the feeling. We've never been interested in getting rich, have we, Scratch?"

"Speak for yourself," the silver-haired Texan replied. "I reckon I could have me a little hacienda somewhere and be perfectly happy to do nothin' the rest of my life."

"Sure," Bo said, his tone of voice making it clear that he didn't believe that for a second.

When they had all the gold back in the cabin, they unsaddled the horse in the corral. Smoke still rose from the chimney. There were a lot of tracks in the snow, but when the outlaws returned they wouldn't be able to tell that those tracks hadn't been made by the men they had left here. For the most part everything looked like it had when the rest of the Devils left for Deadwood, except for the horses belonging to the cavalrymen. A couple of the troopers led the animals back up the ledge and picketed them well away from the rim, where they wouldn't be seen.

With that done, Bo, Scratch, and Gustaffson discussed their strategy again. "Olaf, I think you should take four of the men up there in the rim and wait with them there. We'll put three men over in the trees, and Scratch and I will wait in the cabin. We'll confront the Devils first."

"You'll take the most dangerous job, in other words," Gustaffson said.

Bo shrugged. "Or the easiest, depending on how you look at it. We'll have a good position to defend if we have to, and once the Devils see that we've got their loot and they're caught in a crossfire, maybe they'll surrender. *Quién sabe?*"

Gustaffson let out a skeptical grunt and said, "Yeah, sure they'll surrender. You really think that bunch of murdering thieves will give up?"

"Probably not," Bo admitted.

"Likely it'll take shootin'," Scratch said.

"Call in your sentries," Bo went on. "We'll all get in position, and then we'll be as ready as we'll ever be. All we can do then is wait."

Gustaffson nodded. "All right. I still think you two are running the biggest risk, but I don't suppose there's any point in arguing."

"None at all," Scratch said with a grin.

Even with the snow on the ground, the Devils ought to be able to make better time today than they had the night before, Bo thought. Added to that was the fact that they might have a posse on their trail, which would make them move even faster. Despite that, it would take them at least half the day to get back from their raid on the bank in Deadwood. Bo didn't expect them to show up at the hideout until sometime in the afternoon.

That gave everyone time to take advantage of the supplies stored in the cabin and have a hot meal of bacon, beans, and coffee. After that, the cavalrymen took their positions, and Bo and Scratch settled down to wait in the cabin.

Scratch opened the shutter on the window a couple of inches so he could keep a watchful eye on the approach through the canyon. As he stood there, he asked, "You given any more thought to who's really behind all this trouble, Bo? We know the Devils are workin' for somebody."

"Yeah, I've thought about it a lot," Bo replied. "I'd still say Nicholson is the mostly likely suspect, but something about the whole situation makes me think he's not the hombre in charge."

"Maybe we can take one or two of those owlhoots alive. Most fellas get mighty talkative when they're starin' a hangrope in the face."

"That's what I'm hoping," Bo said. "The law would need evidence to convict the ringleader, and the testimony of a couple of the Devils might be enough."

Scratch tapped a fingertip against the ivory-handled butt of one of his Remingtons. "This law don't need a lot of evidence. Just the truth."

Bo shrugged. A lot of times, gunplay was what it all came down to. Someday the frontier would be completely civilized, he supposed, and such rough justice would no longer be needed. But that day was still a long way off, he sensed, and even when most people *thought* it had arrived, there would still be evil out there that required good men to take up the gun and face it down. Bo wasn't sure that would *ever* change.

The hours dragged, as they always did when violence loomed but the time of its arrival was uncertain. The sky brightened slightly as the sun climbed to its highest point, but the clouds never really broke. And then the light began to dim again.

Bo and Scratch took turns watching from the window. Bo was standing there when a flicker of movement from down the canyon caught his eye. Earlier he had seen a couple of birds flitting around, and once a rabbit had hopped across the canyon floor. This was different. This was a bigger shape moving around down there.

This was a man on horseback.

"Scratch," Bo said quietly.

Scratch was sitting at the table. He got up and came over to join his old friend at the window. "One rider," Bo went on. "About three hundred yards down the canyon."

"Yeah, I see him," Scratch said. "You reckon he's alone?"

"He's probably a scout. Since we can see him, that means he can see the cabin. It'll look to him like nothing's changed since the gang left."

The Texans continued watching as the man rode closer. A moment later he reined his horse to a halt and sat there motionless in the saddle.

"Could be studyin' the place through field glasses," Scratch said, pitching his voice quietly even though the rider was well out of earshot.

"Yeah," Bo agreed. "I hope all those troopers stay out of sight."

"At least the sun ain't shinin' bright. It won't reflect off a rifle barrel or anything like that."

The rider took his time assessing the situation in the canyon. The minutes that he sat there on his horse passed even more slowly than they had while Bo and Scratch were waiting for someone to show up.

Finally, the man turned his horse around, drew his rifle from its saddle boot, and raised the weapon over his head, pumping it up and down three times. It was an unmistakable signal to someone who was still out of sight.

Not for long, though. Several more men on horseback appeared and joined the first one. They rode toward the cabin at a fairly leisurely pace.

"I only count four of 'em," Scratch said. "You reckon the others got killed when they hit the bank in

Deadwood? That'd make things easier for us. They might give up for sure when they see we got 'em outnumbered more than two to one."

"Maybe," Bo said. "Or maybe they're just being careful."

A moment later, more riders came into view, and Bo knew his second speculation had been right. From the looks of it, the whole gang had survived, which meant that the odds had tipped slightly to the outlaws' side.

It was even worse than that, Bo realized as a frown creased his forehead. He did a quick head count again and said, "Something's funny here, Scratch. It looks to me like there are two more riders than left here last night. They brought a couple of people with them."

"Who do you reckon that could be?"

"I don't know. It might be that ringleader the Devils are working for, or they could have grabbed some hostages and brought them along—"

Bo stopped short as shock coursed through him. The second group of riders was close enough now that he could make out more details. Two figures who rode in the center of the group, surrounded by the outlaws as if they were being guarded, were hatless. Blond hair and red hair stood out as splashes of color against the snowy background. Scratch recognized the riders, too, and ripped out a curse.

"Is that—"

"Yeah," Bo said. "Marty Sutton and Sue Beth Pendleton, and it looks like they're prisoners."

CHAPTER 23

Bo's hands tightened on the rifle he held as he went on. "Those young troopers better not have itchy trigger fingers. It wouldn't take much to get those women killed."

"I reckon not," Scratch said, just as tense as Bo suddenly was. "One shot would start the ball."

Bo's brain worked furiously. Everything had changed in the blink of an eye. Now a shootout with the Devils was the last thing they wanted.

"We're going to have to make a trade," he said.

"What sort of trade?"

"Gold and safe passage out of here in return for the women."

"Safe passage for who?" Scratch asked. "Those murderin' owlhoots?"

"I don't like it any more than you do," Bo said, "but the first consideration is saving the lives of those hostages. When the Devils see that we've got them covered, maybe they'll let Sue Beth and Marty go."

Scratch shook his head. "I don't think so. They'll

know that as soon as the gals are clear, all hell's liable to break loose."

"Probably, but we've got to try." Bo took a deep breath. "I'm going out there."

"They'll shoot you on sight!"

"Maybe not. Somebody's got to negotiate with them, and they're more likely to pay attention to me if they can see me."

"Well, then, I'm comin', too."

"No need for both of us to get killed in a fool play."

"Save your breath," Scratch said. "If we're goin', let's get out there."

He was right, Bo thought. The four men in the lead were only about twenty yards from the cabin now, and the rest of the group was about ten yards behind them. The showdown couldn't be postponed.

"Follow my lead," Bo said as he moved to the door, pulled the latch string, and swung it open. He stepped out into the gray light with his rifle held ready.

The Devils probably expected the two members of the gang they had left behind to greet them, so they didn't react instantly when two figures emerged from the cabin. Only a heartbeat went by, though, before they realized that the Texans weren't the ones they were expecting.

By that time, Bo and Scratch had lifted their rifles to their shoulders and drawn beads on the men in the lead. "Hold it!" Bo shouted, his voice echoing back from the canyon walls and reaching the cavalry troopers in the trees and those on the rimrock. "Everybody hold your fire and stay calm!"

That order was meant as much for Gustaffson and his men as it was for the Devils.

Several of the outlaws started to reach for their guns. It was an instinctive reaction when they were threatened. But one of the riders who had led the way up the canyon flung out a hand and gestured sharply.

"Hold it!" he echoed Bo. "They wouldn't step out in the open like that if they didn't have more guns pointed at us!"

"You're right about that, mister," Bo said as he peered at the man over the barrel of his Winchester. "There are enough rifles pointed at you right now to shoot all of you into little pieces."

The outlaws weren't wearing their bandana masks now. Their faces were uncovered, and they were a hard-looking bunch. The one who seemed to be the boss was tall and powerfully built, with a close-cropped dark beard and mustache. Something about him was familiar, and Bo had a pretty good hunch what it was. He stole a look at the man's left hand holding the reins and saw that the little finger was missing.

A smile crept across Black Tom Bardwell's craggy face. "Includin' those two women?" he asked. "Because I guarantee you, Tex, if we get shot to pieces, they will, too."

"Maybe nobody has to get killed," Bo suggested. "Let the women go and we'll talk about it."

Bardwell snorted. "Like hell! We let the women go and your bushwhackers'll open up on us a second later." He frowned at Bo and Scratch. "That's assumin' you've even got any bushwhackers hid out. Maybe the whole thing's just a bluff after all. Maybe it's just you two trouble-makin' pieces of Texas trash tryin' to get in our way."

"Mister," Scratch warned, "you better watch what you say about Texas."

"Or what?" Bardwell shot back with a sneer. "You can't start the ball any more than we can. Not without those gals gettin' killed."

"Here's the deal," Bo said. "Let the women go, and you can take the gold that's in the cabin and ride out of here. I give you my word on that."

Up there on the rimrock, Gustaffson was probably seething at the possibility of the men who had nearly wiped out the patrol getting away, but right now Bo's only concern was saving the lives of Martha and Sue Beth.

"If we kill you, what's to stop us from just takin' the gold?" Bardwell demanded.

A few minutes earlier, Bardwell had accused Bo of bluffing. Now Bo was ready to run a real bluff, one that had just occurred to him based on what was most important to these outlaws.

"You'll never be able to get to it," he said with a confident smile. "It'll be blown to kingdom come. There are five kegs of blasting powder in there, and the fuses attached to them are already lit. They've got maybe another two minutes to burn. Maybe."

Bardwell stiffened in the saddle and let out a curse. "You can't . . . You fools! The blast'll kill you, too!"

"We'll chance it," Bo snapped. "Now what's it going to be?"

He saw Bardwell wavering and knew the man was about to agree to the deal. But bad luck chose that moment to crop up, as Sue Beth Pendleton's nerve finally broke under the strain of being a prisoner. She screamed, "Oh, my God! We're all going to die!" and yanked her horse around. She drove her heels into the animal's flanks and sent it lunging against the horse of one of the outlaws surrounding her and Martha

Sutton. The man cursed and instinctively jerked his gun up toward her.

The muzzle of Scratch's rifle tracked swiftly to the side and gouted flame as he fired. The .44-40 round smacked cleanly through the head of the outlaw threatening Sue Beth and exploded out the other side, taking a fist-size chunk of skull with it and killing the man instantly. He toppled out of the saddle.

The explosion of the shot set off a frenzy of violence. Several of the outlaws jerked their guns out and started blazing away at Bo and Scratch, who had no choice but to return the fire as they backed hurriedly toward the door of the cabin.

At the same time, Gustaffson and the rest of the troopers opened up on the gang. Some of the Devils twisted in their saddles to return that fire as well. Not Black Tom Bardwell, though. He whirled his mount and spurred back down the canyon, obviously trying to escape the deadly crossfire. As bullets whipped around him, he leaned over and grabbed the trailing reins of the horse belonging to the man Scratch had shot.

The Texans had reached the doorway and crouched just inside it, using the jambs as cover while they battled with the outlaws. Bo caught a glimpse of Bardwell leading that riderless horse and knew the packs on the animal must hold some of the loot they had taken from the bank in Deadwood. Some of the other men were fleeing, too, including a couple who had hold of the reins attached to the horses carrying Sue Beth and Martha.

Bo tried to line up a shot at them, but he held off on the trigger as he realized he couldn't risk it. There was too great a chance of hitting one of the women instead. Grimacing, he switched his aim to one of the outlaws who was firing a six-gun at him and blew the man out of the saddle.

The roar of the shots was deafening and seemed to go on forever, but in reality the battle lasted only moments. Bo and Scratch held their fire as they realized that five of the outlaws were down, and the others, along with Sue Beth and Martha, were already a considerable distance down the canyon and getting farther away by the second.

"We gotta go after 'em!" Scratch said as he lowered his rifle.

"Yeah," Bo agreed. As he came out of the cabin he shouted, "Hold your fire! Hold your fire!"

Some of the troopers were still throwing lead after the fleeing outlaws and their hostages. As far as Bo had been able to tell, neither Sue Beth nor Martha had been hit, but he couldn't be sure of that. The way lead had been flying around, it was a pure miracle neither of the women had been killed.

Gustaffson bellowed for his men to stop shooting, too. As the firing finally died down, Bo and Scratch ran for the trees where their horses were hidden along with the other mounts. There was no time to waste.

One of the cavalrymen who had been concealed in the trees was down, thrashing around. Another lay close by, motionless. Splashes of blood crimsoned the white snow around them. The third trooper knelt beside the wounded one, trying to help him. Bo wished he and Scratch could stop and help, but the lives of the two women were still at stake.

They jerked their reins loose and swung up into

the saddles. As they rode out of the trees, they saw Sergeant Gustaffson running toward them. "Wait a minute!" the non-com yelled. "Where are you going?"

"After the Devils," Bo said.

"I've got wounded men——"

"Then tend to them and guard the gold in the cabin," Bo snapped. "We're going after the Devils."

"Blast it, I'm coming with——"

The Texans didn't wait any longer. They thundered after the outlaws, leaving Gustaffson behind them with his mouth still open.

"That was a hell of a bluff you came up with!" Scratch called over the pounding hoofbeats. "For a second there you almost had me believin' we was about to get blowed up! That boss outlaw believed it, too!"

"Yeah, I know!" Bo replied. "I just wanted to get the women out of the line of fire!"

"Almost worked!"

Yes, Bo thought, almost . . . but not quite. And for now, at least, that made all the difference.

It was easy to follow the trail left in the snow by the fleeing outlaws and their prisoners. Bardwell must have decided to cut his losses. He had most of the loot the Devils had taken from the Deadwood bank, and he had a couple of hostages. Leaving behind the gold in the cabin must have been a bitter pill to swallow, but it was better than staying and getting shot.

Bo wondered if a posse had followed the outlaws from Deadwood. If it had, there was a chance he and Scratch could catch the Devils between them and the townsmen.

They reached the mouth of the canyon, where the trail swung to the left, away from Deadwood and deeper into the rugged hills. They hadn't run into a posse along the way, so the possibility of closing the jaws of a trap on the Devils was gone.

He and Scratch would continue the pursuit anyway, Bo thought. The Texans had faced long odds before and managed to survive.

As best he'd been able to count in the heat of battle, seven of the outlaws had escaped. That would take some whittling down, Bo told himself, but he and Scratch could do it. It might have been better if they had let Gustaffson come along, maybe with a couple of troopers. The other cavalrymen could have been left to guard the gold in the cabin. But Bo had never been one for second-guessing himself, so he shoved those thoughts aside.

The horses were starting to flag a little after the hard run down the canyon. Bo and Scratch reined them back to a walk. It was frustrating, knowing that the outlaws might be opening up a larger lead on them, but it would be even more disastrous if they ran their horses into the ground. A man who galloped his mount until it died underneath him usually stood a good chance of winding up dead himself.

"Them Devils have been around here for a while," Scratch said. "They probably know this part of the country better than we do right now."

Bo nodded. "More than likely. But with this snow on the ground, they'll have a hard time giving us the slip. They probably know that, too, so we'd better be on the lookout for an ambush."

The trail rose steadily, climbing toward a rugged-looking, snow-covered mountain several miles away. There would be plenty of places for the outlaws to hide in the rough country around it. If they managed to give Bo and Scratch the slip, it might take another cavalry patrol weeks of searching to find any trace of them . . . and by that time, what was left of the gang would be long gone, taking the hostages with them.

Either that, or they would leave the women behind, more likely dead than alive, Bo thought grimly. The best chance of saving Sue Beth and Martha was to catch up to the outlaws today. Every minute the women spent as prisoners increased the odds against them.

Both Texans checked their back trail from time to time, out of habit. Scratch glanced back now and said, "Riders comin' up fast behind us, Bo."

Bo reined in and turned to look. He saw the men Scratch had spotted. Half a dozen of them came across the snow-covered landscape, pushing their horses hard so that the powdery white stuff flew up around the animals' hooves.

"One of 'em's wearin' a uniform," Scratch said. "Bet a dollar to a doughnut that's Olaf."

"No bet," Bo said. "But who are the others?"

There was only one reasonable answer to that, and as the riders came closer, Bo saw that his hunch was right. He recognized the lean, hawk-faced figure of Sheriff Henry Manning and knew the lawman was leading a small posse from Deadwood.

The identities of a couple of the other men were surprising, though. Reese Bardwell and Phillip Ramsey were riding with the sheriff. Bo stiffened at the sight of the big mining engineer. Bardwell's brother was one of the men they were pursuing. Did Bardwell know that?

"Son of a gun," Scratch said. "The old-timer's with 'em."

Bo nodded, having also recognized Chloride Coleman. The final member of the posse was Andrew Keefer, the superintendent of the Golden Queen mine.

The Texans waited while the posse caught up to them. As the riders reined in, Olaf Gustaffson said, "I told you I was coming with you."

"Where's the rest of the patrol?" Bo asked.

"I left them at the hideout. I lost three men in that fight, and a couple of the others were wounded. I figured there needed to be two healthy men guarding that gold, at least."

Bo nodded. "You're right. Have you filled in the sheriff on what happened?"

"The sergeant told me about the fight with the Devils," Manning answered before Gustaffson could say anything. "We ran into him at the mouth of that canyon where the hideout is located. We'll go back there and pick up the gold once we've rescued the women and dealt with the Devils."

"You sound mighty sure about that, Sheriff."

"Why shouldn't I be?" Manning demanded. "From what Sergeant Gustaffson tells me, the odds are about even."

"Yeah, but there's something you don't know." Before any of them knew what was happening, Bo drew his Colt and leveled it at Reese Bardwell. "You've got one of the Devils riding with you."

CHAPTER 24

Bardwell stared at Bo in apparent shock. For a moment he didn't seem able to speak. When he got that ability back, he burst out angrily, "What in blazes are you talkin' about? By God, Creel, I'm gettin' tired of you pointin' a gun at me!"

Coolly, Bo said, "You don't have much room to complain, considering that just a little while ago, your brother and his men were doing their best to kill us. They did kill three of those troopers, and we don't know yet if the women are still all right."

"My brother!" Bardwell repeated. "You're crazy. My brother's dead. He was killed in a shootout with marshals down in Kansas."

"Then you don't deny he's an outlaw?"

"Why should I? Sheriff Manning already knows about it. He's seen the wanted poster on Tom. I never lied about it to anybody who was man enough to come up and ask me." Bardwell's lip curled in a sneer. "Most people would rather just sneak around and spread gossip, though."

"Just how sure are you that Tom Bardwell is dead?"

The ridge above Reese Bardwell's eyes became even more prominent as he frowned. "I heard that he was badly wounded when a posse chased down him and his gang. He dropped out of sight after that, and everybody figured he was dead . . ."

"But you don't know that for certain," Bo said when Bardwell's voice trailed off. "I saw him with my own eyes this afternoon. He matches the description and the drawing on the wanted poster, right down to the missing finger on his left hand."

Bardwell grimaced. "You know how he lost that finger?"

"I don't have any idea," Bo said.

"I cut it off with an ax. I didn't mean to. We were just kids, and I was trying to split some wood for the fireplace. I was havin' trouble with it, so Tom went to grab the chunk of wood and steady it. The ax slipped . . . Lord, I never will forget seeing that finger go flyin' in the air . . ."

"Put your gun away, Creel," Sheriff Manning said. "I believe Bardwell. Maybe his brother *is* the leader of the Devils, but if that's true, Bardwell didn't know anything about it."

Bo lowered the Colt but didn't holster it. "You're betting a lot on a hunch, Sheriff."

"Don't you do the same thing sometimes?" Manning snapped.

Bo had to admit that he did.

Phillip Ramsey spoke up, saying, "Far be it from me to defend the man, but if you'd seen how he was carrying on when he heard that Marty had been taken prisoner, you'd believe him, Mr. Creel."

Bardwell's head snapped toward Ramsey. "I've got

just as much right to be worried about her as you do, Ramsey. What are *you* doing here, anyway? And don't call her Marty."

Bo and Scratch glanced at each other in surprise. What they had just heard in that exchange was the unmistakable sound of two men who both were in love with the same woman. So Bardwell and Ramsey, both employees of Martha Sutton's biggest rival, wanted to court her?

Romance usually didn't pay any attention to business or much of anything else, Bo reminded himself. A fella's heart did what it wanted, sometimes to his great regret.

Ramsey was saying, "I have just as much right to call her Marty as you do, Bardwell. A woman like that needs a man with culture and intelligence."

"I'm smart enough to run a blasted mine, and not sit around all day scribbling numbers in a book," Bardwell shot back with a sneer.

Chloride moved his horse over next to Bo and Scratch and said, "It's mighty good to see you boys again. I reckon you've figured out by now them two are both moonin' over the same gal."

"Yeah, and it don't seem likely Bardwell would feel like that if he was mixed up with his brother robbin' the gold wagons," Scratch said.

Bardwell looked at them and said, "I know we haven't gotten along, but I give you my word, this is the first I've heard about Tom being anywhere in this part of the country. I was in Deadwood this morning, but I didn't see the robbery take place. Even if I had, I might not have recognized him since he was masked. It's been years since we've seen each other."

Scratch looked over at Bo and asked, "Are we gonna believe him?"

Bo slid his revolver back in its holster. "I reckon. We ought to let the horses rest for a few minutes longer. While we're waiting, how about somebody telling us exactly what happened in town this morning?"

"We've already wasted enough time," Ramsey objected. "I think we should push on after them right now."

Manning shook his head. "Creel's right. We've ridden hard all the way from Deadwood. I don't like letting them get any farther ahead of us than you do, Ramsey, but if we kill these horses, the bastards will get away, and there's no doubt about that."

"What about the robbery?" Bo prodded as they all dismounted.

"They must have gotten into town just before dawn and broken into the bank somehow. The first anyone knew something was going on was when they blew the door off the vault. There was no way to hide that. I was in my office when I heard the blast. I grabbed a shotgun and headed toward the bank. Figured that was where the explosion had to come from."

"I was in my room at the boarding house," Ramsey said. "I heard the explosion, too, and came out to see what was going on. I had to dive for cover a minute later, because when the outlaws came out of the bank, they came out shooting."

"How'd they wind up with the women?" Scratch asked.

Manning said, "Some of them must have gone

across the street to the Red Top earlier to grab some hostages. I had taken cover behind a parked wagon and was trading shots with them by then, but I had to hold my fire when they came out dragging Mrs. Pendleton and Miss Sutton."

One of Reese Bardwell's hands clenched into a massive fist. "I saw that, too," he said. "I rode into town last night to talk to Mr. Nicholson, and it was so late when we finished up, I spent the night on a cot in the back room of the office. The explosion and the shooting woke me up. I wasn't armed then, so there was nothing I could do, but when I saw they had Marty, I wanted to charge them anyway."

"How gallant," Ramsey said with a sneer.

Bardwell turned toward him and might have swung that big fist if Manning hadn't stepped between them. "Fighting each other isn't going to accomplish anything," the lawman said sharply. He turned back to Bo and Scratch. "Some of the townspeople had joined in the fight, but once the Devils had the two women as hostages, everyone had to hold their fire. They made it to their horses, stole a couple of mounts from a hitch rack for the women, and galloped out of town. I put together a posse and came after them as fast as I could, but it took a little while."

Bo looked at the five men and said, "No offense, Sheriff, but this isn't much of a posse."

"People are still afraid of the Devils, some of them even more so now that they've dared to invade the town itself. I had more men with me when we left, but they dropped out during the day, one or two at a time, and headed back. It's cold and it's going to be dark after a while, and like I said . . . people are afraid of the Devils."

"But the trail went past the Golden Queen," Chloride put in, "so me and Andy here joined up when the posse came through."

"You didn't see that the outlaws had Miss Sutton with them?" Bo asked.

"We didn't actually see 'em," Chloride explained. "Heard some horses this mornin', but they were on the other side of the canyon, out of sight of the mine."

"We didn't know what had happened until Sheriff Manning stopped to tell us," Keefer added.

"We followed the trail on up here, ran into Sergeant Gustaffson, and then caught up to you two," Manning told the Texans. "Now you know as much as we do. We'd better mount up and get after them again."

Bo nodded. "You're right, Sheriff. We don't need to push the horses too hard, though. Save something for a hard run later if we need it."

"Makes sense," Manning agreed. "Let's go."

They swung up into their saddles and set off after the Devils. The posse was seven men strong now, which matched exactly the number of outlaws who had fled from the hideout. It would be an even fight once they caught up.

Except for the fact that the Devils still had two hostages, and as much as the members of the posse wanted the gold back and wanted to bring the outlaws to justice, they wanted to save the lives of Sue Beth Pendleton and Martha Sutton even more.

* * *

The wind began to pick up late in the afternoon, which added to Bo's worries. "If it starts to snow again, those tracks we've been following could fill up," he said quietly to Scratch as they rode side by side just behind Henry Manning, who continued to lead the posse.

"Yeah, I thought of that, too. We need to get in front of 'em somehow. I wonder how well Chloride knows this part of the country."

"Let's ask him," Bo suggested.

The old-timer was bringing up the rear on his mule. Bo and Scratch dropped back, letting Gustaffson, Bardwell, Ramsey, and Keefer go past them, and fell in on either side of Chloride.

He looked back and forth at them with narrowed eyes. "You boys got somethin' in mind," he said. "I can tell by lookin' at you."

"You have any idea where those varmints might be headin'?" Scratch asked.

"How should I know? Do I look like a bandit to you?"

"We thought maybe you'd know a good place for them to set up an ambush," Bo said. "They've got to have a pretty good idea that we're on their trail, and they're bound to want to get rid of us."

"Well . . ." Chloride scratched at his beard. "Back in my prospectin' days, I wandered up and down a bunch of these canyons and climbed some of the mountains, includin' that one it looks like they're headin' for. There's a place called Wolf Head Rock that got the name because—"

"It's shaped like a wolf's head," Scratch guessed.

Chloride glared at him. "Are you tellin' this story, or am I?"

"Go ahead, Chloride," Bo told him.

The old-timer snorted and said, "Well, anyway . . . There's a pass on the south side of the mountain that's the easiest way to get through to the other side, especially now with this snow. The other passes are narrow enough they're gonna be drifted up so's it'd be hard to make it through 'em, even though this wasn't that bad of a storm. Thing of it is, Wolf Head Rock sorta sits there overlookin' the trail to the pass, so you can't get up there without ridin' by it. Once you go past there's a trail that loops back around to the top."

"And some riflemen hidden up there could pick off anybody who rode past," Bo said.

Chloride nodded. "If I was on the run and tryin' to get shut of a posse, that's the way I'd go, sure enough."

"The Devils ride past the rock and leave plenty of tracks so the posse has to follow 'em," Scratch mused, "then they circle around, get above the trail, and wait to bushwhack whoever's followin' 'em."

"Yep," Chloride said. "It's just a guess, mind you, but if the trail we're followin' goes past Wolf Head Rock, I'd bet my last dime those varmints'll be up there layin' for us."

Bo thought about it for a moment and then asked, "Is there any way to get up to the rock without going past it and then doubling back?"

"Yeah," Chloride said. "If you're a—"

"Don't say mountain goat," Bo interrupted. "Please."

Chloride frowned at him. "How'd you know that's what I was gonna say?"

Bo sighed. "Because I keep having to climb, and I don't like it much."

"But you could climb down to Wolf Head Rock from the back side of it?" Scratch persisted.

"Maybe," Chloride said. "With this cold and snow and the fact it'll be gettin' dark soon . . . I don't know. Sounds to me like a good way to get killed."

"There are a lot of good ways to get killed out here," Bo said. "Do you know a shortcut that might get us there before the gang, so we can be waiting for them?"

"I can get you there, but not before the Devils. They've got too big a start on us."

Scratch looked across the old-timer at Bo. "It's gonna be dark soon. If the posse makes camp, the Devils'll have to wait for 'em to come along in the mornin'. That'd give us time to slip in the back and maybe get those gals outta there."

"You mean to take the women back up that rock wall you'd have to climb down?" Chloride shook his head. "You can't do it. They'd never have a chance."

"Then we could take the Devils by surprise while they're waiting for the others," Bo suggested. "We'll hit them from behind and distract them while the rest of you gallop past, circle around on that trail, and come at them from that direction. We can cut down the odds, grab the hostages, and get them out of harm's way while the rest of you charge up there and finish off the outlaws."

"Yeah, that's a mighty fine plan . . . if it works," Chloride said.

"All plans are fine when they work," Scratch said. "You got any better ideas, old-timer?"

Chloride squinted at him. "I ain't gonna sink to your level and dignify that with an answer." He looked over at Bo. "I reckon if you want to give it a try, I can show you where to go."

Bo nodded. "Let's talk to Manning and the others."

He rode forward and asked the sheriff to call a halt while they discussed the plan. Manning did so, and Bo laid out the idea.

"You'll just get Marty and Mrs. Pendleton killed," Bardwell protested.

"That's if you even get there," Ramsey said. "You'll probably fall and break your necks."

Manning asked Chloride, "Have you ever been to the top of this Wolf Head Rock, Coleman?"

"Yeah, I been up there," Chloride said. "The rock sticks out in front and narrows down so it looks like a wolf's snout. There are a couple of spires, one on each side, that form the ears. Back of that is the open ground that's at the top of the trail from down below, and back of *that* is an even bigger rock that forms a cliff." He looked at Bo and Scratch. "I been thinkin' about it. That rock sorta pooches out. You can't climb down it. Not even a mountain goat could. You'd have to be a fly to make it."

"How about lowering us on ropes?" Bo asked.

Chloride thought about it. "Maybe. You can't get horses up there. You'd have to make it on foot and find places to tie the ropes. I reckon it could be done. But one slip and you're a dead man."

"We're willing to take that chance." Bo looked at Manning. "What do you think, Sheriff?"

"We don't even know for sure they'll be up there to try to ambush us," Manning said.

"The Devils love to bushwhack folks," Chloride pointed out. "They've done it over and over again."

Manning thought it over and slowly nodded. "If you're wrong, though, we've lost some time and let them get even farther ahead of us. That could turn out to be fatal for those women."

"It's a chance we have to take," Bo said. "If the Devils wipe us out, Sue Beth and Marty are done for."

"We can't let that happen," Bardwell said.

"I agree," Ramsey added. "We have to try it, Sheriff."

"All right," Manning said. "The rest of us will find a place to camp, and the three of you—" He looked at Bo, Scratch, and Chloride.

"We'd better get goin'," the old-timer said. "There ain't no time to waste."

Manning gave them a curt nod. "Just remember that more than the safety of the women depends on you. We'll be riding past Wolf Head Rock in the morning, and if you're not up there to hit the Devils from behind, we'll be right in their sights. It'll be like they're taking target practice on us."

"Then you'd better wish us luck," Bo said with a faint smile.

"And a happy day after Thanksgivin'," Scratch added, "because otherwise it's liable to be a black Friday for all of us."

CHAPTER 25

As the posse took up the trail again, Bo, Scratch, and Chloride veered away from the rest of the group. Since the decision had been made to head for Wolf Head Rock, they didn't have to worry anymore about following the tracks left by the Devils. They could reach the place by the shortest, quickest route possible. Chloride knew some shortcuts through the rugged landscape, but he warned the Texans that they wouldn't be easy.

That certainly turned out to be true. Chloride led them through brush-choked gullies, along knife-edge ridges, through gaps between giant rocks that were barely wide enough for a man on horseback to get through them, and down slopes that would have been steep and slippery under good conditions. The coating of snow just made them worse. More than once, Bo thought he and his mount were about to tumble to their deaths.

Somehow, though, they always made it where they were going. As dusk began to close in around them, Chloride paused and pointed across a valley that cut into the side of the mountain now looming close and menacing above them.

"Look over yonder," the old-timer said. "That place stickin' out is Wolf Head Rock."

The light was bad enough that Bo and Scratch had trouble making out the landmark. Finally they saw it, and Scratch said, "How in the world are we gonna get there once it's dark?"

"Oh, don't worry, I know the way," Chloride said.

"If it's like the way we've come so far, we'll never make it without being able to see," Bo said.

Chloride snorted. "There's seein', and then there's *seein'*. I know where I'm goin', dadgum it. The trail won't be too bad from here as long as you fellas just follow me and don't stray off."

Scratch looked over at Bo and shrugged. "We don't have much choice in the matter, do we?"

"Nope," Bo said. "Go ahead, Chloride. We'll be right behind you."

"Dang well better be."

The men set off again, Chloride in the lead, Scratch following him, and Bo bringing up the rear. The warmth of the cabin at the Devils' hideout seemed like something experienced in another life. Bo was chilled through and through, right down to the bone, and he wondered if he would ever be anything but cold again.

Chloride led them down into the valley. When they reached the bottom, they found a good-size creek rushing through it. Chloride reined in and said, "All right, take a look."

"Take a look at what?" Scratch asked. "I can't see

a dang thing, it's so dark. I can hear the stream, but I can't really see it."

"Right there," Chloride insisted.

Bo and Scratch had moved up alongside the old-timer. Bo's eyes made out a snow-covered shape arching up and out, but he couldn't discern any details. "What is it?" he asked.

"It's a rock bridge, a natural bridge over that creek," Chloride explained. "You don't want to slip off of it, neither. As cold as it is, if you go in the water you're liable to freeze to death 'fore we could build a fire to thaw you out."

"Are you sure that's a bridge?" Scratch asked. "It looks more like a rock that just sticks up a ways and ends in nothin'."

"It goes all the way across," Chloride insisted. "Leastways, it did the last time I was in these parts."

"How long has that been?" Bo wanted to know.

"Oh, a couple o' years, I expect."

"So the other side could have collapsed since then?"

"Could have, I suppose," Chloride said. "But I don't believe it did."

"You don't believe it did," Scratch repeated. "I'd feel a whole heap better about this if you knew for sure."

Chloride snorted. "How much do folks ever really know for sure in this life? How do you know the sun's even gonna come up in the mornin'? You don't, that's how!"

"All right, you made your point," Bo said as he lifted his reins. "I'll go first—"

"No, you won't," Chloride said. "I been leadin' the

way so far. I'll go. That way, if I fall off you'll know you better turn around and go back."

Before either of the Texans could argue with him, the old-timer nudged his mule forward. The animal seemed reluctant to start out on the stone bridge, but Chloride banged his heels against the mule's flanks and kept it moving. The mule picked its way up the arching bridge, and after only a moment, the Texans lost sight of Chloride in the gloom.

Bo and Scratch heard the iron shoes on the mule's hooves striking the rock with each step, so they could follow Chloride's progress that way. The hoofbeats were slow and steady, but after a moment they came to a halt. The Texans couldn't hear anything except the rushing of the icy water in the creek.

"Chloride?" Bo called. "Chloride, are you all right?"

"Yeah," the old-timer's voice came back. "Looks like the bridge is all still here. You'd best dismount and come across on foot, leadin' your horses. The snow's made the rock mighty slick. This ol' mule o' mine almost slipped."

"Why don't you dismount where you are and go ahead on foot?" Scratch asked.

"No room to do that. Just got to hope the jughead can make it, that's all."

"Be careful, Chloride," Bo called. He and Scratch listened tensely as the hoofbeats resumed.

After a minute or so that seemed more like an hour, Chloride shouted, "Made it! I'm on the other side. Come ahead, boys, slow and easy and mighty careful-like."

The Texans dismounted. Scratch didn't wait to discuss who was going to go first. He just gripped his horse's reins and started across the natural bridge. Bo's nerves grew taut as he waited to see if his friend was going to make it.

Again the crossing seemed interminable, but just when Bo was about to call out and ask Scratch if he was all right, the silver-haired Texan raised his voice and said, "Come ahead, Bo! It's no worse'n that time down Sonora way when we had to cross that big ol' canyon on a rope bridge."

"As I recollect, we almost wound up dead that day," Bo called back.

"Yeah, but we didn't!"

Bo couldn't argue with that logic. He gave a grim chuckle, grasped his horse's reins a little tighter, and started up the slope of the bridge, leading the animal behind him. The soles of his boots slipped a little on the snow that coated the rock, and he cautioned himself not to get impatient and rush things.

You would think that somebody who had lived as long and done as many things as he had wouldn't be all that upset about the prospect of dying, he mused. But every time his feet slid a little on the snow and his hand tightened on the horse's reins, his heart pounded a little harder and he knew that more than anything else he wanted to see the sun come up in the morning, guaranteed or not. Life had never been perfect for him, far from it, in fact, but he wasn't through with it yet.

He reached the top of the bridge's arch and started down the far side, being even more careful now. He began to be able to make out Scratch and Chloride at the other end. A moment later he was beside them, his pulse hammering in his head and his breath seemingly frozen in his throat. He forced himself to start breathing again and calm down.

"This was the hard part, right?" Scratch asked the old-timer.

"Actually, yeah, it was," Chloride replied. "Until we get to Wolf Head Rock, that is. That's liable to be even worse."

The three of them started making their way out of the valley, and as Chloride had said, the going wasn't too difficult. A few minutes later, snow began to fall again. It wasn't coming down very hard, but Bo was glad it waited until they had crossed that stone bridge, anyway.

Chloride followed a narrow game trail that zig-zagged up the mountainside and then curled around it. The snow-covered ground had a certain luminos-ity to it that allowed the three men to see where they were going despite the pitch-black skies. After what seemed like half the night, Chloride called a halt and said quietly, "We can't take the horses no higher. We'll have to leave 'em here. You'll want a rope."

"Got one," Scratch said as he unfastened his lasso from the saddle.

They tied the reins to the trunk of a stubby pine beside the trail. Then Chloride started climbing a rock-studded and brush-littered slope that was steep enough to have all three men breathing hard after only a few minutes.

"How'd you find this place?" Bo asked when they finally paused to rest.

"I was followin' a big horn sheep," Chloride ex-plained. "Got me the idea I wanted a set o' them curly horns as a trophy. Don't know why. It was a durned fool notion. And I never did get a good shot at the blasted thing, but after a while I come out on a ledge where the trail ended and realized I was up above Wolf Head Rock. Don't know if anybody ever set foot up there besides the Injuns. Probably ain't anywhere in these hills they ain't been at one time or another." Chloride bent over, rested his hands on his knees, and took several deep breaths. When he straightened, he went on. "You ready to go some more?"

"Yeah," Scratch said. "Let's go."

They resumed their climb. In places it was so steep they had to reach out and give each other a hand. But in time they came to the ledge Chloride had mentioned. It was narrow, maybe ten feet deep and twice that long. The Texans pressed their backs against the cold rock wall and rested there, catching their breath again.

"We're gettin' . . . a mite too old for this," Scratch said in a whisper.

"Yeah," Bo agreed, "but I reckon it's better than not living this long."

"Amen."

They took their hats off, stretched out on the snow-covered ledge, and bellied up to the edge so they could look over. Bo had already smelled smoke, so he wasn't surprised when he saw a small fire built in a ring of rocks that had been stacked up to hide the flames. No one would be able to see the fire from the main trail below. Bo and his companions had a bird's-eye view from up here, though.

The orange glow from the flames filtered out over the big, level area that formed the top of the so-called wolf's head. Men moved around down there, talking quietly and drinking coffee from the pot sitting at the edge of the fire. The horses were off to the left, tied to a rope that was strung between two trees. Half a dozen pines bordered the open space on that side.

Sue Beth Pendleton and Martha Sutton were sitting with their backs to two of those trees, huddled in their coats. Bo couldn't tell if they were tied to the pines or if the outlaws had left them loose because there was no place for them to go if they tried to escape. The Devils were between the women and the narrow path that led down to the main trail.

Scratch leaned his head close to Bo's and whispered, "If we can get down there without them seein' us, we can grab the gals, hustle 'em behind those trees, and throw down on the varmints. Maybe ventilate a couple of 'em before they even know what's goin' on."

"That's the way I figure it, too," Bo replied, his voice so quiet that only Scratch and Chloride could hear him. "That was a good guess you made about them being here, old-timer."

"Now don't *you* start—" Chloride began. "Ah, never mind. You gonna shoot without givin' 'em a chance to surrender?"

"After all the things they've done, you really reckon we ought to worry about that?" Scratch asked.

"I ain't goin' to. I was just askin' if you were."

"We're not officially deputized," Bo pointed out, "so Sheriff Manning doesn't need to know every little detail about what happens up here."

"That sounds good to me," Chloride said. "I ain't forgot how that big varmint carved those pitchforks

on my friends. Don't know if I ever will forget it."
The old-timer gave a little shake of his head, as if to
get that image out of his thoughts. He pointed and
went on. "You can see what I mean about the rock
bulgin' out a little. Ain't no way to climb down."

"And even using the lasso, it's going to be hard to
get down there quietly," Bo said. "We're going to
have to rig a loop under the arms of one of us, dally
the rope around a rock, and let him down slow and
easy."

"That'll work while there's still two hombres up
here to hold the other one's weight and lower him,"
Scratch pointed out. "Chloride ain't big enough to
handle that chore by himself."

"I'm willin' to give it a try," Chloride said.

Bo shook his head. "No, we'd just wind up making
a racket and alerting the Devils, and the second man
would probably fall fifty or sixty feet, to boot. It
looks like this is going to be a one-man job."

"Blast it, Bo—" Scratch said.

"The second man can get in the fight from up
here," Bo cut in. "And that'll be you, Scratch."

"How come?"

"I'm a little lighter than you are."

"Not so's you'd notice," Scratch insisted. "I'll bet
there ain't ten pounds' difference between us. Never
has been."

"Ten pounds can be a lot when you're lowering a
fella on the end of a rope," Bo said. "Don't worry,
you'll still get to shoot some of those road agents. In
fact, you'll have an even better shot at them from
up here."

"Well . . . you got that right, anyway." Scratch

sighed. "All right. Me and Chloride'll lower you down there. When are you goin'?"

Bo thought it over and said, "Probably be better to go ahead and do it now. If we wait for morning, they'll be more likely to spot me. I see some rocks down there where I can hide until I'm ready to make my move. That won't be until the rest of the posse gets here. Everything has to seem normal until then."

"All right," Chloride said. "Let's find some place to dally that lasso."

Bo couldn't see the grin on Scratch's face, but he could hear it in his friend's voice as Scratch said, "I always knew at least one of us would wind up at the end of a rope, Bo, but I always figured it'd be me!"

CHAPTER 26

Bo took off his hat and coat and set them aside on the ledge. He would be cold down there without his coat, but he wanted the rope to have a nice secure fit around his chest and under his arms while Scratch and Chloride were lowering him.

Chloride had found a little pinnacle of rock at the back of the ledge that would work as a place to secure the rope. He passed one end around it, gripped both parts of the rope, and leaned hard on it to make sure it would stand the strain of Bo's weight. The rock didn't budge.

Meanwhile, Scratch fashioned the loop in the other end of the rope and lowered it over Bo's up-raised arms. He snugged it tight under Bo's arms and said, "All right, you're ready to go."

Bo went over to the brink and sat down. Scratch and Chloride took up their positions, back a few feet from the rock spire. They gripped the rope tightly as Bo turned around and wriggled backward, letting his legs go off the ledge first. Carefully, Scratch and Chloride let the rope slide a little around the rock.

Supported by the lasso, Bo slipped completely off the ledge and dangled there just under the rim. He nodded to Scratch and Chloride to let them know he was all right, although he wasn't sure they could see the gesture in the thick darkness. He gave the rope a sharp tug, the signal for them to let it down some more.

It was a very uncomfortable feeling, having nothing but fifty or sixty feet of empty air under your boots. Without really thinking about it, Bo held his breath during the slow descent. He managed to turn around so he could look down and see what was going on in the camp below him. Several of the outlaws had turned in for the night, brushing snow off the ground so they would have clear spots for their bedrolls. Three men hunkered beside the little fire, drawing what warmth they could from the flames. Over by the trees, the prisoners appeared to be asleep now, too, huddled at the base of those pines.

Bo had let himself over the edge above a small cluster of rocks. They weren't quite big enough to be called boulders, but he thought they would do to keep him hidden unless one of the outlaws decided to walk over there to relieve himself or something like that. If Bo was discovered, he and Scratch and Chloride would have to give as good an account of themselves as they could. With the other two covering him, Bo thought he at least stood a chance of making it to the trees and getting Sue Beth and Martha behind the pines.

With luck, though, the remaining Devils wouldn't stumble over him and he wouldn't have to make his move until morning, when the rest of the posse would be close by to pitch in.

Bo made the descent at a slow but steady pace. A feeling of relief went through him when his feet finally touched the ground. Quickly, he loosened the loop around his chest and took it off over his head. Scratch and Chloride would have felt his weight leave the rope. He gave the lasso a couple of quick tugs to let them know he was all right and that they should pull the rope back up. It made a faint slithering sound, a little like a snake, as it went up a lot faster than it had come down.

That left Bo crouched behind the rocks about fifty yards from the fire. The women were slightly to his left, also about fifty yards away but at a different angle.

Bo's impulse was to try to reach them now, to let them know they were going to be all right, but he couldn't risk being spotted so soon. He would have a lot better chance to get to the prisoners when all the remaining Devils were getting ready to ambush the posse. The outlaws' attention would be focused then on the trail up to the pass.

Using a gloved hand, Bo brushed a clear spot behind one of the rocks and sat down. The cold from the rock seeped into him and made the chill even worse, although he wouldn't have thought that was possible. He clenched his jaw to keep his teeth from chattering. It didn't seem likely they would make enough racket for the outlaws to hear them, but he didn't want to take that chance.

A few flakes of snow still drifted down from time to time. Bo felt them hit lightly on his face. Luckily the wind had died down, so it wasn't blowing to add to his misery.

Mexico, he thought. Next fall he and Scratch would head south a lot earlier, for sure. Some sleepy little town across the border with a hotel and some cantinas . . .

Bo didn't even realize he had fallen asleep until his head jerked up an unknowable time later. That had been a mighty stupid thing to do, he chided himself. As uncomfortable as the weather was, he didn't think it was cold enough for a man to freeze to death, but going to sleep was a step in that direction. Not to mention the fact that he couldn't keep up with what the outlaws were doing while he was asleep. He was lucky none of them had stumbled over him.

He looked at the sky and saw a slowly widening band of gray light on the horizon. Dawn wasn't far off. According to the plan hatched the day before, Sheriff Manning and the rest of the posse would be riding past Wolf Head Rock in about an hour if nothing had happened to delay them.

Bo heard men talking and moving around. Carefully, he raised his head enough to look over the rock at the camp. A couple of the Devils hunkered next to the fire, getting some coffee boiling. The rest of the outlaws were over by the jutting rock that formed the wolf's "snout." One man crouched behind an "ear," keeping an eye on the trail.

Bo looked toward the trees and saw that Sue Beth and Martha were awake again and sitting up. One of the men at the fire stood up and walked toward them carrying cups of coffee. Bo hoped the women hadn't been trifled with. So far it appeared there was a good chance they had been left alone.

When they took the coffee, Bo saw that their hands were tied together in front of them. That wasn't too bad. As long as their ankles weren't tied, he would be able to get them up and onto their feet without too much trouble.

Having checked out the camp, Bo turned his head and tilted it back so he could look at the cliff looming above him. With the rope pulled back up, he couldn't see any sign of Scratch and Chloride, which was what he expected. As long as they stayed away from the rim, the chances of the outlaws spotting them were pretty small.

Bo stretched as much as he could while staying hidden, trying to loosen up muscles grown stiff from sleep and cold. He caught the scent of the coffee and craved a cup of the hot, black brew. Although it would probably take at least a whole pot to thaw him out, he thought.

Now it was just a matter of waiting.

The snow had stopped during the night, and as the sky grew lighter, Bo saw that there were openings in the clouds. The overcast promised to break at last. It might even warm up enough during the day to melt some of the snow. The first real storm of the season was over. Bo hoped that was a good omen. He was going to take it for one, anyway.

He could tell now that the man who had taken the coffee to the women was Tom Bardwell. He was still standing there talking to them. After a moment Bardwell threw his head back and laughed, obviously amused by something he had just said.

Bo didn't feel much like laughing. He would have much rather drawn his Colt and put a bullet through the outlaw's head.

Bardwell turned and walked back to the fire. The other man had some breakfast ready by now. Bo's stomach growled as he watched the Devils take turns eating. He didn't remember the last time he'd had any food. It was the middle of the day before, at the hideout, he figured out.

This was hardly the first time in his life he'd been hungry, he reminded himself. And it probably wouldn't be the last . . .

Unless he didn't live through the next hour or so, of course.

Bardwell took what appeared to be biscuits to the women. They were able to handle them with their hands tied. Bardwell was still standing there talking to them when one of the other men called, "Tom!"

Bardwell swung around and hurried to join the rest of the gang. They all picked up rifles and moved closer to the point that overlooked the trail. Bo knew what that movement had to mean.

The outlaws had spotted Manning and the other members of the posse riding toward Wolf Head Rock.

Bo could imagine what was going through the heads of the posse members right now. They didn't know whether the Texans and Chloride had managed to get into position to disrupt the ambush. For all they knew, they were riding right into a trap that was about to slam shut on them. But for the plan to work, Manning, Gustaffson, Ramsey, Keefer, and Reese Bardwell had to keep moving as if they weren't worried about anything except catching up to their quarry.

Bo wondered briefly what Reese Bardwell would do when and if he saw his brother again. Would he take part in the battle, knowing that it might be his own bullet that ended his brother's life, or would he hang back because of that?

Or would he betray the men who were supposed to be his allies?

The chill inside Bo deepened even more as that thought went through his head. It might have been smarter to send Reese back to Deadwood. But it was too late to do anything about that now. The Devils were hiding behind the rocks and aiming their rifles down at the trail. None of them looked toward the trees where the women sat. It was time for Bo to make his move.

Cold, cramped muscles caused him to stumble a little as he came out from behind the rocks and broke into a crouching run toward the trees. His eyes cut toward the outlaws. He expected one of them to spot him and let out a shout of alarm at any second, but they continued staring down at the trail. Thirty yards, twenty, ten . . . Sue Beth and Martha saw him coming by now and stared at him in wide-eyed shock. To them it must have seemed as if he had appeared out of thin air.

Martha was closer. He dropped to a knee beside her and pulled the clasp knife from his pocket. His gloved fingers fumbled with it as he tried to open it. The fact that his fingers were half-frozen didn't help matters. Despite the cold, he yanked the glove off his right hand and finally managed to open the blade. So far neither of the women had said a word.

They had to know that the longer it was before the Devils realized Bo was there, the better.

That was what Bo thought, anyway. But sometimes he was wrong, and this was one of those occasions. Wrong about a lot of things, in fact, but when he heard the metallic ratcheting of a gun being cocked and looked up to see Sue Beth Pendleton holding a small revolver in both hands and pointing it at him, everything snapped into place in his brain. All the questions that had bothered him had answers . . . now that it was too late.

"Drop the knife, Bo, and don't reach for your gun," Sue Beth said. "I'll kill you both if I have to."

CHAPTER 27

A gaping Martha managed to gasp out, "My God, Sue Beth! What are you—why—"

"Because she's the real leader of the Deadwood Devils," Bo said. "Isn't that right, Sue Beth?"

The friendly, attractive woman was gone, replaced by a hard-faced killer. She ignored the questions and grated, "I said, drop the knife."

"Short-barreled guns like that aren't very accurate," Bo said.

"You're four feet away! I can't miss at this range."

Bo knew that was true. Sue Beth could kill him and Martha in a heartbeat. He was a little surprised she hadn't already done so.

But he smiled faintly as he realized why she hadn't pulled the trigger. "A gunshot right now will spoil your little ambush, won't it?" he asked. "You want Bardwell and the rest of your hired killers to wipe out the posse from Deadwood."

Sue Beth's lips were faintly blue from the cold. They pulled back from her teeth in a grimace as she said, "Why wouldn't I want them dead? The whole town could burn to the ground with everybody in it and I wouldn't shed a tear. I haven't cried since the day they came and told me my husband was dead."

"That's not the town's fault."

"No, but it was the mine's fault, and the town wouldn't be there if it weren't for the mines!"

Bo wanted to keep her talking. As long as she was venting her rage and hatred in words, she wouldn't be pulling the trigger.

"So you decided to ruin the mines, and you used Black Tom Bardwell to do it."

"That's right. He showed up in Deadwood looking for his brother, but he stopped at the Red Top for a meal first. I could tell that he was a hard, violent man, even though I didn't know at the time he was an outlaw. I had a hunch he was the sort of man who could help me. I didn't know how right I was, but I found out the next morning, after he'd spent the night at my place. He told me who he was and that his gang was hiding outside of town. They were the ones who had been pulling those stagecoach robberies. That's when I laid out my plan and invited Tom to join forces with me. I was able to help him with information." She sneered. "Everybody in Deadwood comes into my café, and you'd be surprised what people will let slip over pie and coffee!"

That was the way the picture had sprung into Bo's mind as soon as he saw the gun in Sue Beth's hands. When he had considered who had a reason for wanting to hurt the mines around Deadwood, he hadn't even thought about her, but he knew now he should have. What better motive for revenge than the death of a loved one?

She had fooled everybody, including him and Scratch. That knowledge made a sour, bitter taste well up under Bo's tongue. Usually he and Scratch were pretty good judges of character, but not this time. Not by a long shot.

"Bardwell and the others didn't take you hostage after that bank robbery yesterday," he said. "You wanted to come along. That was your way of getting out of Deadwood without anybody knowing what you've done. Bardwell wanted to take the gold and move on, and even though you hadn't caused enough trouble to make the mines shut down yet, like you planned, you know you couldn't keep going without him and the rest of the gang. So you *pretended* to be a prisoner. Why bring Marty along?"

"She happened to be in the café, and Tom thought he might need a real hostage before this was all over." Sue Beth shrugged. "I kept the pose going up until now, just in case this bitch somehow got away. I don't want the law after me. Which means, as soon as Tom and the others have taken care of the posse, both of you will have to die, too. In fact, I think I'll just go ahead and kill you as soon as the shooting starts."

Martha was still staring at the older woman. In a voice that trembled with emotion, she said, "I . . . I thought you were my friend."

"Maybe I would have been," Sue Beth said, "if it hadn't been for the lust for gold that fills all of you mine owners."

"But I never did anything to hurt you! I was sorry when your husband died—"

"Sorry's not good enough! Sorry won't bring him back!"

Bo said, "Neither will killing anybody else."

Sue Beth's face twisted. Maybe somewhere deep inside her, she knew that what she had done was wrong. Maybe there was a constant struggle going on between the woman she had been and the woman she had become. Bo didn't know.

All he knew was that time had run out, because Sue Beth extended her arms, pointing the gun right at his head, and her finger started to tighten on the trigger.

Before the hammer could fall, Martha Sutton suddenly lunged toward Sue Beth and lashed out with arms that were bound together at the wrists. She hit Sue Beth's arms and drove them upward just as the little revolver exploded with a wicked snap. Martha kept moving, lowering her shoulder and barreling into Sue Beth with enough force to knock the older woman over backward.

The posse had to be close now. Close enough for the plan to work, Bo hoped. But he no longer had any choice about whether to wait.

The time had come to fight.

As Martha and Sue Beth struggled, Bo surged to his feet and whirled toward Wolf Head Rock and the Deadwood Devils. The shot had alerted them that something was wrong, and several of them spun around as Bo palmed his Colt from its holster. The gun roared and bucked in his hand as he fired.

Shots blasted from the rifles held by the outlaws. Bo felt the heat of a bullet as it whipped past his ear. Crouching, he fired again and saw one of the Devils double over as the slug punched into his midsection. Clutching his belly, the man staggered backward and took one step too many. With a scream, he toppled off the edge of Wolf Head Rock and plummeted toward the trail below.

More shots rang out from the ledge above the camp as Scratch and Chloride joined in the fight. The Devils had thought they held the high ground, but now they saw they were wrong about that. They scattered and sought cover among the rocks.

From the corner of his eye Bo saw Martha slam clubbed fists across Sue Beth's face. The older woman sagged, obviously stunned. Bo triggered another shot, then bent to grab Martha's arm and haul her to her feet. At the same time, he kicked away the little revolver Sue Beth had dropped.

"Get behind the trees!" Bo told Martha as he pushed her in that direction. He snapped a fourth shot toward the rocks where the Devils had taken cover and then darted behind one of the pines as soon as he saw that Martha was safe behind one of the thick-trunked trees. Gun thunder still echoed from the slopes around them as the battle continued.

Bo took a moment to thumb fresh rounds into the empty chambers of his gun. While he was doing that, he heard the swift rataplan of hoofbeats from the trail. The posse was running the gauntlet down below, but with most of the Devils shooting at him, Scratch, and Chloride, the chances of the lawman's entourage making it past Wolf Head Rock were a lot better.

Bo snapped the Colt's cylinder closed and thrust the gun past the tree trunk. He slammed out three shots just as one of the outlaws tried to dart from one rock to another. The man went down writhing in pain from a bullet-shattered shoulder.

The hoofbeats grew louder. Bo glanced toward the path that led up from the main trail and saw the members of the posse surge into sight with their guns blazing. Two more of the Devils went down, but Phillip Ramsey pitched out of the saddle as a bullet tore through his arm. Sergeant Gustaffson jerked as he was hit, but he managed to stay on his horse and kept firing the rifle clutched in his hands.

Reese Bardwell's horse suddenly went out from under him as a bullet struck it. The big engineer was thrown clear, slamming to the ground and rolling over several times as he landed. His rifle had flown out of his hands when he fell.

Reese came up within arm's reach of one of the outlaws. The man fired at him at such close range that it seemed impossible for him to miss. Reese kept coming, though, swinging one of his huge fists in a sweeping blow with so much power behind it that when the punch smashed into the outlaw's jaw, he was lifted clean off his feet and thrown backward. He sprawled on the ground, limp and motionless, either dead or out so cold that he was no longer a threat.

Bo was watching as Reese Bardwell started to turn around. He saw the black-bearded figure leap out from behind one of the rocks and line his gunsights on Reese. Tom Bardwell might have hesitated for just a split second when he recognized his brother, but then the gun in his hand roared and spouted flame and smoke anyway. Bo fired at the same instant and saw Tom Bardwell jerk under the impact of the slug that drove into his chest. Bardwell stumbled back a step and fell to his knees.

Reese was still on his feet, holding a hand to

his side now. Bo saw crimson welling between the engineer's fingers. Reese took a step toward his wounded brother. Tom Bardwell, his face a twisted mask of hate, struggled to lift his gun and shoot his brother again, but his strength suddenly deserted him. The revolver slipped from his fingers and thudded to the ground. Bardwell followed it, flopping face-first.

Reese turned and looked at Bo for a second. Then he gave the Texan a curt nod of thanks.

The shooting was over. The rest of the posse dismounted, and Sheriff Manning moved quickly to check the bodies of the outlaws who lay sprawled here and there on Wolf Head Rock.

While Manning was doing that, Bo stepped over to a groggy Martha Sutton, who was shaking her head as she struggled to get to her feet.

Sue Beth Pendleton was gone.

Bo took Martha's arm and helped her stand up. "Are you all right?" he asked her. He didn't see any blood on her, but a bruise was already starting to show on her jaw.

"Yes, I . . . I'm fine," she said. "Mrs. Pendleton walloped me pretty good, but I—" She stopped short and looked around. "Where did she go?"

"She must have slipped off during the ruckus," Bo said. He saw that the revolver Sue Beth had had hidden somewhere in her clothes still lay on the ground where he had kicked it. He picked it up and tucked it behind his belt while he looked around for her.

"Bo!"

The shout from above made him look up. Scratch

stood on the ledge with Chloride. He called down, "Are you all right, Bo?"

Bo was waving to indicate that he wasn't hurt when hoofbeats suddenly sounded close by. Martha cried out a warning. Bo jerked around and then leaped aside as one of the horses belonging to the Devils loomed up, practically on top of him. He caught a glimpse of Sue Beth riding the unsaddled animal as he threw himself out of the way just in time to avoid being trampled. He pushed himself to his knees as she galloped toward the path leading down to the main trail.

Before she could reach it, Andrew Keefer leaped in her way, yelling and waving his arms. The horse veered away from the stocky mine superintendent. Then Henry Manning shouted, "Mrs. Pendleton, wait!" He tried to grab the bridle Sue Beth had slipped onto the horse, but she frantically jerked the animal away from him.

The horse was already spooked from all the gunfire and powder smoke. Neighing shrilly, it reared up and danced backward. Out onto Wolf Head Rock it went, plunging and bucking, and Sue Beth screamed as she fought to bring the horse under control. That scream turned into a shriek of terror as hooves slipped on snow-covered rock and the horse's legs skidded out from under it. Bo and everyone else watched in horror as the horse slid off the edge, taking Sue Beth with it.

"My God," Martha said in a shocked, hollow voice. A big hand fell on her shoulder, and she turned to find herself standing next to Reese Bardwell. She buried her face against his massive chest as a shudder went through her.

A few yards away, Phillip Ramsey stood with his right hand clutching his bloodstained upper left arm. He glared at Reese and Martha and then shook his head. The young bookkeeper wasn't hurt too bad, Bo thought . . . at least not physically.

He left Reese Bardwell comforting Martha while Ramsey looked on in disgust. Bo had spotted Olaf Gustaffson sitting propped up against a rock, and now he hurried toward the sergeant.

"How are you, Olaf?" Bo asked as he knelt beside the non-com.

"I think I'll live," Gustaffson replied. "A bullet got me in the side and knocked out a chunk of meat, but it went on through and didn't hit anything too important, I hope." He looked toward the protruding rock where Sue Beth and the horse had fallen. "I'm sorry about Mrs. Pendleton. What a tragedy."

"You don't know the half of it," Bo said.

By evening, everyone was back in Deadwood except the troopers who had been left to guard the loot at the Devils' hideout. The next day, Chloride and several other drivers would take wagons up there to retrieve the gold and bring it back to town, where somebody would have to sort out which part of it belonged to who. Bo was glad he wasn't going to have anything to do with that job.

Reese Bardwell, Ramsey, and Gustaffson had had their wounds patched up by one of the local doctors, and they were all expected to make a full recovery.

Sue Beth Pendleton's broken body was down at the undertaker's, along with the bodies of the outlaws. John Tadrack was going to be busy for a while.

It didn't seem right that those varmints would be laid to rest properly while Lieutenant Holbrook and the other soldiers killed in the avalanche would probably sleep for eternity under those tons of rock . . . but that was the way of the world, Bo knew. Justice was a relative thing, and often incomplete.

The Texans and Chloride were striding along the boardwalk when the door of the Argosy Mining Company opened and Lawrence Nicholson stepped out in front of them. The mine owner smiled and said, "Good evening, gentlemen. I've been hoping you'd come along so I could have a word with you."

"What do you want?" Chloride asked, not bothering to be overly polite about it.

"Why, I'd like to offer you your job back, Mr. Coleman," Nicholson said. He looked at Bo and Scratch. "And I'd like for the two of you to work for me as well."

Scratch shook his head. "We're a mite too old to swing a pickax."

"Don't worry, I'll find something better than that for you. I'm sure I'll need some good men to guard our gold shipments."

Bo said, "You shouldn't have any more trouble. All the Deadwood Devils are either dead or behind bars in Sheriff Manning's jail."

"The Deadwood Devils aren't the only bandits in the world, you know," Nicholson said. "I'm sure there'll be more trouble in the future."

"Yeah, well, you'll have to find somebody else to handle it," Scratch said. "We're makin' a run for Mexico, soon as the snow melts."

Nicholson sighed. "I can't persuade you to change your minds?"

Bo shook his head. "I'm afraid not."

"That is too bad. I can't get you to work for me, and I'm going to be losing my chief engineer and superintendent, too. Possibly even my bookkeeper."

"How do you figure that?" Bo asked with a frown.

"Now that Marty Sutton knows how Reese and Phillip feel about her, I fully expect both of them to resign from the Argosy and go to work for the Golden Queen, so they can continue their rivalry for her affections."

"Now *that* could cause some problems," Bo said.

"But somebody else'll have to handle that fracas, too," Scratch added.

Nicholson chuckled. "To tell you the truth, I'm not really that upset about it. I figure that sooner or later, Marty will decide between the two of them and then settle down to get married and have children, and she'll let me buy her mine at a reasonable price. If you put the Argosy and the Golden Queen together, you know, it would be the biggest mining operation in this part of the country."

"That thought crossed my mind," Bo said, not mentioning that at the time he had been trying to decide whether or not Lawrence Nicholson was really the ringleader of the Deadwood Devils.

Nicholson nodded and bid them a good night. As the three men strolled on down the street, Scratch asked, "How would you feel about comin' to Mexico with us, Chloride?"

"What, you mean you want to associate with an *old-timer* like me?" Chloride asked with a disgusted snort.

Scratch grinned. "I reckon we've sorta got used to havin' you around."

"Well, thanks but no thanks. I got a job drivin' for Miss Sutton, and I intend to keep it." Chloride grinned under his bushy mustache. "Besides, I got a feelin' that bein' around the Golden Queen's gonna be pretty entertainin' once those two young fellas are all healed up."

"You're probably right about that," Bo said. He paused and looked across the street. The Red Top Café sat there, closed and dark. Bo couldn't help but think about how nice it would have been to walk into the warmth of that place, to have a bowl of stew and a piece of pie and a cup of coffee, to look across the counter and see Sue Beth Pendleton with a friendly smile on her face . . .

"'Smile and smile, and be a villain,'" he murmured.

"What's that?" Scratch asked.

Bo shook his head. "Nothing." He paused. "Wind's turned around to the south. It feels a little warmer already. Won't be long before the snow's all gone, and we can light a shuck for Mexico."

Built on dreams. Forged in blood. Defended with bullets. The town called Fury is home to the bravest pioneers to ever stake a claim in the harsh, unforgiving land of Arizona Territory.

In William W. Johnstone and J. A. Johnstone's blockbuster series, the settlers take in a mysterious stranger with deadly secrets— and deadlier enemies . . .

Turn the page for an exciting preview of

A Town Called Fury: Redemption

Coming in July 2011

Wherever Pinnacle Books are sold

PROLOGUE

29 October, 1928
Mr. J. Carlton Blander, Editor
Livermore and Beedle Publishing
New York, New York

Dear Carlton,

Thank you so much for pointing me toward
this Fury story! I know you didn't mean for me
to get a "wild hare" (or is that "wild hair"?)
and just go charging out to Arizona at the drop
of your not-inconsequential hat, but that's
exactly what I did. The story runs deeper than
you could have known—or the sketchy
reference books say, for that matter—and I
found a number of the participants still alive
and kicking, and best of all, talking!

As you know, the story actually begins long
before the events you provided me to spin into
literary fodder. They begin in 1866, when
famed wagon master Jedediah Fury was hired

*by a small troupe of travelers to lead them
West, from Kansas City to California.
Jedediah was accompanied on this mission by
his twenty-year-old son, Jason, and his fifteen-
year-old daughter, Jenny, they being the last of
his living family after the Civil War. Jedediah
was no newcomer to leading pilgrims West.
He'd been traveling those paths since after the
War of 1812.*

*I have not been able to ascertain the names
of all the folks who were in the train, but what
records I could scrounge up (along with the
memories of those still living) have provided
me with the following partial roster: the
"Reverend" Louis Milcher, his wife (Lavinia)
and seven children, ages five through fifteen;
Hamish MacDonald, widower, with two half-
grown children—a boy and a girl, Matthew
and Megan, roughly the ages of Jedediah's
children; Salmon and Cordelia Kendall, with
two children (Sammy, Jr. and Peony, called
Piney); Randall and Miranda Nordstrom,
no children (went back East or on to
California—there is some contention about
this—in 1867); Ezekiel and Eliza Morton,
single daughter Electa, twenty-seven (to be the
schoolmarm) and elder daughter Europa
Morton Greggs, married to Milton Griggs,
blacksmith and wheelwright (no children);
Zachary and Suzannah Morton (no children),
Zachary being Ezekiel's elder brother; a do-it-
yourself doctor, Michael Morelli, wife
Olympia, and their two young children*

(Constantine and Helen); Saul and Rachael Cohen and their three young sons. There were a few other families, but they were not listed and no one could recall their names, most likely because they later went back East or traveled farther West.

The train (which also contained livestock in the forms of a number of saddle horses and breeding stock, a greater deal of cattle, goats, and hogs—mostly that of Hamish MacDonald and the Morton families—and, of all things, a piano owned by the Milchers) left for the West in the spring of 1866. It was led by Fury, with the help of his three trusty hirelings. I could only dig up one of the names here: a Ward Wanamaker, who later became the town's deputy until his murder several years later (which follows herein).

Most of the wagon train members survived Indian attacks (Jedediah Fury was himself killed by Comanche, I believe, about halfway West, several children died, and Hamish MacDonald died when his wagon tumbled down a mountainside, after he took a trail he was advised not to attempt), visiting wild settlements where now stand real towns, and withstanding highly inclement weather. About three-fifths of the way across Arizona, they decided to stop and put down stakes.

The place they chose was fortunate, because it was right next to the only water for forty or fifty miles, both west and east, and it was close enough to the southernmost tip of the

Bradshaws to make the getting of timber
relatively easy. There was good grazing to be
had, and the Morton clan made good use of it.
Their homestead still survives to this day as a
working ranch, as do the large homes they
built for themselves. Young Seth Todd, the
last of the Mortons (and Electa's grandson)
owns and runs it.

South of the town was where Hamish
MacDonald's son, Matthew, set up his cattle
operation, which had been his late father's
dream. He also bred fine Morgan horses, the
only such breeder in the then territory of
Arizona. His sister, Megan, ran the bank both
before and after she married, she having the
head for figures that Matthew never
possessed.

For the first few years, everyone else lived
inside the town walls, whose fortress-like
perimeter proved daunting to both Indians
and white scofflaws, and the town itself
became a regular stopover for wagon trains
heading both east and west.

But I'm getting ahead of myself. What
concerns us here is the spring of 1871, the
year that gunfighter Ezra Welk went to meet
his maker. Former marshal Jason Fury
(now a tall but spare man in his eighties, with
all his own teeth and most all of his hair, and,
certainly, all of his mental capacities) was
very much surprised that I was there, asking
questions about something "so inconsequential"
as the demise of Ezra Welk.

"*Inconsequential?!*" *I said, as surprised by his use of the word as its use in this context.*

"*You heard me, boy,*" *he snapped.* "*Salmon Kendall was a better newsman than you, clear back fifty or sixty years!*"

I again explained that I was a writer of books and films, not a newspaperman.

This seemed to "settle his hash" somewhat, however, it was then that I changed my mind about the writing of this book. I had planned to pen it pretending to be Marshal Fury himself, using the first-person narrative you had asked for. However, in light of Marshal Fury's attitude (and also, there being other witnesses still living), I decided to write it in third person.

And so, as they say, on with the show!

CHAPTER 1

The black, biting wind was so strong and so fierce that Jason feared there was no more skin left on his upper face—the only part not covered by his hat or bandána.

His nostrils were clogged with dust and snot, despite the precautionary bandana, and his throat was growing thick with dust and grit. Whoever had decided to call these things dust storms had never been in one, he knew that for certain. Oh, they might start out with dust, but as they grew, they picked up everything, from pebbles to grit to bits of plants and sticks. He'd been told they could rip whole branches from trees and arms off cacti, and add them into the whirling, filthy mess, blasting small buildings and leaving nothing behind but splinters.

He hadn't believed it then.

He did now.

He could barely see a foot in front of him, and just moving was dangerous—his britches had turned into sandpaper, and his shirt was no better.

At last he reached his office—or at least, he

thought it was—and put his shoulder into the door. He hadn't needed to. The wind took it, slamming both the door and Jason against the wall with a resounding thud that must have startled folks as far away as two doors up and down, even over the storm's howling, unending roar.

It took him over five minutes to will both his body and the door into cooperating, but he finally got it closed. Slouching against it, he went into a coughing jag that he thought would never quit. He would rather have been cursing up a storm than coughing one up, but when it finally stopped, a good, long drink from the water bucket put the world right-side up. Well, mostly. He still couldn't breathe through his nose, but a good, long honk—well, six or seven—on his bandana put that right again.

With the wind still howling like a banshee outside and flinging everything not tied down against his shutters and door, he thanked God for one thing: the storm was, at least, keeping everyone inside, which included Rafe Lynch—wanted for eight killings in California, across the river—and currently ensconced at Abigail Krimp's bar and whorehouse, up the street.

He didn't know much about Lynch, other than that he was clean in Fury, and for that matter in the whole of Arizona, and Jason was therefore constrained by law to keep his paws off Lynch, and his lead to himself. Actually, he felt relieved. He didn't feel up to tangling with someone of Lynch's reported ilk. Still, he was worried. What if Lynch tried to stir up some trouble? And what if he or Ward couldn't handle it? Ward was a good deputy, but he wouldn't want to put him up against Lynch in a card game, let alone a shoot-out.

He sighed raggedly, although he couldn't hear himself. Outside the jailhouse walls, the storm pounded harder and harsher. Dust seeped in everywhere: around the door and the windows, even up through the plank floor. Jason knew damn well that the floor only had a two-inch—or less—clearance above the dirt underneath, and this occurrence left him puzzled.

He'd managed to make his rounds, although a bit early. It was only three in the afternoon, despite the dust and crud-blackened sky. Everyone was inside, boarded up against the wind and wrapped in blankets against the storm's detritus and the sudden chill that had accompanied it.

Couldn't they have just gotten a nice rain? Jason shook his head, and two twigs and a long cactus thorn fell to the desk. He snorted. He must look a sight. At least, that's what his sister Jenny would have said, had she been there to see him. But she was nestled up over at King's Boarding House with her best friend Megan MacDonald, or she was at home, madly trying to sweep up the dust and grit that wouldn't stop coming.

His thoughts again returned to Rafe Lynch. It gnawed on him that Lynch was even in town. In his town, damn it! Well, not actually his. The settlers had christened it Fury after his father, Jedediah Fury, a legendary wagon master who had been killed on the trail coming out from Kansas City. He supposed the place's name was attractive to scofflaws, but they seemed drawn to the tiny, peaceful town in the Arizona Territory out of all proportion. Why couldn't they ride on over to Mendacity or Rage or Suicide or Hanged Dog or Ravaged Nuns?

He shivered. Now, there was a town he didn't want anything to do with!

His sand-gritted eyes were weary and so was he. He glanced up at the wall clock again. 3:30. No way that Ward was going to make it down here on time, if he came at all. It wouldn't hurt him to get a little shut-eye, he figured, and so he put his head down on his dusty arms, which were folded on the desk.

Despite the battering storm outside, he was asleep in five minutes.

Roughly twenty-five miles to the west of Fury, a small train of Conestoga wagons fought their way through the dust storm. Riley Havens, the wagon master, had seen it coming: the sky growing darker to the east, the wind coming up, the way the livestock skittered on the ends of their tie ropes, and the occasional dust devils that swirled their way across the expanses on either side of them.

But now the edge of the darkness was upon them, and if Riley was correct, they were in for one whip-tail-monster of a dust storm. He reined in his horse and held up his hand, signaling for the wagons to halt.

Almost immediately, Ferris Bond, his ramrod for the journey, rode up on him and shouted, "What the devil is that thing, Riley? Looks like we're ridin' direct into the mouth a' hell!"

"We are," Riley replied grimly. "Get the wagons circled in. Tight."

"What about Sampson Davis? He rode off south 'bout an hour ago."

Riley didn't think twice. "Screw him," he said, and turned to help get the settlers, with their wagons and livestock, in a circle.

Down southeast of town, the storm wasn't as much sand and grit as twigs and branches, and Wash Keogh, who'd been working the same chunk of land for the past few years, was huddled in a shallow cave, along with his horse and all his worldly possessions. Well, the ones that the wind hadn't already taken, that was.

But despite the storm, Wash was a wildly happy man, because he held in his hand a hunk of gold the size of a turkey egg. It wasn't pure—there was quartz veining—but it sure enough weighed a ton and he was pretty sure that pay dirt was just upstream—up the dry creek bed, that was—a little ways. If this damned wind would just stop blowing, well, hell! He might just turn out to be the richest man in the whole Territory!

That thought sure put a smile on his weathered old face, but he ended up spitting out a mouthful of mud. The grit leaked in no matter how many bandanas he tied over his raggedy old face.

Well, he could smile later. The main thing now was just to last out the storm.

Like him, his horse waited out the wind with his back to it and his head down. Smart critters, horses. He should have paid more attention when the gelding started acting prancy and agitated. But how could a man have paid attention to anything else when that big ol' doorstop of gold was sitting right there in his hand. He'd bet he would have missed out on the second coming if it had happened right there in front of him! And, blast it, he didn't figure Jesus would be mad at him, either! 'Course, he'd probably "suggest" that 10 percent of it go to the Reverend Milcher or some other Bible thumper.

Fat chance of that!

He hunkered down against the howl of the storm to wait it out.

But he was happy.

Back inside the stockaded walls of Fury—walls that had used up every tree lining the creek for five miles in either direction and used up most of the wagons, too—the wind was still whistling and whining through the cracks between the timbers. Solomon Cohen, who had been known as Saul until he changed it back to Solomon during a crisis of faith several months back, was huddled in the mercantile with Rachael, his wife, and the boys: David, Jacob, and Abraham. The back room of the mercantile was fairly tight, and so they had planted themselves there for the duration.

Solomon's crisis had come after a long time, a long time with no other Jews in town, no one else who spoke Yiddish or understood Hebrew, no one with an ancestry in common with himself or Rachael. Oh, there was she, of course, but it wasn't like having another Jewish man around to share things with, to complain with, to laugh with, and to spend the Sabbath with. How he wished for a rabbi!

And now Rachael was with child once again. He feared that they would lose this one, as they had the last two, and each night his prayers were filled with the unborn child, wishing it to be well and prosper. He didn't care whether God would give him a boy or a girl, he just heartily prayed that Jehovah would give him a child who breathed, who would grow up straight and tall, and who would be a good Jew.

Still, he wished for another Jewish presence in Fury. A man, a woman . . . a family at best! His children had no prospects of marriage in this town filled with goyim.

If they were to marry, they would likely have to go away to California, to one of the big cities, like San Francisco. It was a prospect he dreaded, and he knew Rachael did, too. They had talked of it many times. They had even spoken of it long before the children's births, when they first met in New York City and Solomon spoke of his dreams of the West and the fortunes that could be made if a man was smart and handy and careful with his money.

It had taken him over ten years (plus his marriage to Rachael and three babies, all sons) to talk her into it, but at last she relented. Although he always remembered that she had cautioned that they didn't know if the West held any other Jews that their children could marry—or even, for that matter, would want to!

As always, she had been right, his Rachael.

He looked at her, resting fitfully on the old daybed they kept down here, her belly so swollen with child that she looked as if she might pop at any second, and he felt again a pang of love for her, for the baby. She was so beautiful, his wife. He was lucky to have her, blessed that she'd had him.

The wind hadn't yet shown any signs of lessening, and so he slouched down farther in his rocker and carefully stuck his legs out between David and Abraham, who were sound asleep on the floor. Glancing over at Jacob to make sure he was all right, too, Solomon said yet another silent prayer, then closed his eyes.

He was asleep in less than five minutes.

The Reverend Milcher angrily paced the center aisle between the rows of pews. Not that they had ever needed them. Not that they'd ever been filled. Not that anybody in town appeared to give a good damn.

Even though he hadn't spoken aloud, he stopped immediately and clapped his hand over his mouth. From a front pew, Lavinia, his long-suffering wife, looked up from her dusty knitting and stared at him. "Did you have an impure thought, Louis?" she asked him.

"Yes, dear," he replied after wiping more sand from his mouth. "I thought a sinful word."

"I hope you apologized to the Lord."

"Yes, dear. I did."

He began to pace again. They were running out of food, and he needed to fill the church with folks who would donate to hear the word of the Lord. That, or bring a chicken. He had tried and tried, but nothing he did seemed to bring in the people he needed to keep his church running. And now, this infernal dust storm! Was the Lord trying to punish him? What could he have possibly done to bring down the Lord's wrath upon not only himself, but the town and everything and everyone around it?

Again, he stopped stock still, but this time his hand went to the side of his head instead of his mouth. That was it! The dust storm! Oh, the Lord had sent him a sign as sure as anything!

"Louis?"

"What?" he replied, distracted.

"You stopped walking again."

He pulled himself up straight. "I have had a revelation, Lavinia." Before she could ask about it, he added, "I need some time to think it through. Good night, dear." Soberly, he went to the side of the altar, opened the door, and started up the stairs.

Lavinia stood up and began to smack the dust out of the garment she'd been knitting, banging it over and over against the back of a church pew. She kept on whacking at it as if she were beating back Fury, beating back her marriage and this awful storm, beating back all the bad things in her life.

At last, she wearily stilled her hand and started upstairs.

When Jason woke, he still found himself alone, surrounded by unfettered wind whipping at the walls. And it was, according to the clock, 10:45. And there was no Ward in evidence.

He let out a long sigh, unfortunately accompanied by a long sandy drizzle of snot, which he quickly wiped on his shirtsleeve. Well, he should have expected it. He gave himself credit in foretelling that Ward wouldn't brave the storm in order to come down to the office, though. Jason just hoped he'd found himself a nice, secure place to hole up in.

Jason reminded himself to hike up to the mercantile and see if they had any calking. That was, when the storm let up. If it ever did. He was going to make this place airtight if it killed him.

There was still dust coming in around the windows and the front door, and right up through the floor. He didn't want to see what was happening around the back door, but he knew it'd be bad. It wasn't nearly as tight as the front one.

Just then, a loud bang issued from the back room, and he shot to his feet, accompanied by the soft clatter of thousands of grains of sand falling from his body and hitting the floor.

Whispering, "Dammit!" he went to the door to the back room and threw it wide. He had expected to be met by the full force of the storm and the outer door hanging off its hinges, but instead he found Ward, struggling to close the back door.

He fought back the urge to laugh, and instead helped Ward. The two men succeeded in closing and latching the door, and Ward leaned his back against it, his head drooping.

Jason grinned. "You look like you been rode hard and put up wet, man."

"Feel worse," Ward replied after a moment. Then he looked Jason up and down. "You don't much look like a go-to-town slicker, yourself, boss."

Jason smiled, then led him into the main part of

the office. "There's clean water in the bucket. You want coffee, you're gonna hafta make it yourself."

Ward went to the bucket and had himself two dippers of water, then splashed another on the back of his neck. "You ever seen a storm like this?"

Jason said, "I never even heard a' one." He hadn't, either, not one like this!

"Well, I heard about 'em, but this one's sure a rip-snorter. Don't believe I ever heard tell a' one lastin' so long or goin' so hard. Oh—what I come to tell you. One a' the Milcher kids is missin'. Found the Reverend out lookin' for him, but you know him—he's like buttered beef in a crisis. Made him go on home."

Jason nodded. "When'd he go missing?"

"Sometime between seven and nine thirty. The Reverend thinks he's out lookin' for the cat. She's missin', too." During the passing years, the Milcher's original cat, Chuckles, had been replaced several times. The latest one was . . . well, he couldn't remember at the moment. But it was either a grand kitten or a great-grand kitten of Chuckles.

"Shit." Jason put his hands flat on the desk, then pushed himself up. "I reckon now's as good a time as any." He shook out his bandana and tied it over his nose and mouth. "You rest up. Come out when you're ready."

But Ward was on his feet, his clothes dribbling sand on the floor. "Naw. I'll go with you. Four eyes are better than two. Or so they tell me."

Jason nodded. "Appreciate it. Pull your hat brim low."

He opened the front door. He had a firm hold on the latch, but the sudden influx of wind shoved Ward off his feet and into the filing cabinets.

"You wanna warn a fella afore you do that?" he groused.

Jason didn't blame him. "Sorry, Ward."

Muttering something that Jason was glad he couldn't hear, Ward slowly got back to his feet, using his feet and hands and back for traction. He made it to the desk, and finally to the door.

Jason shouted, "We're gonna hafta get outside, then pull like crazy, okay?"

Ward nodded, and they did, each bracing a boot on either side of the door frame. It took them nearly five minutes just until Jason lost sight of the wall clock, but eventually it was closed and latched.

"Which kid was it?" he asked Ward over the howling wind.

"Milcher!"

"Which Milcher kid?" There were a bunch of them.

"Peter. The five-year-old!"

Great, just great. A five-year-old kid lost in this storm!

A storm a grown man could barely keep his footing in, and that seemed intent on staying around until the end of time. Maybe it *was* the end of time.

But Peter was a tough little kid. If he had survived the trip out West in his mother's belly, he could survive anything. At least, that's what Jason hoped.

He tried to think like a five-year-old following a cat . . .

"Follow me!" he said to Ward, and set off, staggering against the buffeting wind, toward the stables.

Down at the stable, they found several cattle and a couple of saddle horses standing out in the corral, all with their heads down and their butts into the wind. Jason wondered if they could get them inside once they found the Milcher boy.

It didn't take them long at all. Once they pulled the barn door closed after them and called out his name a couple of times, they heard soft sobbing coming from the rear of the barn. Well, it would have been loud wailing, if not for the roar of the storm. Ward heard it first, and Jason followed him back to a rear stall, where Jason uncovered the boy, hiding beneath a saddle blanket.

"Peter?" he asked.

"My daddy's gonna kill me!" came the answer. When the boy looked up, his face was streaked by the trails of tears through the crust of dust and grit on his face. "But I had to find Louise! She's gonna have kittens, and she's having them right now!" He pointed down next to him in the straw, and there was the Milcher's cat, with a third or fourth kitten just emerging.

"Get a crate, Ward," Jason said, and put an arm around the boy. "Don't worry, Peter. Your daddy's not gonna kill you. In fact, he was out looking for you, he was so worried."

Ward handed him an apple crate, in which he'd already placed a fresh saddle blanket.

"H-he was?" Peter asked.

"He was indeed. Now let's see . . ."

Jason gently lifted the mother cat while Ward stooped over him, carefully bringing the still attached kitten along, and they placed them in the apple crate. "Good," Jason said. "Now let's see who else is here."

He found not three, but four other kittens. Three were tabby and white, and one was all white. By the time the men got them all back with their mother, she had finished giving birth to the fifth kitten, had cut the cord, and was busy licking it clean. "Good kitty," Jason murmured, "good momma." The kitten was tabby and white, too, although with more white than the others.

Jason and Ward stood up, and Jason held his hand down to the boy. "Guess we'd best get the lot of you back home!" Ward shifted through the stack of saddle blankets and dug out a relatively fresh one, covering the box snugly.

"But the baby cats can't go back!" Peter said as he grabbed Jason's hand and pulled himself to his feet. "Daddy doesn't like them. He says he doesn't like the smell of birth."

"Reckon he's just gonna have to get over it," Jason said, trying to hide a scowl. He didn't much like the smell of Milcher, either. And if Milcher objected to those kittens in his damned house, then Milcher was going to find himself in jail. For something or other.

Jason lifted Peter up into his arms, then threw a blanket over him. "You all snugged up in there?" he asked.

A muffled, "Yessir," came from beneath the

blanket, and with Ward carrying the box of kittens and their momma, the men pushed their way out into the storm again.

The wind hit Jason like a slap in the face, but behind him, he heard Ward say, "Believe it's lettin' up some!"

Jason didn't reply. He just forged ahead, toward the Milcher's place. Thankfully, it wasn't far, and when he rapped on the church door Mrs. Milcher threw it wide, then burst into tears. "Is he all right?" she cried, pulling at the boy in Jason's arms. "Is he—"

"I'm fine, Momma," Peter said after he wiggled out of the blanket. And then he broke out in a grit-encrusted grin. "Louise had her babies!"

Ward set the box down and lifted the cover. A purring Louise looked up with loving green eyes, and mewed softly.

Mrs. Milcher cupped her boy's face in her hands. "Is that why you went out, honey? To find Louise?"

"Yes'm. And I did, too! She was in the stables."

Mrs. Milcher looked up at Jason. "She always wants to hide when she feels her time is here. What a night to pick!"

"Mrs. Milcher, ma'am? I know you've given away kittens before, and I was wonderin' if—"

"Certainly, Marshal! Any one you want!"

Jason smiled. "I kind of fancy the little white one. Got a name for him already and everything."

She cocked her head. "But you don't even know if it's a boy or a girl! Do you?"

"No, ma'am. Wasn't time to check. But I figured

to call it Dusty. Name works either way, I reckon, and I'll never forget when he was born."

Mrs. Milcher smiled back at him. "No, I don't suppose you will! Thank you, Marshal, thank you for everything. My husband would thank you as well, I'm sure, but he has retired for the night."

Jason lifted a brow but said, "I see. Well, take care of young Peter, here, and watch over my kitten until it's ready to leave its momma." He and Ward both tipped their hats, and both stepped through the doors at once. But instead of the whip of wind that Jason was expecting, they stepped out into cool, clear, still air.

"What happened?" Ward said, looking around him.

"I guess it quit."

"Guess so. You wanna go up and get a drink?"

"Nope. Wanna go home and wash up."

Ward nodded. "Reckon that sounds good, too. Well, you go on ahead, Jason. I'll have a drink for both of us."

Jason laughed. "Just one, Ward. You're on duty, y'know."

Jason turned around and started the walk back to his house. The air felt humid, as if rain was coming. He hoped it was. Nothing would feel better right now than to just strip off his clothes and stand out in his front yard, nekkid. He chuckled to himself. Yeah, there'd be hell to pay if Mrs. Clancy saw him, but on the other hand, she wasn't likely to be awake at eleven at night, was she?

Jenny'd skin him, though. It was a terrible thing, he thought, to be ruled by women. Then he pictured

Megan MacDonald. Well, there exceptions to every rule, he thought, and grinned.

It did rain, and while Jason was outside, beaming and standing nekkid in his front yard with a bar of soap in his hand, miles away the wagon train was getting the worst of the dust storm. The wagons had been tightly circled and all the livestock had been unhitched and brought to the center, but the wind screeched through the wagons like a banshee intent on revenge. Young Bill Crachit thought that maybe God was mad at them for giving up on the dream of California, and he huddled inside his wagon, praying.

The Saulk family, two wagons down, held their children close, hoping it would just stop. Well, Eliza Saulk did. Her husband, Frank, had the thankless job of trying to hold the wagon's canopy in place: the train had lost three already to the torrent of grit and dirt and cactus thorns. He was around the far side when, out of nowhere, an arm of saguaro hit him in the back like a bag of nail-filled bricks. He went down with a thud, but was helped to his feet a moment later by Riley Havens, who yanked the cactus, stuck to Frank by its two-inch spines, free.

Blood ran down Frank's back in a hundred little drizzles, soaking his shirt, and Riley helped him back up inside the wagon.

"Saguaro!" he shouted to Eliza. "Get those thorns out!"

Never letting go of the children, she moved back

to her husband, gasped, "Oh, Frank!" and immediately began to ease him out of his shirt.

Riley left her to take care of her man and struggled next door, to the Grimms's wagon. Their canopy had blown off earlier. It had taken four men to chase it down and get it tied back in place. And that had been before the wind came up so damned hard. He doubted they could repeat their performance.

All was well with the Grimms, except that their dog wouldn't shut up. He was a cross between a redbone hound and a Louisiana black-mouthed cur, and the wind had brought out the hound side of him, in spades. While he yodeled uncontrollably, the Grimms had covered their heads with blankets and quilts, trying to hold off the noise of him and the storm. Riley hollered, "Shut up!" at him a few times, but it made no difference, and so he moved on to the next wagon and left the howling beast behind.

The raw wind still raked at his ears, though, even though he'd tied his hat down with one scarf, then covered his nose and mouth with a second one. But the crud still got through somehow, worked its insidious way up his nose and into his mouth. His eyes were crusted with it, and even his ears were stuffed. *I must look like hell,* he thought, then surprised himself by smiling beneath the layers. The whole world looked like hell tonight. He wasn't the only one.

The wind picked up—although how it managed, he had no idea—and one of the horses reared. He felt it more than saw it, because the horses were circled twenty feet away, in the center of the ring of wagons, but he knew what had happened. Somebody's gelding or mare had fallen prey to another of those thorny chunks of cactus that the wind seemed intent on throwing at them.

He made his way through the roar, falling twice in the process, but at last reached the distressed animal. Lodged on its croup was a fist-size chunk of jumping cholla, which, in this case, might have jumped all the way from Tucson as far as Riley knew.

He pulled it free, then pulled out what spines he could see. It was all he could do, but the horse seemed grateful.

Slowly staggering, he made his way to a new wagon to check in and give what reassurances he could. Which weren't many. He swore, this was the last train he was going to ferry out or back.

He was done.

CHAPTER 2

Back in Fury, it was still raining come the morning, although it had settled into a slow but steady drizzle. And it didn't take much water for an Arizona inhabitant to forget the dust, Jason discovered. When he walked up the street to the office, he didn't pass a single water trough that wasn't filled to the brim. And grimy from gritty, dusty cowhands helping themselves to a free bath. Jason pitied the horses that had to drink from those troughs.

Surprisingly, there hadn't been that much wind damage. To the town, anyway. Ward Wanamaker told him, before he went home for the day, that the east side of the surrounding stockade wall looked like God had been using it for target practice.

Jason didn't feel like walking around the outside of the town, so he walked past the office and all the way down the central street, to the steps that would take him to the top of the wall. Every wall, his father had taught him, had to have places from which men could defend the interior, and this one did, around all four sides. When he reached the top, he stood on the rails that also ran around the perimeter and looked down.

Ward had been right.

Cactus—clumps, arms, and pieces—covered the outside of the wall, and at the base was enough vegetation to start a small forest. If anybody in their right mind would want a forest of cactus, that was. And then he got to thinking that a forest of cactus just might be a good thing for the outside of that wall. He knew cactus would just send down roots and take off, if you threw a hunk of it down on the ground. And they sure had a good rain last night, that was for sure. The stuff was probably rooted already.

He decided to leave it. It'd be just one more deterrent for Apache, and he was all for that.

He figured the stuff stuck to the wall would eventually fall off, leaving spines and stickers behind to discourage anyone who might try to climb in, too. If they made it past the cactus forest, that was.

"Oh, get a grip on yourself," he muttered to himself. "Stuff only blew in last night, and here you've got it six feet tall in your head!"

Shaking his head, he went back down the steps and started up toward his office. But he paused before going inside. He wondered if he should have a word with Rafe Lynch. He decided he should, but he put it off. Frankly, he didn't want it to turn into a confrontation, and he was afraid that Lynch could do that pretty damn fast.

Actually, he was afraid that Lynch could rope, tie, and brand him before he even knew he was in the ketch pen.

So he turned and walked into the office, expecting

one hell of a mess that'd need cleaning up. But to his surprise, Ward had spent a busy night with the push broom and the cleaning cloths.

Hell, Jason thought, this place ain't been this clean since we built it! When he stepped out back, he found that even the bedding from the cells had been hung out in the rain!

"Wash and dry in one move," Jason said with a chuckle. "That's Ward."

Southeast of town, Wash Keogh was looking like mad for his gold vein, the one he was certain was going to make him rich, and the one of which he carried a goose egg–size chunk in his pants pocket.

He'd been searching all morning, but nothing, absolutely nothing showed up. It wasn't raining now, but it had drizzled long enough after sunrise that the desert was still wet, washed free of its usual cover of dust. He had expected to find himself confronted with a shimmering wall of gold, the kind they wrote about in those strike-it-rich dime novels.

But no. Nothing.

Had somebody been in here before him and cleaned it all out? It sure looked that way. Maybe the chunk he'd found had simply been tossed away like so much trash. He growled under his breath. Life just wasn't fair!

"What did those other boys do right that I done wrong?" he asked the skies. "I lived me a good life, moved settlers back and forth, protected 'em from the heathen Indians! I worked with or for the best— Jedediah Fury, Whiskey Hank Ruskin, and Herbert

Bower, to name just three. All good, godly men! I brung nuns to Santa Fe and a rabbi to San Diego, for criminy's sake, and I guarded that preacher an' his family to Fury. All right, I do my share of cussin', some say more. And I like my who-hit-John, but so do them priests a' yours. What more do you want from me?"

There was no answer, only the endless, clear-blue sky.

Another hour, he thought. Another hour, and then I'll have me some lunch.

He set off again, his eyes to the ground, keenly watching for any little hint of glittering gold.

Jason had let his sister, Jenny, sleep in. She was probably tuckered out from the storm—he knew he was.

The girls—Megan MacDonald was with her—woke at nine, yawning and stretching, and both ran to the window at the sound of softly pattering rain.

"Thank God!" Jenny said, loudly enough that Megan jumped. Jenny didn't notice. "Rain!" she said in wonder, and rested her hand, palm out, on the windowpane. "And it's cool," she added in a whisper. "Megan, feel!"

She took Megan's hand and pressed its palm against the pane, and Megan's reaction was to hiss at the chill. "My gosh!" she said, and put her other hand up next to it. "It's cold!"

Ever down-to-earth, Jenny said, "Oh, it's not cold, Meg, just cool. I wonder if Jason's up?"

She set off down the hall to wake him, but found

his room empty except for an absolutely filthy pile of clothes heaped on the floor, dead center!

"He's gone," she said to nobody. Meg hadn't followed her. Turning, she grumbled, "Well, I hope he had the good sense to take a bath," and walked up the hall toward the kitchen, where she heard Megan already rooting through the cupboards.

A little while later, after both girls had washed last night's grime out of their hair and off their bodies, and had themselves a good breakfast, they walked uptown toward Solomon and Rachael's store.

The storm—long gone by now—hadn't shaken Jenny's hens, who had taken shelter in the low hay mow of Jason's little barn, and subsequently laid a record number of eggs. The girls' aim was to sell the excess eggs and find a new broom and dustpan, which Jenny had needed for a coon's age, but hadn't got around to buying yet. This seemed like the time, what with the floors of the house nearly ankle-deep in detritus.

They had barely reached the mercantile and were standing, staring in the window, when the skies suddenly opened again! Rain began to pelt them in huge, hard drops, and Megan grabbed Jenny's hand and yanked her. "C'mon!" she hollered.

But Jenny had put the brakes on, and just skidded along the walk behind Megan, the egg basket swinging from her hand. "Wait! The door's back the other way, Meg!"

"Come on!" Megan insisted, and tugged Jenny for all she was worth. "The mercantile's closed, Jenny!"

"It is?" Jenny began to run alongside Megan then, and what Megan was headed for wasn't a very nice place—it was Abigail Krimp's. But any port in a storm, she told herself. It surely beat standing out here. Her skirt was already almost soaked!

Abigail was holding the door for them, and they ran directly inside, laughing and giggling from the race, not to mention where it had ended. It was the first time either one of them had so much as peeked inside a place like Abigail's—just the location made them giddy!

But Abigail was just as nice as Jenny remembered from the trip coming out. Why, she didn't look "sullied" at all! That's what Mrs. Milcher always called her. And then it occurred to her that she didn't even know what "sullied" meant. And Jenny had the nerve to call herself Miss Morton's assistant schoolmarm!

Abigail put a hand on each girl's shoulder and said, "Why don't you young ladies have a seat while you wait it out? I declare, this weather of late is conspirin' to put me outta business!" She led them to the first of three tables and sat them down. "You gals like sarsaparilla?"

Jenny's mouth began to water. It had been ages! She piped up, "Yes, ma'am!" and Megan nodded eagerly.

But Jenny's money sense moved in. "We don't have any money, Miss Abigail. But thank you anyway."

Megan looked at her as if she'd like to toss her over the stockade, and Jenny stared down at her hands.

"Not everything in here's for sale, you sillies!" Abigail laughed. "I thought we'd just have us a nice, friendly sody pop. Been forever since I just got to sit and socialize." And she was off, behind the bar.

Megan and Abigail exchanged glances, but Abigail was back by then, with three bottles of sarsaparilla, three glasses, a bottle opener, and a small bowl of real ice! The ice itself opened up the first topic of conversation, and Abigail told them that she had a little cellar dug far underground, under the back of the bar, where she kept a barrel full of ice when she could get it. This was the last of her current stash, which had come down from the northern mountains with the last wagon train to stop in Fury.

Jenny was transfixed, but Megan was halfway through her first glass. If you put enough ice in the glass, your bottle was enough to pour out twice. Jenny looked away from Abigail long enough to ice her glass, then fill it with sarsaparilla. It bubbled up into fizz when it hit the ice, and she was giggling out loud, which started Abigail, then Megan, laughing as well.

Abigail lifted her glass. "To old friends," she said.

Jenny and Megan followed suit, then clinked all three together and drank.

Until her dying day, Jenny would swear that was the best sarsaparilla she ever drank.

"What the hell's goin' on out here? A hen party?" asked a new voice, male and jovial, but pretending to be cross.

Both Jenny and Megan twisted in their chairs to see the speaker. He was coming out of the mouth of the hall behind him, all clanking spurs and hip pistols and worn blue jeans and nothing up top except his long johns. And his hat, of course. Jenny didn't understand why in the West, nobody took off his hat, not even to greet a lady. Not even in church. Just a touch of the brim was the most she'd seen since they left Kansas!

But this man—who Jenny liked already, just on general principle—not only took his hat clear off, but bowed to the table! Then he swept his hat wide, and said, "Good morning ladies! I trust everyone came through the night in one piece?"

While the girls tittered, he looked at Abigail, raised his brows, indicated the empty chair at the table, and asked, "May I?"

"Certainly," she said. She was on the edge of laughter, herself.

The man sat down—right next to Jenny, who nearly fainted.

He was tall, over six feet, and had wavy, sandy hair, and it was cut fairly short. His eyes were blue, but not regular blue, like hers, nor sky blue, like Jason's. They were a deep, deep blue, as blue as she imagined the ocean would be if you swam down so far that your lungs were ready to burst. And he was, well, gorgeous, if you could call a man that.

"Allow me to introduce myself," said the vision sitting beside her. "My name is Lynch, Rafe Lynch, and I'd appreciate it if you'd call me Rafe."

Jenny stuttered, "Hello, Rafe. I'm Jenny Fury."

"Like the town!" He smiled wide. "Coincidence?"

She barely had her mouth open when she heard Megan say, across her, "Her father was the wagon master who started us West and her brother is our marshal, and I'm Megan MacDonald and my brother owns the bank."

Megan ran out of air, and Jenny just said, "Yes. What Megan said, I mean." She felt herself flush hotly and took a quick sip of her soda pop.

It was Abigail who saved her. She reached over and put a hand on Rafe's arm. "Can I get you somethin', honey?"

Rafe picked a little chunk of ice out of the bowl and ran it over his forehead. "A beer, if you wouldn't mind, Abby."

She said, "No problem at all," and stood up. Before she left, though, she said, "Rafe, honey, why don't you tell the girls, here, how you just beat the dust storm to town? I swan, I would'a been scared to death!"

He grinned. "Don't take much to scare you, does it, Abby?"

She laughed, and he just kept grinning, even as he turned back toward the girls. "How old are you two? Unless it's uncalled for to ask, I mean."

Megan said, a little too proudly, "I'm twenty-one. Jenny, here, is only nineteen."

Oh, terrific. Now she was marked as the baby of the group. She was going to have a word or two with Megan later. That was for sure! As calmly as she could, she said, "But I'll be twenty come June."

There. That was better.

"And your brother's the famous Jason Fury I been hearin' so much about?"

Jenny had never heard that he was famous, but she said, "Yes, I guess so. But he's just my brother."

Rafe Lynch ran the last of his ice over his forehead again, then popped it into his mouth. He pointed an index finger at Jenny and said, "You're funny. Why, I

heard about him back in California! Somethin'
about a couple a' Indian attacks. And yeah, somethin' else . . ." He smiled and thumped his temple.
"It's gone right outta my head for the time bein'."

Abigail was back, and slid his beer across the table
before she sat down again. "You tell 'em yet how you
beat the dust storm?"

Jenny wanted to know what the other thing was
that he'd heard, but held her tongue while Rafe took
the first sip of his beer. Megan, she noticed, was leaning forward eagerly. Way too eagerly for somebody
who was supposed to be soft on her brother, Jason,
she thought. That was something else she was going
to have to talk to Meg about later on.

Rafe started talking about the storm, how he saw
it coming on the horizon and nearly stopped. But
then he saw signs of Apache far to the south, and
hightailed it . . .

Jenny listened as raptly as Megan. He was so
handsome and charming, and had little lines that
fanned out from the corners of his deep blue eyes
when he smiled or laughed. Even his name was wonderful. She'd never known anyone called Rafe before.

She was smitten.

Over in California, near the Pacific coast and
the upstart town of Los Angeles, Ezra Welk sat at
the back of his room at Maria's place, listening to
the morning birds singing over the desert while he
smoked a cigar. He was a tall man, although he preferred to think of himself as compact, and studied

the ash on the end of his cigar before he rolled if off on the edge of the sole of his boot.

He was alone in the room, and had been ever since seven, when the little spitfire he'd spent the night with had left. Her name had been Merlina, he thought. Hell. She was probably servicing some caballero downstairs right now, behind the back bar.

That's where he'd found her, anyway. Quite the little bucking bronca, that gal.

He hoped her next "rider" was as satisfied as he was. He rolled the ash off the end of his cigar in the ashtray, this time—cut glass pretending to be crystal, he thought—and let out a sigh. He wasn't that tired. Well, maybe a bit tuckered out from Señorita Merlina, but that'd pass. No, if he was tired of anything, he supposed it was just life itself.

That was a funny thing, wasn't it? He couldn't think of another way to put it, though, when a feller was sick and tired of, well, everything.

He took another drag on his cigar, then put it out before he stood up and gave his collar a tug. He supposed he'd best see about finding himself some breakfast, and then think about what to do.

This is all Benny Atkinson's fault, he thought unpleasantly as he left his room and started downstairs. Why in hell did Benny have to show up in the first place?

West of Fury, the wagon train sat forlornly, broken and wind-whipped. Two of the wagons had blown clean over during the night, killing the occupants of one of them. The Banyons had managed to fall asleep somehow, Riley Havens guessed, and when their wagon went over, they were crushed by Martha's chifforobe.

Ferris said it had taken two men with shovels to scrape up Darren's skull.

Three of the other men had set off to dig a couple of holes, and it wouldn't be very long before he was asked to come out and say some words over the dearly departed. What could he say? That Darren Banyon was the second to the cheapest cheapskate he'd ever met, but that he was a good man with his horses? And Martha Banyon . . . That she could be sharp tongued and had already caused more than one blowup in the troupe, but that she could sing so sweet and pretty that it could make a grown man go all gooey?

He supposed he should just say the best parts. He'd leave the Bible-thumping to a couple of the other travelers. They sure enough had a crop of them on this journey, including a real Catholic priest.

But he supposed that Sampson Davis, wherever he was, leveled the field, good and evil-wise. There was something just plain nasty about the man. It wasn't in his voice or his looks or the way he carried himself, and so most people in the train liked him all right. But there was something . . . evil, that's what it was, downright evil . . . lurking behind those eyes. Riley seldom wished any man ill, but, may the good Lord forgive him, he hoped Sampson Davis had died in the dust storm.

"Mr. Havens?" Young Bill Crachit, a sixteen-year-old on his own, and with his own wagon, stepped around to the tailgate where Riley was sitting. "I guess we're ready for you, sir."

Riley hopped down, then ground out his smoke under his boot. "Thanks, Bill," he said as the two of them started toward the burial site. "Sampson Davis show up yet?"

"Oh, yeah," Bill said. "Rode in a half hour ago. Why?"

"No reason," Riley answered. "Just keepin' tabs on the train members, that's all."

They came to the site of the graves. Somebody had found the wood and twine to tie together some crude crosses, and the bodies had already been lowered. When the gathered crowd saw Riley and Bill coming, they stopped their low hum of conversation and looked toward Riley.

He took off his hat. "I'm not one for Bible verses," he said. "I'll let you, Fletch, or you, Father, take care of that part. But I can tell you about the Banyons. I didn't know 'em long, but long enough to know that Darren was the best I've seen for soothing a colicky mare or knowin' how to hitch his team just right, so they didn't ever sore. Martha was a beauty, and when it came to singin' a tune, I doubt anyone would say she wasn't the best they'd ever heard, especially in a wagon camp when people need some of the civilized things around them, fine things like music and manners."

Someone in the crowd tittered at that, and he cleared his throat. "Well, maybe I made a bad choice of words right there. But I think you all know what I meant. And now, if one of you more religious gents will take over?"

He stepped aside, and Fletcher Bean took his place between the head markers. Solemnly, he bowed his head, opened his Bible, and began, "Let us pray . . ."

Jason got up the nerve to go talk to Rafe Lynch around two in the afternoon, long after the girls had gone home. He found himself walking slower and slower as he neared Abigail's place, though, and had to mentally kick himself in the rump for being so scared. Lynch wasn't going to do anything, he told himself, not and ruin his harbor in a whole fresh territory!

That helped a little, so he was walking faster when he came up to Solomon's store. He knew full well that it was Sunday, but that had never before stopped Solomon from being open. Curious, he stopped and peeked in the front window, cupping a hand over his eyes to cut the glare.

What he saw surprised him. He saw the backroom door open, and Dr. Morelli step out and shake hands with Solomon, who'd been kneeling against a counter. The look on Solomon's face was ecstatic, and he pushed Morelli aside to go into the room, but Morelli blocked his passage, speaking to him very seriously. Solomon nodded just as solemnly, and then burst out in a fresh grin. He leapt up in the air, laughing, and finally Jason could make out some words through the glass.

"A girl! It's a girl!" Solomon shouted, and then gave Morelli one of those big bear hugs of his.

Morelli freed himself after a moment, and when he walked outside again, Jason was standing there on the boardwalk, smiling at him.

"Lived, didn't it?" Jason asked with a grin on his face.

The doctor allowed himself a small smile. "Yes, she did. I'm very happy for them, but . . ."

"But what?"

"The baby isn't quite right, Jason. I think there's something wrong with her heart." Morelli shook his head slowly. "But it was a tad early. Sometimes these things just fix themselves with time, if there is any. This may have been what killed the boys, too, but since their religion prohibits any sort of postmortem . . ." He stared at the ground for a moment, then looked up. "Well, I must go. My wife's waiting dinner for me." He tipped his hat and cut across the street, making a beeline for his house.

Jason leaned back against the storefront, and shaking his head, muttered, "Well, I'll be dogged." He hoped Morelli was right about time fixing things. The last thing he needed was Solomon shooting up the place again.

He was just opening the doors into Abigail's place when someone fired a gun—and not too far from him! He whipped around and saw that it was Solomon Cohen himself, gun in hand, and screaming, "It's a girl! It's a girl!" He fired up into the air once again, then took off at a dead run, right down the center of town.

Jason took off right after him.

He caught up with Solomon only about six or seven steps later (Jason having the longer legs of the two, and not being nearly so giddy with joy) and wrested the gun away from Solomon.

"Yes, we know it's a girl! I reckon even the Apache, practically down on the Mexican border, know it, too!"

Solomon wasn't easily calmed or stilled, though. "But it's a girl, Jason, and she's alive!" he shouted, so loudly that it hurt Jason's ears. He blinked, and had to quickly change position when Solomon tried to take his gun back.

"There'll be none a' that, now. Why don't you come on over to the office, and we'll toast her with a cup a' coffee. I made it, Ward didn't," he added as an incentive. Ward made terrible coffee.

Solomon stood up straight. "Why, Jason! You're not goin' to arrest me!?"

"Just until you settle yourself down. I can't have you runnin' all over town, shootin' and maimin' folks."

"I'm not—"

"I know, Solomon," Jason said as he began to get them aimed toward the jail. "I know you're not tryin' to harm a soul. But you gotta admit that you ain't the best shot. What if you was to shoot somebody by accident and they died? Think about how bad you'd feel then! And think how bad I'd feel, havin' to hang you after all we been through together!"

By this time, Jason had Solomon nearly to the office, and Sol wasn't fighting him. But in the half-second it took to let go of his arm and open the office door, Solomon snatched back the pistol, jumped away, and fired twice (down toward the open ground by the stockade wall), hollering, "Yahoo!"

Jason grabbed him from behind, shaking his wrist until the gun fell into the dirt. "Jesus Christ, Solomon, gimme a break, all right?"

"You shouldn't be taking the name of a prophet in vain," Solomon scolded.

"And you shouldn't be allowed anywhere near firearms when your wife's havin' a baby!" Jason shoved him back toward the jailhouse. This time, he got him clear through the front door and locked in a cell, then had to run outside again to pick up his gun.

The first thing Solomon said to him, once he came back inside, was, "So, I was promised coffee, already?"

Across the street, the Reverend Milcher sat alone in his church. Lavinia and the children were nowhere to be seen, and even the shooting and the shouted news that Solomon Cohen's child had lived—this time—wasn't enough to make him take his eyes from the broken clay–tiled floor.

Again, no one had come for Sunday service. No one except his family, and you could hardly count them.

How would he feed his children without some funding? How could he pass a collection plate when there was no one there to hand it to?

They had their milk cow, still, and she was heavy with calf. She'd calve any day, and then they could be sure of having milk. But he couldn't slaughter the calf until fall, until it had put on enough beef-weight to make it worthwhile. Lavinia had the few vegetables she could coax from the desert floor, but that was it.

This was indeed the wilderness, but there was no manna from heaven.